KT-599-081

ROTATION
PLAN
EAST SUSSEX COUNTY COUNCIL
WITHDRAWN
15 APR 2024

03644567 - ITEM

ANGEL FROM HELL

Christopher Nicole titles available from
Severn House Large Print

Cold Country, Hot Sun
A Fearful Thing
The Falls of Death
The Followers
The Voyage

ANGEL FROM HELL

Christopher Nicole

Severn House Large Print
London & New York

This first large print edition published 2008
in Great Britain and the USA by
SEVERN HOUSE PUBLISHERS LTD.,
9-15 High Street, Sutton, Surrey, SM1 1DF.
First world regular print edition published 2006 by
Severn House Publishers, London and New York.

Copyright © 2006 by Christopher Nicole.

All rights reserved.
The moral right of the author has been asserted.

British Library Cataloguing in Publication Data

Nicole, Christopher
    Angel from hell. - Large print ed.
    1. World War, 1939-1945 - Secret service - Germany -
    Fiction 2. Suspense fiction 3. Large type books
    I. Title
    823.9'14[F]

ISBN-13: 978-0-7278-7686-7

Except where actual historical events and characters are being described
for the storyline of this novel, all situations in this publication are
fictitious and any resemblance to living persons is purely coincidental.

Printed and bound in Great Britain by
MPG Books Ltd, Bodmin, Cornwall.

'Angels and ministers of grace defend us!
Be thou a spirit of health or goblin damn'd,
Bring with thee airs from heaven or blasts from
hell,
Be thy intents wicked or charitable
Thou comest in such a questionable shape
That I will speak to thee.'
                    Hamlet, William Shakespeare

EAST SUSSEX COUNTY LIBRARY	
03644567	
Bertrams	18/02/2011
CRO/CRO1	£19.99
10/16 8/11	UCK LEW 12/14 10/15

Prologue

I parked the car before the large, wrought-iron gates. The mountain rose in front of me. It had once been terraced to grow vines but these had long been abandoned and it was now a wilderness of overgrown shrubs and pine trees. The drive beyond the gate curved up to the house, only just visible through a screen of weeping willows. From the small stone hut, just within the gates, I could hear the hum of the pool circulating pump, although from below I could not see the water. I pressed the phone button.

'Si?'

My Spanish is not very good. 'My name is Christopher Nicole.' I spoke very slowly and carefully. 'I have an appointment with the Countess.'

'Ah, yes, si, si. The Countess is expecting you.'

There was a click and the gates slowly swung open. I got back into the car and drove up to the small parking area behind the house. There I faced the rear of the building, which appeared to be all on one level. I got out and the back-

door opened to reveal a short, dark-haired young woman. 'Come in, please, Señor Nicole.'

I entered a spacious kitchen and then a comfortable lounge with a dining area. To my left a corridor led away, presumably to the bedrooms. In front of me, glass doors gave access to an equally comfortable naya, from which there was a magnificent view of the Jalon Valley and river, several hundred feet down. In the foreground, some twenty feet below me, there was a large swimming pool in which the water was bubbling. I also saw at a glance that off this lower terrace there was another living area.

But this evidence of refined, comfortable living was quite insignificant beside the woman.

She sat in a cane armchair looking out over the view. She wore pale blue pants with a loose white shirt and sandals, and looked cool; because of the glare she also wore dark glasses. I knew she had to be well into her eighties, and her hair was both thinning and absolutely white; she wore it cut short, in some contrast to the old photographs I had seen of her. But her bone structure remained flawless, her feet were still shapely, and even sitting down there could be no doubt that she was a tall woman.

I had searched for Anna Fehrbach for several years. This was as much to gratify my curiosity as for my desire to write a book about her. She had, no doubt wisely, elected to disappear after her last great exploit. That was a long time in

7

the past. But there had always been strands in the wind. The search had not, of course, been a full-time occupation; I have a living to earn. But whenever I had a few weeks off, I had hunted through archives, newspapers and even talked to people who claimed to have known her – however truthfully, I could not tell.

And now there I was, actually standing before her. I could hardly believe that my quest might have ended.

She smiled at me, took off her sunglasses and the day suddenly felt even brighter; I had heard so much about her eyes. They were a soft blue, welcoming, almost summoning: could they really suddenly turn into shafts of steel? She extended her hand; she wore several valuable rings as well as a diamond-encrusted gold bracelet on her wrist. 'Forgive me for not getting up,' she said, her voice low. 'I get a little stiff nowadays. Do sit down. Encarna, bring some...?' She looked at me. Instinctively I looked at my watch, and she gave a throaty gurgle of amusement.

'Of course, you are English. My first real lover was English,' she said nostalgically. 'But it is eleven o'clock. I am sure you could have a glass of champagne.'

I sat opposite her. 'That would be very nice, Countess.'

Encarna hurried off.

'It's very good of you to see me.'

She shrugged. 'I felt in the mood. Have you come to kill me?'

8

My head jerked. *'Eh?'*

Another of her gorgeous smiles. *'It has to happen, eventually. Although they may leave it too late.'*

'They? You mean you know them?'

'Oh, I do not know them individually. I only know they are there.'

'But you know who, or where, they are coming from?'

Encarna placed two glasses of champagne on the table between us.

'I do not even know that,' Anna Fehrbach said. *'It could be any of a hundred sources, a hundred people out for revenge. I have made a lot of enemies, as I think you know, Mr Nicole.'* She raised her glass. *'Your health.'*

'And yours, Countess.' I sipped. *'But, knowing that there are people out there who wish you dead, you can sit here calmly, in an isolated villa, with a single maidservant?'*

'I am not very easy to kill. A lot of people have found that out.'

'And if I had come here to kill you...?'

Her hand moved so quickly it was hardly discernable, and I found myself looking down the barrel of a small automatic pistol. *'Oh, you would die first.'* She smiled. *'But I was only joking. I know you are not an assassin.'* She restored the pistol to its original position beside her cushion. *'When you wrote me asking for this interview, I had you investigated. Besides, I have read some of your novels. Do you intend to write about me?'*

9

I was still catching my breath. 'I would like to.'

'Well, then, I think it is about time. You have a tape recorder?'

I took it from my briefcase and laid it on the table.

'Excellent. You will stay for lunch, and perhaps for dinner, and I will talk to you. But you must let me tell my story in my own way. Do not fear, it will be the whole truth, I promise. But I must not be interrupted by questions.'

'Agreed. But before you start, may I ask three questions?'

'Certainly.'

'Were you truly the most beautiful woman of your time?'

'My contemporaries are all dead. You will have to look at old photographs and form your own judgement.'

'I have some of them here.'

'Well, then?'

'You are the most beautiful woman I have ever seen.'

'Thank you. What a pity I did not meet you sixty years ago. There were two other questions?'

'Have you really had a hundred lovers?'

'I have never kept a record. You will have to add them up as we go along. And your last question?'

I drew a deep breath. 'And have you really killed more than a hundred people?'

Anna Fehrbach smiled.

10

One

The Angel

The tramp of booted feet rumbled through the streets of Vienna. It shrouded the Schonbrunn, rose amongst the many other palaces and churches which filled the ancient capital of the Holy Roman Empire. It obliterated thought and memory, left no doubt in the minds of the citizens – not only of Vienna, but of all Austria – that a new era had arrived: the Anschluss!

Few ordinary Austrians wished to be united with Germany, and certainly not with Nazi Germany, yet such was the immensity of the event, and the fascination with the thousands of uniformed men, marching in perfect goose-stepping discipline and unison, steel helmets straight on their heads, their officers with drawn swords, that the streets were packed with spectators. Some were weeping; some merely looked dejected; others thought it prudent to wave swastika flags and cheer. All were well wrapped up against the chill breeze in this early March of 1938, and all were inquisitive as well as apprehensive: it was rumoured that the Fuehrer himself would soon arrive.

Annaliese Fehrbach could not help but share in the excitement, even if, although she herself was not interested in politics, she knew that her father was against the union. But all those handsome, dedicated young men ... She stood at the back of the crowd, her five feet ten inches of height enabling her to see over most of them. And now, when she turned away to go home, those around her willingly parted, happy to have the opportunity to look at her.

Annaliese was quite used to this, and smiled at them all, even those louts who sought to brush up against her or tried a surreptitious squeeze of her hips. As it was a Saturday she was wearing a dress rather than her convent uniform. In the new coat she had been given for Christmas, with its fake-fur collar, she looked older than her seventeen years, her beauty enhanced by her self confidence. She knew she was beautiful. She had been told so often enough, even had she not had the evidence of her own mirror. Her flawlessly carved, slightly aquiline features, her waist-length dark yellow hair, her height indicating her long legs – no less than the fullness of her blouse – suggested the maturity of her body. A look from her huge, soft blue eyes could turn a man's knees to water. Mama often said that she was the direct descendant of a Valkyrie, although Annaliese hoped that her mission in life would be less dramatic.

Because, for all her looks, the most striking thing about her was her smile, which lit up her face and turned those eyes into glowing sapphires. That smile she was using now, to ease her passage until she gained a side street and could hurry home, arriving slightly breathless.

'Where have you been?' demanded Papa, who had also taken the day off work, no doubt to concentrate on another seething editorial in the privacy of his study.

'I went to see the parade,' Annaliese explained, taking off her coat.

'You went to see the blackest day in Austrian history,' Papa announced.

'Well, Papa, if it is so, then it is also surely an historic day, and should be remembered.'

Johann Fehrbach snorted. But he knew it was impossible to argue with his eldest daughter: he understood her intellectual superiority. As for disciplining her, he had not even been able to shout at her, much less strike her, since she had been ten, when he had sought to spank her and had found himself impaled upon those suddenly flint-like blue eyes, the flaring nostrils that were the only signs of anger he had ever seen in her. He put it down to her Irish mother. Many people, most of all her own family and colleagues, had been amazed and concerned when such a distinguished journalist as Jane Haggerty had decided to abandon her career in order to marry an obscure Viennese reporter. But Vienna in 1919 had been a strange, chaotic, tragic place, where people had been dying of starvation in the streets because of the continuing Allied blockade, and great businesses lay

13

empty amidst the financial rubble of the collapsed Habsburg Empire. It had been a cauldron that a famous investigative reporter like Jane Haggerty had been unable to resist. But Jane, possessing all the passion of her ancestors, had been as eager to investigate life itself as the misery of the aftermath of the greatest of wars. Johann did not suppose Vienna itself had had anything to do with this; he had discovered that she was not a virgin on the night they had first shared her bed. That meant nothing to him. To be allowed to lie in the naked arms of the most vibrantly exciting and beautiful woman he had ever met, to be allowed to forget for one night the horror with which he had been surrounded, had been a glimpse of paradise.

Having been given so much, he had yet been astonished when, a month later, her assignment completed, on the night before she was due to leave for Paris, and he had been bracing himself for a return to misery, she had said, quite casually, 'You know, Jo-Jo, I'd like to pack it in and stay here. If you'll have me.'

'Why?' he had asked in bewilderment. 'You are everything. I am...'

She had placed her finger on his lips. 'You are everything that I wish.'

Obviously there had been more to it than that, even if he well understood that her animal instincts were often uppermost and he had been a handsome and virile man. He had only slowly realized that her principal aim in life was

14

creation. Jane's dream had been to take a man of her very own and make him into a star. Johann had never objected to that, even if he had always been astounded by her energy, the way she had taken pregnancy and the mothering of her two daughters in her stride without, it seemed, even drawing breath. It had been a roller-coaster ride, as with her always at his elbow he had soared up the ladder of investigative and denunciatory journalism, often running foul of the government of the moment, especially during the Dollfuss dictatorship, when he had more than once narrowly escaped a prison term. But Jane had always assured him that no sane government would ever lock up a prominent newspaper editor, and she had been right, as with the coming of Schussnigg the threat had receded.

Until now. He looked at his wife, framed in the doorway. 'You'll have gathered that they are actually here.'

'I have ears.' Jane Fehrbach was forty-eight, but remained a strikingly handsome woman, even if there were grey wisps in her yellow hair. 'And you went out to see them, miss?'

'Well, it's an event, isn't it?' Annaliese was apprehensive. If she had no fears of her father, she had a healthy respect for her mother's temper.

'What did they look like?' asked Katerina who, at fourteen, still suffered from puppy fat, but showed some promise of looking like her sister one day.

15

'Oh, tremendous,' Annaliese said, without thinking.

'They are our enemies,' Jane declared. 'Union? Austria has been invaded and conquered.'

'This copy is ready.' Johann stood up. 'I must get down to the office and see that it goes to press. We may be closed down tomorrow.'

'They wouldn't dare,' Jane said. 'They—'

The doorbell rang. The Fehrbachs looked at each other. Then there came a heavy knock.

'Oh, my God!' Johann said.

Another knock, this time thunderous.

'If we don't let them in,' Annaliese said, 'they will break it down.' She waited a moment for someone to disagree, but as no one did, she went to the door, turned the key ... and was hurled backwards as it burst inwards. The backs of her knees struck the wing of an armchair and she tumbled over it into the seat, legs scattered into the air in a most un-lady-like fashion, her skirt riding up to her thighs to expose her stockings. But the four uniformed policemen and their plain-clothes commander ignored her to advance on the three remaining members of the family.

'Johann Fehrbach?' the inspector demanded.

Johann stepped forward. 'I am he. What is the meaning of this outrage?'

'You are under arrest.' The inspector turned to Jane. 'You are Frau Fehrbach?'

'Is that not obvious?' Jane inquired.

'You are under arrest.' He snapped his fin-

16

gers, and two of his men came forward, taking the handcuffs from their belts.

'On what charge?' Jane demanded.

'Treason.'

'Treason? Are you crazy?' Her arms were pulled behind her back and the handcuffs snapped into place. 'We are loyal citizens of Austria.'

'But not of the Reich,' the inspector pointed out, and gestured at the desk. 'Bring all those papers,' he told his men. 'Anything you can find. They will prove their subversive activities.'

Johann's wrists had also been secured behind his back. 'My wife has both Irish and British nationality,' he said.

'As she is married to you, she is also now a citizen of the Third Reich, and as she assists you in producing your anti-Nazi propaganda she is equally guilty of treason. Take them out.'

Katerina screamed.

'Shut that brat up,' the inspector snapped.

A policeman stepped forward and slapped Katerina across the face. She gave another shriek and staggered.

'You bastard!' Jane shouted.

'Oh, get them out,' the inspector said.

'And the children, Herr Inspector?'

'Bring them along. A whipping will do them good.'

A policeman grasped Katerina's arm to drag her forward. There was a bruise spreading across her cheek and she was weeping. Another man turned his attention to Annaliese, who had been so horror-stricken by what had been happening that she was only just swinging her feet to the floor and straightening her skirt. Now she muttered, 'Don't touch me!'

He stared at her, but it was more in appreciation than apprehension. 'Herr Inspector,' he said, 'do you not think these girls should be searched? They could be carrying concealed weapons.'

'You are a pederast, Rohmer,' the inspector remarked. 'Get them out of here. Then I want this house searched from top to bottom.'

'Yes, Herr Inspector,' the policeman said regretfully. Katerina was already being marched to the door, sobbing loudly. 'Come on, darling, up you get.'

He tucked his fingers into the bodice of Annaliese's dress, pressing the back of his hand against the soft flesh beneath, and she swung her hand, fingers curved. Her nails slashed into his cheek and blood spurted.

'Bitch!' he snarled, releasing her bodice to swing his own hand, and have his wrist grasped from behind with a force that nearly jerked him off his feet. The inspector had joined them.

'I do not wish her marked.'

The policeman snorted. 'She has cut my cheek. I will have a scar.'

'So you can pretend you went to university.' The inspector stood above Annaliese, who had retreated as far as she could into the chair, drawing up her legs and clutching her skirt

18

around her knees. Now he stared at her for several seconds, while she started to pant. 'She is not to go with the others. Take her to my office. Handcuff her, but do not injure her in any way.'

His men exchanged glances and waggled their eyebrows.

'Now, Fraulein ... what is your name?'

'I am Annaliese Fehrbach,' Annaliese said, her voice still low. 'And I will never submit to you.'

The inspector smiled. 'I am sure we will be able to come to some arrangement. Now go with these men. Behave yourself, and you will not be harmed.'

Slowly Annaliese stood up. One of the policemen had the handcuffs waiting. 'Am I allowed to put on my coat?'

Neither her parents nor Katerina had been granted that privilege. But to her surprise the inspector nodded. 'We do not wish you to catch a cold.'

She pulled on her coat and then put her arms behind her back. 'What will happen to my family?'

'I have said I am sure we will be able to come to some arrangement.'

'Ah, Gunther,' Colonel Glauber said. 'Come in. Sit down. I think yesterday went off very well. Do you know, I really felt there might be some trouble. But the people seemed quite happy. I can tell you that the Fuehrer is very pleased.'

Gunther Hallbrunn cautiously lowered himself into the seat before the desk. Glauber was a large, friendly-looking man, who could beam, as he was now doing. But he could also explode into a violent rage when things did not go exactly the way he thought they should. 'So, tell me,' he now said. 'You had no trouble?'

'No, Herr Colonel, there was no trouble. The usual protests, expressions of outrage, hysterics from the women ... we are used to that.'

'And now they are all safely behind bars. But my secretary told me you requested this interview on an urgent matter.'

'Not urgent, Herr Colonel. But I thought it might be of interest to you.'

'Indeed?'

'I have a present for you.'

Glauber raised his eyebrows. 'I hope you have not been looting.'

'No, no. This is one of our prisoners. I put her in the interview cell,' Hallbrunn explained. 'Would you care to look at her?'

Glauber regarded him for several seconds. 'Why should I wish to do that, Captain?'

'Because, as I say, I think she will be of interest to you.'

Another moment's consideration, then Glauber stood up. Hallbrunn hurried in front of him to open the door, and they passed the eyebrow-raising secretary into the outer hall of the central police station that had been appropriated as Gestapo Headquarters, and went down the stairs and along the corridor to the cell block.

20

The cells were crowded with people, men and women, and even some children, all part of the preventive arrest of known subversives carried out by the police. Some of the inmates asked or shouted questions, but most recognized Glauber's rank and prudently kept quiet. Beyond the cells was the interview room. Here a guard stood to attention.

'Would you care to look, Herr Colonel?'

Glauber glanced at him, then slid the inspection hatch aside and looked into the room.

'Is she not magnificent?' Hallbrunn asked.

Glauber closed the hatch. 'She is a handsome girl, and it is good of you to think of me, Hallbrunn, but I have a beautiful and demanding wife in Berlin, and an even more beautiful and much more demanding mistress in Hamburg. I am actually enjoying this interlude in Vienna as a period of rest and recuperation from the requirements of the flesh. As for a young girl ... she would laugh at me.'

'I am sure she would not, Herr Colonel. But it is not just a matter of her looks, although they are exceptional. I have had her examined by Molder, who tells me that her body is as flawless as her face. But I have also made inquiries about her. She is intellectually brilliant; according to her Mother Superior she has an IQ of a hundred and seventy-three.' Glauber looked sceptical.

'She is the head girl of the convent,' Hallbrunn went on, 'and she is the best athlete in the school as well; she is the captain of hockey,

21

netball and athletics. She is also a strong swimmer. She has an Anglo-Irish mother, and speaks English like a native. She is also fluent in French.'

'You will be telling me next that this paragon is a mathematical genius.'

'I do not know about that, sir. But you told me to keep my eyes open for anyone unusual, anyone who might be of use to the Reich. Surely the SS can find a use for someone with a combination of such looks and such intellectual capacity.'

Glauber turned back to the hatch, slid it open again. 'You expect her to work for us, when you have just arrested her entire family?'

'She understands the situation, Herr Colonel. I have told her that if she co-operates with us, her parents will neither be shot nor sent to a concentration camp. If she does not ... well...'

'And what does she suppose you meant by "co-operation"?'

'I imagine she assumes that she is to be some Party official's mistress.'

'And she is prepared to accept this?'

'As I said, sir, she is very intelligent. She is prepared to do anything to protect her family.'

'Has she been raped?'

'Good heavens, no, sir. I would not permit that, at least until you had seen her.'

'Not even by you?'

'Certainly not, sir.'

'Ah, yes,' Glauber agreed. 'I had forgotten. Therefore, in your opinion, she is a virgin.'

'Molder says she is. Anyway, she comes from an eminently respectable family, and attended a convent.'

'You make her sound too good to be true, Hallbrunn. Very good. You may leave the girl. I will find something worthwhile to do with her.'

'Yes, sir. Ah...'

'I said, you may leave the girl,' Glauber repeated.

'Of course. Heil Hitler!'

Annaliese heard the clicking of the hatch being moved to and fro, but she refused to turn her head to try and discover who was looking at her, nor could she hear anything that was being said beyond the glass.

She was desperately trying to compose herself for whatever might soon happen to her, formulate at least a mental plan to deal with it. But this was next to impossible when the past twenty-four hours had been so confusing, so filled with the unexpected. The way the policeman had attempted to manhandle her had been a total shock; nothing like that had ever happened to her before. Her reaction had been instinctive, but she had not intended to scratch his cheek wide open, and when she had looked into his eyes she had realized, with a curious sense of detachment accompanied by a lightness in her stomach, that she was about to be hurt, very badly.

But it hadn't happened; the inspector, who was apparently a captain in the mysterious and terrifying SS, had intervened, and while she had been handcuffed, no violence had been offered to her. No one had even attempted to touch her intimately. But she had known it could only be a matter of time, very little time, before ... Sex was of course a recurring subject at school, the topic of recurring speculation, but for all the claims of some of the girls, none of them had known a great deal about it. She had known less than most, because the subject had never been discussed by her mother and father, at least in front of her. Even when she had begun to menstruate, Mother had merely produced the requisite towels and said, 'Well, now you are a woman,' and left it at that. It was impossible to suppose, looking at her, watching her move – quite apart from the fact that she had borne two children – that Mother was not, even now, a sexual woman, but her sexuality was confined to her bedroom; out of it only politics mattered. As a result, Annaliese had never been very interested in the subject, and in view of her responsibilities at school she had regarded it as her duty to quash too much discussion, certainly when it became too earthy. Of course she had her romantic dreams. None of the nuns had any doubt that she was certain to make university, and there she would meet some handsome young man, preferably wealthy – Mother and Father had never seemed to have quite sufficient money – who would fall in love with her. They would then marry, have children, and live happily ever after in the approved manner.

24

That enticing prospect had now disappeared. Thanks to whatever crime Mother and Father had committed, she was now also being treated as a criminal. And she was surrounded by men who, even if they had not yet touched her, looked at her like hungry wolves, while she was utterly at the mercy of this hard-faced SS officer, who also stared at her constantly. When would it happen? And what would she do when it started? If only she had some idea of what 'it' would be like. It was the majority opinion at school, encouraged by the nuns, that physical sex was a painful and unpleasant business, even when inflicted by someone one liked or might even love. To have such a thing inflicted by a man – or men – one did not even know and was well on the way to hating was unthinkable. Yet it was obviously going to happen, no doubt as soon as this car got wherever it was going.

She had had an urgent desire to scream, and had begun drawing deep breaths, when to her consternation the captain had placed his hand on her arm and given it a gentle squeeze. 'I have told you, there is nothing for you to be afraid of, as long as you do what you are told.'

She had licked her lips. 'What do you want of me?'

'I wish you to be loyal to the Reich. Just remember that.'

Loyal to the Reich, she thought. When the Reich has just locked up my mother and father, and my sister? But now her attention was caught by her surroundings, as the car turned into the courtyard of what she recalled had been the central police station, but which now flew, instead of the red and white of Austria, the swastika flag of Nazi Germany, while the yard itself was filled with black-uniformed men. The car stopped and someone opened the door for her. She glanced at the captain, who gave a quick nod. She got out, and he followed her, escorting her across the yard to one of the many doorways. Again she was aware of hunger in the eyes about her, but still she felt protected by the presence of the captain.

Once she was inside the building, however, everything had changed. She had been delivered into the hands of a uniformed woman, to whom the captain had given instructions in a low voice that Annaliese had been unable to overhear. The woman had stood to attention and said, 'Heil Hitler!' and the captain had turned to Annaliese.

'You will go with Frau Molder. Obey her in all things.'

Annaliese had looked at Frau Molder, who had looked at her, and suddenly the captain had seemed almost a friend. The woman was not very old, certainly a good many years younger than Mother, and was quite good-looking, with dark hair and sharp features. She did not look vicious, but her eyes were hard. She was chunkily built and several inches shorter than Annaliese, a situation she obviously did not appreciate. 'Come,' she said.

Annaliese followed her along a corridor, past

26

more hungry eyes, and then down a flight of stairs into a cell block. Most of the cells were occupied, and most, as before, by at least four people – men and women and even children. Annaliese did not like the look of any of them; the thought of being shut away with such companions made her skin crawl. She prayed for a sight of Mother and Father, or even Katerina, but they were not to be seen. Then her gaoler opened a door and gestured her to go in. Annaliese drew a deep breath; unlike the cells further down the corridor, this room was not barred but had a solid wall, save for an inspection hatch in the door, and so whatever happened in here could not readily be overlooked by any of the other prisoners or by any guard in the corridor. But it was empty. Slowly she released her breath, and then realized that once the door closed this woman could do anything she liked to her, without fear of comment, much less interruption.

'Good, eh?' Frau Molder asked. 'You are privileged.' She produced a key and unlocked the handcuffs, hanging them from her belt.

Annaliese rubbed her wrists as she looked around herself. The cell could almost have been described as comfortable, if you had never known anything better. In addition to the cot bed there was a table and a chair, and a slop bucket with a lid. But the only light was a naked bulb suspended from the ceiling, and the room smelled of disinfectant. Still, it was better than she had expected, and it could do no harm to be

27

friendly. 'I hope it is not the condemned cell,' she ventured.

Frau Molder gave a cold smile. 'All cells are condemned cells, when you are condemned,' she said.

Annaliese gulped and sat down on the bed. Frau Molder snapped her fingers. 'Up.' Annaliese stood again, somewhat uncertainly. 'Strip.'

'Do what?'

'Undress. Take off your clothes.'

Annaliese bridled, despite her determination to maintain her composure no matter what happened. 'You have no right to make me do that.'

'Fraulein, I have the right to do anything to you that I choose. Captain Hallbrunn has said that he does not want you marked, anywhere visible, and particularly on your face. But this...' From her belt she took a short, thick, rubber truncheon. 'Can cause extreme pain, and the only mark will be a rush of blood to the injured part, and that will fade again in an hour. The pain remains longer. Now stop being a silly little girl. I am not going to harm you, but I am required to examine you.'

Annaliese drew another deep breath. She had not undressed in front of anyone since the age of ten, and that had been her mother. Even after sports at school she had preferred to go home rather than share the shower with the other girls. But she did not wish to be beaten. 'I will tell the captain of this,' she said, as she took off her coat and draped it over the chair.

'You are welcome,' Frau Molder agreed. 'Continue.'

To Annaliese's surprised relief, the ordeal had been entirely asexual, even if it had been the most embarrassing of her life. Frau Molder had made her bend over and parted her buttocks to look between, but she had done nothing more than that. Then she had had to lie on her back with her knees drawn up while the woman had again peered at her genitals. She had also looked into her mouth with great care, seeming to examine each tooth. Actually the worst moment had been when Molder had plucked the small gold crucifix suspended on a chain round Annaliese's neck, given her by her mother on her sixteenth birthday, from between her breasts. Molder had touched her flesh while turning the crucifix over, before allowing it to fall back into place.

'Do you believe in this?' she had asked.

'Don't you?' Annaliese had responded.

Molder had gazed at her for some seconds, and then she said, 'You are a very handsome young woman.'

She had been allowed to dress again, to use a communal bathroom, with Frau Molder at her elbow, and given a good meal. She began to feel almost friendly to her captor. 'Do you treat all your prisoners like this?' she asked.

'No.'

'Then why am I being treated like this?'

'Captain Hallbrunn did not tell me.'

'Is he going to rape me?'

Molder had given another of her cold smiles. 'I think that is very unlikely. Had you been a pretty little boy, now...'

Annaliese had no idea what she was talking about.

That had been nearly twenty-four hours ago. There had been three more very edible meals, three more escorted visits to the toilets, each time by different female guards, and the rest of the time she had spent lying on her cot or sitting at her table. She had been given nothing to read, and she knew nothing of what might be happening outside this prison, or in it, for that matter. During her brief excursions, which had involved passing the open cells, she had been subjected to whistles and shouted comments, but none of those were the least informative; her various guards never spoke at all.

She felt she should pray, especially as today was Sunday, and fingered her crucifix. But the cell did not lend itself to thoughts of God, and she had an uneasy feeling that God had abandoned her, at least for the time being. She had to take Hallbrunn's word that her parents and Katerina were not being ill treated – although she could not believe they were being treated as well as her, and she had continually to brace herself, whenever her door was opened, for some fresh ordeal. She had asked if she could not be returned home, under guard, to pick up a change of clothing and had been rewarded with a brief 'Nein.'

So all she could do was sit, and try not to think, but how could she, with her intensely active brain, not think? What would be happening at school tomorrow morning? What would they be saying? All Vienna would know by now that Johann Fehrbach and his family had been arrested. The girls would be imagining all sorts of horrible, titillating things happening to her ... and she still did not know that they might not yet be proved right.

And now the hatch had been opened and then closed again, several times. There were people out there, looking at her, deciding what to do with her. She simply could not imagine what they might have in mind if they were not going to rape or sexually assault her, but had separated her from her family for some reason ... An hour had passed since the hatch had last been opened. She did not have a watch, but her growling stomach suggested it was close to a meal time, which would also include another visit to the toilets – she had gathered that the bucket was only to be used in case of emergency, and she was young enough and fit enough not to have one of those.

And now the door was opening. She stood up, and found herself looking not at any of the women who were her usual escorts, but at Molder, who she had not seen since the previous day. 'Good morning, Fehrbach,' Molder said. 'How are you today?'

Alarm bells started to ring in Annaliese's

31

brain, but she kept her voice even. 'As well as can be expected, Frau.'

'Good. You will be pleased to leave this place. Come along.'

'Do I bring my coat?'

'Yes. You will not be coming back.'

Annaliese put on the coat and looked around her, but she had no belongings to take. She stepped into the corridor. 'Am I allowed to ask where I am going?'

'You are always asking questions,' Molder said. 'It is a bad habit.' She gestured at the stairs and Annaliese went up them, as before aware of the stares around her. 'Through that door,' Molder said. Annaliese opened the door and found herself in a spacious office, a place of filing cabinets and typewriters and three desks, although there was only one person waiting for her. This was another woman, who also wore uniform – a blue tunic and skirt with a matching side cap. She was tall, stood elegantly, and had a coldly handsome, aquiline face; her yellow hair was gathered in a tight bun. 'Fraulein Fehrbach,' Molder explained to the other woman.

The woman walked round Annaliese, who stood very still, aware that her immediate future was about to be determined. Then she said, 'Thank you, Frau Molder.' The door closed, and the woman walked to one of the desks and sat behind it. 'Sit.'

There was a straight chair before the desk, and Annaliese sat on it. The woman opened the folder on the desk in front of her. 'Annaliese,' she mused. 'That is a pretty name. But it is too long. As of now you will be Anna.'

'Yes...' Annaliese hesitated.

'My name is Commandant Frau Gehrig. But you will call me ma'am.'

'Yes ... ma'am.'

Commandant Gehrig tapped the papers. 'These are remarkable notes. When I read them my immediate reaction was that they had to be exaggerated. But I can see that they have not exaggerated, at least as regards your appearance. If your mental and intellectual capabilities have also been correctly interpreted, you may do very well. The only thing that is lacking is any suggestion of control. Do you have control, Anna?'

'I do not know what you mean, ma'am.'

Frau Gehrig tapped the notes. 'It says here that you slashed open a policeman's cheek. That was an irrational act.'

'He touched me.'

'And you do not like being touched? You may have a difficult path to follow. But you must learn to control your impulses.'

She looked for what she would consider the right answer. 'I think I have control, ma'am. But to be molested by a strange man is an intolerable situation. I think my response was entirely natural.'

'You do have a brain in there, Anna. But no doubt you have also been afraid. Perhaps you are afraid now?'

'I do not know what I have to be afraid of,

ma'am. I have committed no crime. I am afraid for my father and mother. And my sister.'

'Because your father and mother have committed a crime, against the Fatherland. Such a crime invariably involves the children as well.'

'Then should I not be locked up with them?'

'You will serve a much more useful purpose by working for the Reich.'

Work for these thugs, who had conquered her country without firing a shot? 'I do not think I can do that, ma'am.'

Commandant Gehrig raised her eyebrows. 'I was given the impression that Captain Hallbrunn had made your position clear. Perhaps he did not. You have been given to me, to serve me, and therefore the Reich, in the position to which I consider you to be best suited. Having seen you, and talked with you, and read this report, I have already determined that you are suitable for the, shall I say, highest aspect of our work. Should you fail to impress me, through inadequacy, I will employ you at a lower, and, you will find, less rewarding level. However, should you fail to impress me, through contumacy or stubbornness, you will be employed at the lowest possible level. That is to say, you will become an SS prostitute, servicing any man, or any group of men – some of them have unusual tastes – who wish the use of your body.'

The calmly impersonal way in which such an unthinkable future had just been outlined to her had taken Annaliese's breath away. Commandant Gehrig had studied her expression as she spoke. 'And of course,' she went on, 'if you were to fail me, now or at any time in the future, your parents, and your sister, will be immediately executed.'

Annaliese swallowed. 'And if I agree to co-operate? Will they be set free?'

The commandant smiled. 'Well, no. We are not that innocent. They will remain in suitable confinement for the time being. The situation will be reviewed from time to time in the light of your progress.'

'Will I be allowed to see them?'

'In due course, perhaps. But for the immediate future, you will have too much to do.'

'What do I have to do?'

'Just learn. You are going to a finishing school. You will be taught how to wear expensive clothes and jewellery. How to behave at the best dinner parties. How to engage men in conversation. Can you ride a horse?'

'I have received lessons. I do not own a horse.'

'You will be taught how to be an expert horsewoman. All of these assets and accomplishments attract men.'

'You mean I am to be a prostitute after all?'

'Certainly not. At least, not without my permission.'

'You mean, if a man propositions me, I must say to him, I cannot agree until I have telephoned Gestapo Headquarters and obtained permission?'

Commandant Gehrig regarded her for several seconds, then gave one of her wintry smiles. 'One day, Anna, your sharp little brain will get you into trouble.'

'No, no, ladies,' said Sergeant Muller. 'Bend! You must bend. Stretch the backs of your thighs, eh?'

The twelve girls – the eldest was just twenty – duly bent, while he walked round them. The embarrassment of wearing only a thin singlet, shorts and gym shoes in the presence of a man who then proceeded to inspect them at close quarters, had worn off over the past five weeks, but Annaliese – or Anna as she now had to consider herself – still felt uneasy when she was touching her toes and he was virtually touching her buttocks.

'Do you think he'd ever actually do anything?' Gerda asked as they showered afterwards.

'They'd have his nuts,' Martina said. 'And if they thought the girl had co-operated...'

They all looked at Karen, who turned away from them to towel herself. They were all still getting to know each other, and their surroundings, but Karen, a voluptuous redhead, had already been caught having a kiss and cuddle with one of the canteen staff. He had promptly disappeared, and Karen had been strapped naked to the ping-pong table in the games room and given six strokes of the cane, wielded by Commandant Gehrig herself. It was not something any of the other girls, who had been assembled to watch the punishment being carried out, would ever forget; it gave Anna goose pimples to think of it.

She had, in any event, been living in a continual state of mixed embarrassment and apprehension ever since coming here. Having to shower virtually in public had been bad enough, but whereas at home she had always had her own room, she now shared a dormitory with the other girls, her every move – almost, it seemed, her every thought – overseen by the others. She was entirely the outsider. Quite apart from being, she was sure, better bred than any of them – they had been forbidden to discuss their backgrounds – she was the only Austrian, as the other girls had quickly discerned from her accent. She was also the only girl wearing a crucifix; there was no religious instruction or even a church service included in their curriculum. Religion was indeed as taboo a subject as family background, and although she did pray every night, whether God was listening or not, it was not on her knees but in the privacy of her bed, and silently.

The others all appeared to be making friends, but no one had made any overtures to her as yet. She was not sure she wanted them to. Although there was a woman named Hilda who slept in the dormitory and was supposed to keep them under control, she never interfered in anything that went on, particularly after lights out, when the room was filled with rustling and suppressed giggles. Again, no one had yet approached her for a midnight cuddle, but she could not help but feel the operative word was 'yet'. The thought terrified her.

'All right,' Gerda said, drying her hair. 'So we can't have men. But what are we being trained for, if it's not to have sex? They tart us up with lovely clothes, they teach us to dance and walk and sit and stand and eat and ride elegantly, we have elocution lessons every day ... I mean, what is it all for, if not to attract men?'

'The *right* men,' Luisa said, knowingly.

'You mean, the Party?' Alexandra was aghast. They were given lessons in Nazi theory every day.

'Well, it has to be somebody,' Luisa pointed out. 'What do you think, Anna?'

In addition to being the outsider, Anna was by some months the youngest of them, but they had quickly recognized her superiority, not only intellectually, but in almost every other field. She had proved the most adept at the physical training, which, for some reason none of them had understood, included the art of self-defence, using both hands and feet. 'Gives you self-confidence,' the instructor had said in response to their questions, although clearly he enjoyed rolling around on the mat with the girls. But she could only offer them her own resolution. 'I think it is better not to think,' she said. 'We'll find out some time.'

'That could take years,' Gerda sneered.

'Well...'

Gerda licked her lips. For all the daily, and quite severe, physical training they underwent, she remained a trifle overweight, and she looked older than her eighteen years. 'So we just sit here and turn into old maids.'

'Beautiful old maids,' Martina suggested.

Which was true enough, Anna reflected. There was not one of them who was not at the very least good-looking, the more so when they were all in the nude.

'The point is,' Gerda said, 'we're forbidden to have sex with men. But...' She looked from face to face. 'There's no way they could tell if ... well, I mean, we simply can't go on forever without any sex at all.' Now she was flushing. But so was everyone else. Gerda giggled. 'It would be fun. Anna, will you come to my bed tonight?'

Every head turned, and Anna felt her cheeks burning. It could be fun! But she didn't know what 'it' was, or might involve. Besides, if she was desperately lonely, longed for the comfort of another pair of arms – she had never considered a sexual embrace – her instincts warned her that there was no love, or even affection, here, simply unfulfilled sexual desires. She felt that as much as anyone, but she also knew that she was surviving simply by surrounding herself with that suit of mental armour she had assumed on the very first day, that complete withdrawal of emotion, that determination just to take every day as it came, and survive it.

Besides, the thought of being discovered and

stretched on that ping-pong table...

She left the showers and put on her clothes. 'I really don't think that would be a good idea.'

'You are a miserable little prude,' Gerda shouted, running at her. 'I am going to rub your pussy raw.'

Anna stared at her. Her entire body seemed to be aflame, and she was aware of two contrasting emotions, one a feeling of utter outrage that she should be placed in this position, the other a sudden ice-cold fury, a certainty of what had to be done. She stepped forward, and Gerda, staring into her eyes, checked in consternation at what she saw. Anna reached for her, grasping her right arm at wrist and just above the elbow, and threw her to one side. There was a terrible crack and a shriek of the most utter agony from the injured girl as she collapsed on the floor.

'Come in, Anna.' Commandant Gehrig was using her 'I am your friend and confidante' voice, which was not always entirely reassuring. Anna entered the office and stood to attention before the desk. She was wearing the school uniform of white shirt with black tie, black skirt, and black stockings with low-heeled shoes. She was in any event apprehensive, as she had known this moment had to come. 'I am sure you will be pleased to know,' the commandant said, 'that Gerda is not going to lose the use of her arm. But she is going to be in hospital for at least a week, and then she will not be able to train for some time. Are you relieved?'

'Yes, ma'am. I...' Anna bit her lip.

'You were going to say, perhaps, that you did not mean to hurt her so badly as to break her arm in two places and dislocate her shoulder?'

Anna drew a deep breath.

'How did you do that? Who taught you? I have never accepted that it was an accidental fall in the showers,' the commandant pointed out. 'Now I would like the truth.'

Anna stared straight in front of her. 'Nobody taught me, ma'am.'

'Would you like to be caned?'

'No, ma'am.'

'But you will risk it not to betray your ... well, she can hardly be your friend, if she attempted to assault you.'

Anna gave her a quick glance.

'Oh, yes,' the commandant said. 'I do know what happened. You silly little girls do not realize that I know everything that happens, either in your dormitory or out of it. So, she wanted to make love to you, and you resisted her. Why did you do that?'

Anna licked her lips. 'I did not wish to.'

'Because you found Gerda personally distasteful? Or because you are not a lesbian?'

Anna stared at her.

The commandant smiled. 'You don't even know the meaning of the word, do you? Of course, I remember, you do not like to be touched. I warned you that you were choosing a difficult path. And I also warned you that you

41

simply had to control these violent impulses of yours. You say that no one taught you, yet on an impulse you can virtually take someone apart.'

Anna continued to stare straight in front of her. 'I did not lose control, ma'am. I did not wish to be assaulted, and I defended myself. I did not mean to break Gerda's arm, only to resist her. I did what came naturally to me.'

Gehrig again regarded her for several seconds. 'Do you know, I believe you. You really are a most remarkable girl. But it is a difficult situation to avoid when you have a group of healthy adolescents locked up together with no outlet for their emotional and physical needs. You do not seem to have any needs, either emotional or physical. That makes you either very strong, or potentially very weak. You do realize that I can no longer risk locking you up with the other girls. I have no idea what may happen, and I wish no more broken bones; they may be some of yours. However, your progress has been so rapid above any of the others that I think you are ready to move on, and in fact our superiors are anxious for you to do so.' She got up, went to an inner door, and opened it. 'I hope you agree with me, Herr Colonel.'

'Entirely, Frau Gehrig,' Colonel Glauber said, entering the office; he had clearly been listening in the other room. 'She is a treasure. I spotted this the moment I first saw her.'

Anna blinked at him. As far as she could recollect, she had never seen him before.

'A potential treasure, Herr Colonel,' Frau

Gehrig suggested. 'She needs to be treated with care, and restraint. I believe she is capable of breaking even your arm, if you push her hard enough.'

'Ha, ha,' Glauber said. 'Come along, young lady.'

Anna looked at Frau Gehrig.

'You belong to the Colonel now, Anna.'

Anna swallowed. 'My things...'

'You will be given new things. Goodbye, Fraulein. I hope you prosper.'

She sounded almost sorry for her, Anna realized.

Two

The Trainee

Anna sat beside the colonel in the back of the Mercedes saloon as they were driven to the north-east. Her head was still in a spin, as it had been since the afternoon of the assault, although she had done her best to appear unaffected by what had happened. But she had had to be aware that not one of the other girls had been on her side, least of all, perhaps, Hilda. That there had been a fight in her dormitory reflected badly upon her. She had had to prevent any more fighting, even if it had been obvious that the other girls were simply waiting for the opportunity to avenge their friend, who had merely been giving the lead to what they all wanted to do anyway. But they had all had to wait to see what Frau Gehrig would do, whether she herself would punish the stuck-up little bitch, as they considered Anna, or whether she would give Hilda permission to throw her to the wolves.

How they must be seething! Unless they supposed, or were told, that she had been expelled to suffer some far greater punishment than could be inflicted at the school. But where was she going to? She glanced at the man beside her, who was studying her. He did not look vicious, and he was in plain clothes. On the other hand, he had been addressed as colonel, and he seemed to have considerable authority. And she now belonged to him!

He smiled at her. 'Are you glad to be away from that place?'

'I would be, sir, if I knew where I was going. To *what* I was going.'

'One day,' he remarked, 'that pert tongue of yours will get you into trouble.'

Anna swallowed.

'However,' he went on, 'I can appreciate your interest. The immediate answer to your question is that you have completed your preliminary training, and that you are on your way to Berlin, where you will commence your new life.'

'As a whore?' She caught her breath. The

44

question, which had dominated her thinking for the past several weeks, had just slipped out.

'You young women appear to be obsessed by sex,' the colonel remarked. 'I suppose that is an essential part of growing up. Frau Gehrig holds the opinion that you are not interested in sex. But as she cannot tell me what you are interested in, I am forced to form my own opinion. It is not humanly possible for a girl as lovely and as physically well endowed as you not to be interested in sex.'

Anna's cheeks were burning. She looked straight in front of her. 'I might be interested in sex, Herr Colonel. With the right person.'

'Who, for the time being, is yourself?' he suggested.

She turned her head, sharply, and he actually flushed as well.

'Point taken. That is no bad thing, until, as you say, something better comes along. But we would prefer to have your affections remain where they are, for the moment. Your future role is sexual, yes. But not in the coarse way you have just conveyed. You are going to work for the Reich. Not as a whore – at least, not in the sense you have been assuming – but as an observer, a listener, a conveyer of information. Let me introduce myself. My name is Hans Glauber, and I am a colonel in the SD. Do you know what that is?'

'No sir.' She was becoming interested despite herself.

'The initials stand for Sicherheitsdienst, that

45

is, the Secret Service. We are the most secret service in the Reich, far more so than the Abwehr, the SS, or the Gestapo.'

'And you wish to employ me?'

'I am employing you. Now...' From his inside breast pocket he took a thick envelope. 'I want you to read, very carefully, everything that is in this envelope, and memorize it. There is no need for you to burn it. You may keep it to refresh your memory. But I will tell you, briefly, what it contains. We are giving you a new identity. We think it would be inappropriate for you to continue to be an Austrian and the daughter of a convicted seditious newspaper editor.'

'Has he been convicted?'

'Now, you well know, Anna, that whether or not he is condemned is entirely up to you, but I have high hopes that he will not be. To continue, we feel it would be appropriate for you to have a rank and a style more in keeping with your looks, and, if I may say so, your naturally aristocratic demeanour. We have decided to retain the given name of Anna, which we feel suits you, but you are now Countess Anna von Widerstand.'

'That is a name?'

'Anything can be a name, Anna. And we think this is entirely appropriate for someone of your character. I understand you are fluent in English. Say it in English.'

'Anna of Opposition? People will laugh at me.'

46

'It also means resistance. That is your name, the Countess of Resistance. Actually, I doubt many of the people you will be dealing with will know the meaning of the word, but in any event, here in this envelope is a complete explanation of how you came by the name, which you may use as necessary. As for people here in Germany, we will make sure that no one laughs at you, at least no more than once. You are the Countess von Widerstand; your full background is here. But that brings me to my next point. You are half-English.'

'I am half-Irish, Herr Colonel.'

'Well said. But your mother holds an English passport.'

'She was a journalist with an English newspaper, and found it most convenient to accept that nationality. After settling in Austria, she continued to renew her English passport.'

'A devious woman,' Glauber commented. 'Do you hate the English, Anna?'

'I have never met an Englishman, Herr Colonel. Or woman.'

'But all people of Irish blood hate the English. Is that not so? Does not your mother hate the English?'

'She has never told me so, sir.'

'Extraordinary. Well, I can tell you that the English are our enemies.'

'I thought the Communists, the Russians, were our enemies.'

'You are right. They, and the Jews, of course, are the people that we must destroy, for the

47

future of Europe. But the English, and the French, are very likely to interfere with our plans.'

'You mean they will side with the Communists?'

'It is possible. Not because they support Communism, but because they are afraid to let us grow too strong. My point is that not many high-ranking Russian military officers or diplomats visit Berlin, but the city is always full of British and French. As Countess von Widerstand you will attend soirees and receptions, balls and cocktail parties, where you will meet these people. They will be attracted to you, and you will be attracted to them.'

'And they will want to sleep with me.'

'They will want to have sex with you. Sleeping will be the least part of it. Fraulein Mayers will explain it to you. But who you accept as a possible partner will be determined by us. And under no circumstances must you surrender your virginity until expressly commanded to do so. Remember that you are the only daughter of a count, not a slut from the streets. Besides, retaining your chastity may prove an asset.'

Anna looked out of the window, at the suburbs of Berlin. Although she would never let this old bastard know it, the conversation, with its suggestion that she was to be deliberately, deceitfully, wanton – at least by all the standards of her upbringing and schooling – under the aegis of the State, was distinctly titillating. Far from hating the British, she hated these people. But as there was no way she could combat them, certainly in her present circumstances, why not enjoy the life they were offering her to the limit? But ... 'You say I am the daughter of a count ... Do you mean I have a new father and mother?'

'Your mother is dead, but we will provide a father when it is necessary. As we will provide your country estate, when it is necessary. For the time being, you will live in Berlin, in your apartment with your faithful maidservant. It is all in that envelope. But you will obviously have to be an acceptable age to be living alone. I understand that you have just turned eighteen.'

'Yes, sir.'

'Fortunately, you look older.' He chuckled. 'That is an asset in a woman, up to, perhaps, twenty-five, and then it gradually becomes a liability. As of now, you are twenty-two years old.'

'I do not think I know enough to be twenty-two, sir.'

'But we are going to teach you. We are going to teach you to be the most sophisticated young woman in Germany. You will have men falling in love with you all over the place. As I have said, we will tell you which ones to humour.'

'What happens if I fall in love with one of them?' she asked.

'I would strongly advise against it,' Glauber said.

* * *

49

The car stopped on a side street off the Unter den Linden. Anna was impressed, but not overwhelmed. Berlin could not compare with Vienna for beauty; the absence of any large, majestically flowing river determined that, quite apart from the architecture. But she had to appreciate the luxury of the lobby of the apartment building into which Glauber ushered her.

'Is this where you live, Herr Colonel?' she asked.

'No, no, Anna. This is where you live.'

Anna swallowed, suddenly aware that her very plain uniform was the reverse of chic. But the concierge seemed pleased enough with her appearance, and when they entered the elevator, the operator – a boy not much older than herself – couldn't take his eyes off her, and some of her confidence returned; she was beautiful, even if dressed like a schoolgirl.

They ascended five floors before entering another lobby. Here there were three doors. Glauber chose the centre one and gave a brief, sharp knock. It was opened almost immediately by a woman.

'Herr Colonel!'

'Elsa!' He embraced her.

She looked past him. 'And this is Anna.' The apparent warmth of her tone was reassuring, which was more than could be said for her appearance. She was at least as tall as Anna herself, but powerfully built rather than slender. Her face was a series of granite ridges, embedded in which were two dark eyes, while her mouth was a flat gash. To complete the general harshness of her appearance she, too, wore the uniform of black skirt and white blouse. Anna almost felt that she should stand to attention. Instead she watched the woman come towards her, take her hands, and draw her into an embrace. 'I shall enjoy working with you,' she said softly.

Oh lord, Anna thought. She did not feel like she would be able to break this woman's arm.

But again her apprehensions dwindled as she was shown around the apartment, which was quite the most luxurious she had ever seen, or even imagined. Her parents had lived in some comfort, but this was almost sybaritic. The floors were covered in soft-pile carpet, the walls with a variety of prints, mostly of classical scenes. The furniture in the lounge was mainly covered in polished chintz, the dining table in the small alcove was mahogany, the kitchen flawless. But best of all was when she was shown into a bedroom.

'This is yours,' Elsa explained. 'Mine is across the hall.'

'You mean...' Anna bit her lip. She had never expected to have a room of her own again.

'It has an en-suite bathroom,' Elsa added.

Anna's breath was taken away; a bathroom of her very own!

Glauber had been following them. 'I will leave you two to get acquainted,' he said. 'How soon, do you think, Elsa?'

'One month,' Elsa said.

'That will be satisfactory.' To Anna's consternation, he kissed her hand. 'I look forward to our next meeting, Countess.' He clicked his heels and left the apartment.

Anna looked at Elsa, who winked. 'I think a glass of schnapps.' She led the way back into the lounge, opened an elaborate sideboard-cum-bar. 'You have lunched?' she asked over here shoulder.

'We stopped ... I did not know the name of the town.'

'It is not relevant.' Elsa handed her a small glass of clear liquid. 'You have tasted schnapps before?'

'I have never tasted any alcohol before, save for communion wine.'

'Ah. In that case, I suggest you position yourself above that chair, and the moment you have drunk, sit down. Now, schnapps should be taken in a single gulp, like this.' She raised the glass to her lips and drained it, then put the glass down. Apart from a little added colour in her cheeks, it did not seem to have had any effect. 'Now you.'

Anna obeyed, and did indeed sit down, with a thump, gasping for breath. 'I am on fire!' She clutched her throat. 'All the way down.'

'It is an acquired taste,' Elsa said. 'As you will find with champagne, and wines. But it is a taste that must be acquired; gentlemen will expect it of you. They talk more freely when

52

they have had too much to drink, but they expect to be matched by their partners, as they hope you will become more accessible when you have had too much to drink. What you have to learn is how to appear to drink as much as they do, but remain sufficiently sober to remember what is said to you, or in your company.'

Anna did not see how that could be possible.

'Now tell me,' Elsa said. 'Do you like the apartment?'

'I think it is fabulous. I had no idea I would ever live anywhere like this.'

'But is this not where you would expect a countess to live, were you a visiting gentleman?'

'You mean I am to bring these people here?'

'Only if instructed to do so. You will be monitored at all times when working, and instructions will be conveyed to you in a variety of different ways. I will instruct you in this.' She indicated the folder that was lying on the coffee table. 'I have studied your file. You seem to be extraordinarily talented, as well as courageous and determined. I am referring to the way you handled the attempt to rape you. Do not look so alarmed. I am not going to pry into that, but it is in your record. The point I wish you to understand is that for all your obvious assets, the Reich, which is spending a great deal of money on making you into what they require, will expect results. So will I. That means hard work, both physically and mentally.

If you work hard, you will prosper, and, more importantly, you will please me.' That was undoubtedly the main aspect of the situation, certainly from her point of view. As she now proceeded to underline. 'If you do not work hard, that will disappoint me, and if I am disappointed, I will punish you, severely. I have carte blanche to deal with you as I please. Do you understand me?'

Anna felt she had to make some kind of a response. 'Providing you do not mark my face or my body.'

Elsa's smile was every bit as cold as Gehrig's. 'I do assure you, Anna, that you would do far better to be my friend. Now...' She gestured at the full bookcase. 'There will be a lot of reading. You have read *Mein Kampf*?'

'Ah ... no.'

'I see. Well, you will start with that, immediately. It is the Fuehrer's only work. Then you will read the works of Nietzsche, and then Chamberlain.' She gave a quick smile. 'I am speaking of Houston Chamberlain, of course, not the English prime minister. Do you know of him?'

'No,' Anna said. It was irrelevant to which of the two men Elsa was referring: she knew nothing of either of them.

'He was an Englishman who became a naturalized German. He married Eva Wagner, daughter of the composer. He died nine years ago. But his works will be immortal; by many they are regarded as the foundations upon which the Nazi philosophy has been built. You will find them fascinating.'

'Yes,' Anna agreed sceptically.

'Now, tomorrow I have arranged a session with the dressmakers. I understand that you have been taught how to behave in good company, but you must have the clothes to go with the behaviour.'

'Oh, yes,' Anna agreed, far more enthusiastically than when they had been discussing the books. 'Will I have jewellery as well?'

'You will be given jewellery to wear, when it is required. But you will not own it.'

'Oh.'

'There are a great many other things you need to learn as well. And there is still work to be done on that dreadful accent of yours.'

'I can't help speaking like an Austrian,' Anna protested. 'I am an Austrian.' And then she added, 'Is not the Fuehrer an Austrian?'

'The Fuehrer has learned to speak like a German,' Elsa pointed out. 'And you must do the same. Now, have you any questions?'

'I would like to go to church.'

Elsa raised her eyebrows. 'Whatever for?'

'It is over two months since I have confessed.'

Elsa regarded her for several seconds. Then she said, 'You are not in a position to confess anything to anyone except me. But that's enough for the moment. Now go off and have a bath. As of now you must bathe every day. There are some casual clothes already in the

55

closet. Put them on and come back here, and we'll start work this evening.'

Anna stood up, a trifle uncertainly; her brain was still swinging from the schnapps. 'May I ask you another question?'

'You may.' Elsa's tone indicated that she did not feel obliged to answer if she did not choose.

'What am I really being trained for? I mean, these surroundings, the things you tell me I am going to learn ... That cannot be simply to engage visiting politicians and soldiers in conversation, in the hope they may say something of importance to the Reich. That does not make sense.'

'There is a note in your file that says you are inclined to look for answers where you should not,' Elsa said. 'It is a bad habit, and, indeed, a dangerous one. Be grateful that you have been selected to serve the Reich, and that your surroundings have so much improved, so much more than anything you could otherwise have hoped for. You will be told in due course what is required of you.'

Anna lay in the hot tub and gazed at the ceiling, her hair piled on top of her head. It was the most luxurious feeling she had known for a long time; certainly since before she had gone to the training school. But while enjoying the state of total physical well-being, she was also conscious of a whole jumble of mixed emotions, of which the principal was apprehension. Of what? Elsa was undoubtedly a formidable female. But so had been Frau Gehrig, and Anna had survived her. And Elsa, like Frau Gehrig, although clearly of some importance in the SD, had shown no desire, to ill treat her either. That seemed too good to be true.

But she remained at Elsa's mercy, or the mercy of Glauber – and, of course, Glauber's superiors. Who were not, as Elsa had reminded her, doing this with her welfare in mind. One day they would demand a return on their money. And they represented a regime she both loathed and feared, a regime which held her parents' and her sister's lives in their hands. And they had taken away even the solace of her faith, left her drifting soullessly through emptiness. She almost burst into tears. Then she remembered a word she had actually learned from Gerda, even if she had no very clear idea what it meant. Bugger them. She would survive. As long as she did that, her family would survive too. And one day...

'I am Captain Blassermann,' the officer announced.

Anna had been seated in the lounge, reading. For all her apprehensions it had been an almost pleasant month. Being fitted for more new clothes than she had ever had in her life had been a treat. Learning to perform various dances, to eat expensive food and to drink expensive alcohol had been even more so. Her morning rides in the park had been totally enjoyable, and her daily work-outs in the gymnasium had been invigorating; she had never felt healthier. It had been irritating to be forced to speak with a high-German accent, but even that had been stimulating. Even Elsa had proved surprisingly congenial company; Anna had taken great care never to oppose her in any way, but to do everything she was told, immediately. That kept the big woman happy. Anna had no doubt that, if to her great relief Elsa had shown no sexual interest in her, she was entirely capable of carrying out the threat she had made on her first day – and would enjoy doing it. But she was a most conscientious member of both the Nazi Party and the Secret Service – to which, Anna often reflected with some surprise, she herself also now belonged – and to her, duty, the successful completion of the task in hand, was paramount. And right now, the task in hand was turning her into what the Reich required.

The pursuit of this single aim apparently dominated Elsa's every waking hour – and perhaps her dreams as well. She indulged in no social activities, and did not appear to have any friends or even relatives, at least with whom she wished to keep in touch. There was a telephone in the apartment, but it never rang or was used to call out. And all the time Elsa was there, watching her, admonishing her, sometimes – but not too often – encouraging her, above all, dictating every moment of every day.

This meant that she also had to be totally dedicated to becoming whatever the Reich

58

wanted of her. Her problem was that she did not know what they wanted. But suddenly the flutter in her stomach, the tightening in her mind, indicated that she might be about to find out.

She closed the book willingly enough – all the Nazi propaganda she was forced to absorb every day was boring in the extreme – and stood up, looking to Elsa for an explanation.

'You are to go with the captain, Anna,' Elsa said.

Anna looked at the captain. She did not really like the look of him, but perhaps that was because he was in uniform; she had an innate dislike of men in uniform. But then, she also spent most of each day in uniform, as required by Elsa. If hers did not consist of tunic and breeches and jack boots, the regulation 'school' uniform, her hair in a tight bun on the nape of her neck, was far less glamorous. For the rest he was not unattractive, no taller than herself, and slightly built, with crisp yellow hair and equally Aryan features, boldly handsome. Now he clicked his heels and gave a brief bow.

'If you are ready, Fraulein.'

'You will remember what I have told you, Herr Captain,' Elsa said.

'How could I forget?'

'Will I be coming back here?' Anna asked.

'This is your home. You will be back...' Elsa looked at the captain.

'That depends upon how quickly she completes the course to our satisfaction, Fraulein. If she proves to be an apt pupil ... a week.'

'She is an apt pupil,' Elsa assured him.

'Then there should be no problem.'

'A week?' Anna cried. 'But...'

'I have packed a bag for you.' Elsa held up the valise.

Once again she was on the back seat of a Mercedes saloon, beside an officer and behind a uniformed chauffeur.

'I don't suppose it will do me any good to ask what is going to happen to me now?' Anna ventured.

'As I said, Fraulein, you are about to complete your training.'

'I thought my training was just about complete.'

He smiled. 'Your training to be a woman of class and breeding, and perhaps some sophistication, yes. But you will soon be leaving the world of women, and moving into the world of men. This world will welcome you, because of your beauty and that apparent breeding and sophistication, but it can be a lonely and brutal place. The Reich will protect you whenever possible, but there will be times when you will have to be on your own, outside our orbit, as it were. Then you will have to depend on yourself alone, your skill, your courage, and your determination. And your understanding of the people – that is, the men – with whom you will be dealing.'

'You make it sound as if you are going to train me to fight for my life,' Anna said, determined to keep it light for as long as possible.

'Yes, Fraulein,' he said. 'That is exactly what we are going to do.'

Their destination was only a few miles outside the city, and they were there in a few minutes, much to Anna's relief. She had spent the second half of the drive trying to come to terms with what he had said. Certainly she had not felt like asking any more questions, nor had Blassermann volunteered any more information; he obviously understood that he had already shocked her.

But now they were entering a military camp, and this was definitely a world of men. There were male guards on the gates, male squads marching to and fro on the central parade grounds, a group of men obviously just returning from a route march, sweat-stained and exhausted. Blassermann suddenly squeezed her hand.

'They are not going to eat you, Fraulein. Even if they may wish to.'

Anna withdrew her hand and the car stopped outside what appeared to be one of the barracks. Blassermann held the door for her and she got out, went up the short flight of steps into an office. He followed, carrying her valise. Two men sat at desks; both stood to attention as the captain entered. Neither could stop their eyes straying to the woman.

'At ease,' Blassermann said. 'You have accommodation for the Fraulein?'

'She will have to be in a barrack, Herr Captain,' the sergeant said. 'We are very crowded.'

'What?' Anna inquired.

The sergeant smiled. 'You will share with the other woman, Fraulein.'

'What other woman?'

'She is in there now. I will take you.'

Anna looked at Blassermann; suddenly he had become her dearest friend.

'I'm sure you will get on very well. Now, you will attend luncheon at twelve sharp. Your course begins this afternoon. I will see you then.' He clicked his heels and left the office.

The sergeant was waiting. He had made no attempt to pick up her bag, so Anna lifted it and followed him along the corridor. She had her usual sensation of not being quite sure her feet were on the ground, of being uncertain when she would come down with a thump. Then the sergeant stopped walking and indicated a door.

'This is your barracks.'

'You said there was only one other woman here.'

'Don't you like company, Fraulein? It is still a barracks.'

Anna swallowed and opened the door, stepped inside, her valise held before herself like a shield, and gazed at the girl seated on one of the several beds arranged along the wall. Beside each bed there was a locker, and at the far end, to her great relief, the door to a toilet and shower area was open; at least there was some privacy. On the other hand, the windows were set high up in the wall and were barred.

'Anna?' asked the girl, getting up.

'Karen?' Her heartbeat quickened, and then slowed again. She and Karen had never been the least bit close, and if Karen had not taken part in the attempted rape, as was to be expected in view of her record, neither had she made any attempt to help her.

But now she was advancing for an embrace. 'Am I glad to see you! I've been scared stiff.'

Anna gave her a perfunctory hug and then released her. 'How long have you been here?'

'About an hour.'

That was disappointing; Anna had hoped for some information on what might be going to happen to her. 'Which bed is mine?'

'Help yourself. I think it's all ours.'

Anna chose the bed exactly in the centre of the row and looked around her. She would unpack later. She gestured at the bars. 'Looks like they mean to keep us in.'

Karen giggled. 'I think they're meant to keep others out. Or even to stop them looking in.'

'There's a point. So ... are any of the other girls here?'

'I don't think so. They took me out of there only three days after you left. There was the most tremendous fuss. I think poor Hilda was sacked. Certainly she was sent somewhere else.'

'And what happened to the other girls?'

'They were all whipped. One after the other.

They were lined up, made to undress, tied to the table and given twelve strokes each. Oh, how they squealed. It was terrible.' But her eyes were glowing as she spoke.

'But you were not caned?' Anna suggested.

'Well...' Karen flushed. 'I had suffered before. You knew that.'

'Yes,' Anna agreed. 'Do they hate me?'

'Oh, yes. You know, one is supposed to fit in, be part of, well, whatever goes on. Not turn the whole place upside down.'

'Did they ever have a go at you?'

'Oh, yes. It's not half as bad as you thought it was going to be. I found it rather fun.'

'That's fine by me. Just remember that I don't think it's fun, and we'll get along very well.'

'And if I don't, you'll break my arm, is that it?'

'I think we're here to learn to break bigger things than arms. Do you have any idea what time it is?'

But at that moment a bell jangled.

They ate in the central mess hall, in the midst of some hundred men. But they sat at a table to themselves, and although everyone stared at them and some attempted eye contact, the room was overseen by a posse of NCOs, and the only conversation was permitted in low mutters.

'They're all dreaming of getting their hands on us,' Karen whispered.

'Is that all you ever think about?'

'What else is there to think about? And it's

going to happen one day, you know. Even to you.'

Anna couldn't think of a reply to that, because she suspected Karen was right, and perhaps sooner than later. They finished their meal, but there was no indication that they, or anyone else, should leave the tables, until the bell rang. As it stopped, all the men stood up. Karen and Anna did also, but a sergeant spoke through the loudspeaker.

'Ladies will remain seated.'

They sat down again. 'I don't think they mean to let us get too close to those chaps,' Karen grumbled.

Which was a relief, but as the soldiers filed from the room an inner door opened and Captain Blassermann came in. Hastily they stood up again, 'Did you enjoy your meal?' he inquired.

'Yes,' they chorused. Actually, the food was surprisingly good.

'Excellent. Now, you will commence work. Do not worry; there will be nothing physical until you have had time to digest. Come along, now.'

Just as if we were children, Anna thought. But perhaps to him they were. They followed him through the private door, along a corridor past the kitchens, out into the bright summer sunlight, and across a quadrangle to another building, again attracting glances from the various men they passed. Karen couldn't resist smiling at them, and this was observed by Blassermann.

'I think you should understand,' he said, 'that as long as you are in this camp you are subject to military discipline. Sexual activity, at any level, is strictly forbidden, and will equally be strictly punished.'

Karen gulped.

Blassermann led them into the building, which consisted of a single room, something like a schoolroom, with a blackboard on one wall behind a desk, in front of which were several individual chairs and tables. But on the other side it resembled a gymnasium, with parallel bars, a trapeze ring, some weights, and a large, thick mat on the floor. Seated behind the desk was a heavy-set bald man, who, to Anna's surprise, was not in uniform. At the rear of the school half of the room sat another man, this one very young, and wearing what appeared to be a dressing gown.

'Sit down, Frauleins,' the man behind the desk invited, and they did so, in the front row as indicated. 'I am Dr Cleiner. It is my business to complete your education in the task you are about to undertake. So listen to me very carefully, and do everything I tell you to do immediately and to the best of your ability. You will only leave this camp in one of three ways. One is in a van to be taken to prison, where you will spend the rest of your life; you will be sent there if there is any disobedience or insubordination. The second is to go to an SS brothel, where you will spend the rest of your lives, servicing perhaps a dozen men a day, until there is no more use for you.'

I cannot possibly be hearing this, Anna thought. I have got to be having a nightmare. She glanced at Karen, who was staring at the doctor, face rigid.

'That will be because you have failed the course,' Cleiner explained. 'The third way will be as a member of the SD, with a glorious career ahead of you in the service of the Reich. As of now, I am the sole judge as to which of those it will be.'

He stared at them for several seconds, and they stared back.

'Very good,' he said. 'Now, up to this moment you have been trained to be well-bred, sophisticated, extremely attractive women. Your business is therefore to attract ... men. But I am told I may assume that neither of you knows a great deal about your objectives. I should hope not, such innocent young girls as yourselves. Our first business is to introduce you to your ... adversaries. Johann.'

The young man rose and came to stand in front of the desk, while Anna bit her lip.

'This disturbs you, Anna?' Cleiner asked.

Anna caught her breath. 'No, Herr Doctor. It is just that my father's name is Johann.'

'Well, then, you should find it easy to remember. Johann.'

Johann shrugged the dressing gown from his shoulders and let it fall to the floor; he wore nothing else. Now both girls caught their breaths, and Anna could feel a rush of blood to her cheeks. She dared not look at Karen. Johann was a perfectly proportioned young man, and even as she watched, his penis was starting to become erect.

'I am afraid that not all, and possibly only a few, of the men you will encounter in the course of your duties will be as handsome as Johann,' Cleiner warned. 'However, they will all have the same basic attributes, and they will all believe themselves to be handsome, or at least, sexually attractive. Your first duty, in each instance, will be to confirm that belief. Your task will be to make your subject enjoy your company, relax in it, and talk to you. The more attracted he is to you, and the more you can persuade him to drink, the more likely he is to be indiscreet. Indiscretions are what you are seeking. How much you yourself drink is up to you, but you must never become drunk.

'But far more important than drink, a man finding himself alone with you will seek some sexual contact. Let me say right away that you will not find yourself alone with any man unless he has been selected or at least approved by your controller. However, the situation will arise often enough. Now there are four levels of sexual relationships. The first will be the conversation and drinking I have mentioned, and will probably be followed by mutual fumbling and kissing. You may permit tongue kissing.'

Anna swallowed.

'I may say that this low-level activity is often

very productive,' Cleiner said, 'and is quite permissible without authority, if you feel it may accomplish anything. A good deal of heavy breathing is a useful asset in these circumstances. At the other end of the scale, the fourth level, there is sexual intercourse – that is, actual penetration. This is absolutely forbidden under any circumstances, unless it is expressly commanded by your controller. I am informed that you are both virgins. Stay that way, or risk severe punishment.'

Predictably, Karen raised her hand.

'You have a question, Karen?'

'If I may, Herr Doctor. Would not actually ... ah...'

'Fucking?'

She flushed. 'Fucking, lead to even more indiscretion on his part?'

'Our scientists have determined not, for several reasons. Firstly, men do not talk about anything except sex when they are having sex, if they speak at all. Secondly, a woman is not receptive to receiving information while performing sexual acts. Thirdly, she may even, inadvertently, come to a climax. I am sure that, for all your apparent innocence, you have both from time to time masturbated yourselves to orgasm. Then you will know that in the throes of that passion you are no longer in control of yourself, and are therefore at risk of being controlled by any partner who may be present. The fourth point is the most important of all. As a general rule, men who have climaxed immediately lose interest in sex, and their partners, for some considerable time; this applies especially to older men, who will be your more usual companions. What is more, regrettably, their interest does not return in circumstances we may describe as casual encounters. The man has a goal; he achieves it, and then, as he will undoubtedly have a wife and family waiting for him in Paris or London or wherever he will be returning to, he is heartily ashamed of himself, and does not wish to see his erstwhile partner again. There are exceptions to this rule, but not enough to make it worthwhile. So all of your spadework will have been a waste of time, and if you were to become pregnant, well, your career would be over, and you know what that would mean.' He smiled at them. 'Why are you looking so glum, Anna?'

Anna started; she had drifted off into a day-dream as she gazed at Johann. She licked her lips. 'It all seems so cold-blooded, Herr Doctor. Suppose we ... well, form a genuine attachment to the man?'

'That would be a grave, and possibly fatal error. You are being employed to be cold-blooded. Any sign of, shall I say, immature romantic notions will be severely punished. Now,' he said brightly. 'Let us move on to the two other stages of sexual relations. The first is where the man wishes you to fondle him. This is the easiest part of your task, and may even be the most enjoyable. The second is when he seeks to fondle you. This may require more careful ...

handling.' Another bright smile. 'But this is what we are going to teach you.'

'Wow!' Karen threw herself on to her bed. 'That was something.' She raised herself on her elbow. 'Didn't it have any effect on you at all?'

Anna sat on her bed. Any effect at all! She felt ... but she didn't know what she felt, save that she would never be able to look at a man again without blushing. 'No,' she said. 'I thought it was disgusting.'

'Well, it's something you're going to have to get used to. I thought it was heavenly. Didn't it feel like velvet? And when he came...' She gave a heavy sigh. 'And tomorrow they're going to start on us. I can hardly wait. In fact, I can't wait. So if you're really not interested, do you mind ignoring me for the next five minutes? If I don't do something right this minute I'm going to start eating the sheets.'

Anna took off her tie and released the top button of her shirt, then kicked off her shoes and lay down on her side facing away from her companion, and put the pillow over her ears. She felt like eating the sheets herself, but was that sexual frustration? Rather it was despair at the increasing sense of loneliness, of utter isolation in a world full of people. That had nothing to do with her not being German. It was simply that they all seemed to be living in an amoral, hedonistic society totally alien to anything she had been brought up to believe in. The most upsetting thing was that she knew she was

71

going to join them, whether she liked it or not. The pressures being brought to bear, both emotionally and physically, were simply too severe for her to resist for very long. She had already joined them, without wishing to, simply by obeying Cleiner that afternoon.

But soon enough she would wish to. It might be possible to convince Karen that she hated what she had been forced to do. But she could not so deceive herself. She felt as if she were hanging from a precipice, dangling above a huge foetid swamp in which she would not drown, but from which she would not be able to escape, and instead spend the rest of her life wallowing in its filth. She desperately wanted to regain the clean land and air above her, but her fingers were slipping, making it increasingly difficult to hold on, and all the while a voice at the back of her brain was whispering, Why not let go, plunge into the mire, and wallow contentedly with the rest?

From the heavy sighs that penetrated even the pillow, she gathered Karen had achieved at least temporary relief. For the first time in her life she wished she could be like Karen, to have not a care in the world save sensual gratification. But no doubt she was going to wind up just like her. And that was the most terrifying thought of all.

'Now, ladies,' Dr Cleiner said jovially, 'you have enjoyed the past three days, eh?' He looked from face to face, and made his own interpretation of what he saw there, while Anna kept her expression stiff with an effort. To have to fondle a man, to be forced to take his member into her mouth had been bad enough, but to permit a man to fondle her to his heart's content, and in front of this man and Blassermann ... She still felt that she had been turned inside out.

'That is good. But sadly, life is not all pleasure, eh? Now, I have watched you in the gymnasium every morning, and it is obvious that you are very fit. This is good. But fitness is not merely for beauty, eh? It is for use. Now we must see what use yours will give us. I understand that you were given some training in unarmed combat at your school. I also understand that one of you used this training to badly hurt one of your fellow students.' He knew who it was, of course, and looked directly at Anna.

She drew a deep breath. 'It was me, Herr Doctor.'

'Tell me why you did this.'

'We ... we quarrelled.'

'And you attacked her and used your new skill to break her arm in two places, and dislocate her shoulder?'

Anna opened her mouth. She was back at her precipice, but this time the ground beneath her was hard, not soft.

Karen came to her rescue. 'That is not so, Herr Doctor. Gerda attacked Anna, and Anna defended herself, very skilfully.'

'I did not mean to hurt her like that,' Anna

73

said. 'It was an accident. I threw her and she broke her arm.'

'Well, anyone can see that,' Cleiner agreed. 'One does not break someone's arm and dislocate their shoulder intentionally, without a great deal of strength and effort. Still, it indicates that you can react violently when you have to. This is good. But what you have so far learned, while it is useful for self defence in an ordinary way, will be of no use to you if you ever really have to hurt a man.'

Both girls stiffened. 'Are we going to have to do that, Herr Doctor?' Karen asked.

'You never know, and you must be prepared for any eventuality. Now, change your clothes.'

They obeyed without hesitation; after the past three days, appearing naked before this man had become commonplace. He watched them put on their singlets and shorts and then pressed the bell on his desk. Immediately the door opened and two soldiers came in, pushing between them a third man, who was in shirt and pants instead of uniform, and was handcuffed behind his back. He was quite a big man, not very tall but solidly built, and was not very prepossessing, having an unshaven chin and a general air of scruffiness. But his eyes gleamed as he saw the two scantily clad young women.

'He likes you,' Cleiner remarked. 'Well, who would not?' He gave a brief nod, and the two soldiers stepped away. They did not leave the room, however, but stood against the far wall. Anna deduced that they also were enjoying the view.

'Now,' Cleiner said. 'We are assuming that you are not armed. If you were armed, you would use your weapon. We will discuss that tomorrow, as we will discuss your actions if he were to be armed. But today, unarmed. We are assuming also that he is attacking you. Of course for the purposes of this demonstration he cannot as his hands are secured, but we do not want him to take advantage of any mistakes you may make and hurt you. Heaven forbid. Besides, it is possible that you may wish to assault him before he realizes your intention. Now, you may suppose that the quickest way to incapacitate a male opponent is to go for the genitals. This is a sound idea, but not a decisive one, for two reasons. If the man is fully dressed, as here, it may be difficult to locate exactly what you want. And then, while you may hurt him, you will not lay him out or prevent his getting hold of you, and that could be fatal – a man who has been hurt in the balls is liable to become very violent. What you must seek are pressure points. They are scattered all over the body – here, for instance, and here, and here.' He walked round the man, who did not seem to understand what was going on, touching him as he spoke. 'A blow delivered in any of these places will render him incapable of responding, at least for a brief while, sometimes longer.' Another smile. 'Then you may turn your attention to his prick, eh? But there is one thing you must bear in mind. Such a blow, in such a place as I will recommend, must be delivered with all the strength you possess, and it must be delivered accurately. When you are defending your life, there can be no room for compromise. Now, Karen, you go first. Hit him here.' He touched the man's back. 'Underneath here is a kidney. A blow here will paralyse him for several seconds. Take a long swing, and use the edge of your hand. You will receive a severe jar, but it will be nothing to what he will receive. Of course, when it comes to the real thing, you may not have the time or the space for a swing; it will be our business to teach you how to inflict a blow of equal power with a short, concentrated delivery. Come along now, Karen.'

Reluctantly, Karen moved behind the man. 'Won't it hurt him, Herr Doctor?'

'Well, of course it will hurt him, you silly girl. It is intended to hurt him.'

'But won't he object?'

'It does not matter whether he objects or not. He is a condemned criminal. I have given you an order, Karen.'

Karen gave Anna a quick look, drew a deep breath, and swung her arm, crashing the edge of her hand into the man's back. He gave a scream of agony and fell to his knees, while Karen leapt back, clutching her arm with her other hand.

'There,' Cleiner said. 'You see what you can do? But watch.'

Anna stared at the man, who was bent double, straining against the handcuffs to be able to reach the injury, and unable to do so. Saliva dribbled from his mouth, while he continued to moan and gasp. But in a few minutes the moaning stopped, and he seemed to pull himself together.

Cleiner had been looking at his watch. 'You see? Four minutes. Of course in that time you would be able to do him a great deal more damage. But still, if you do not finish the job he will recover from such a blow. Now we shall look at something more permanent.'

Oh, my God! Anna thought. She was next.

'Up,' Cleiner commanded, and kicked the prisoner in the thigh. The man grunted, but did not move. Cleiner snapped his fingers, and the two soldiers came forward, held the prisoner's arms, and lifted him to his feet. 'Stay on your feet,' Cleiner warned him, 'or I will have this lovely child cut off your balls.'

The man raised his head, and Anna swallowed as their eyes met.

'Now, as I have told you,' Cleiner said, 'the blow to the kidney is a temporary measure. The blow to the shoulder is decisive. It must be accurate.' He touched the man's shoulder where it joined the neck. 'Right there. Delivered with sufficient power it will cut off the flow of blood to the brain. This will render him unconscious. For how long depends on the force of the blow – that is, for how long it takes for the blood to start flowing again. A sufficiently powerful blow will kill. I am not sure that you have sufficient strength at this time to deliver such a blow, Anna; we will work on this. But I am sure you can lay him out. Let me see you do that.'

Anna licked her lips and then moved behind the prisoner; he was at least an inch the shorter. She glanced at Karen, who was still massaging her arm, but was staring at her.

Cleiner touched the prisoner's neck again. 'Remember, it must be right there.'

Anna drew a deep breath and swung her arm. This time the man went down without a sound, hitting the floor with his knees before falling full length; his head struck with a terrible crack and blood dribbled from his mouth.

'He's dead!' Anna screamed, tears welling from her eyes, as she quite forgot the pain in her own arm and shoulder.

Cleiner took his pulse. 'No, no. But he will not be active for a while. That was an excellent blow, Anna. I congratulate you. How is your arm?'

'It hurts,' Anna muttered, staring at the unconscious man. Did I really do that? She wondered.

Cleiner nodded. 'We are going to have to toughen you up. Do you know that is one of the most difficult tasks we have, making a girl like you powerful enough to take on anyone, and yet not develop any unsightly muscles in your arms. But we will do it. Thank you, ladies. That will be all for today. Tomorrow we will start on weapons.'

Karen lay on her bed with her hands beneath her head. 'How do you feel?' she asked.

Anna sat with her elbows on her knees. 'Odd. I still can't believe I did that.'

'But how did it feel?'

'It hurt.'

'I mean, in your head. In your heart.'

Anna glanced at her. 'I don't want to think about it.'

'It made me feel sick,' Karen confessed. 'Didn't you feel sick?'

Anna stared at her. No, she thought; I didn't feel sick. I was concentrating too hard on delivering the blow with all my strength and in the right place. With pleasing Cleiner. But I still should have felt sick, at hitting a defenceless man hard enough to lay him out.

Karen was frowning at her. 'Then what did you feel?'

Anna licked her lips. 'It was something I had to do.'

'Because Cleiner told you to?'

'Yes. We have to obey him, don't you see? We're entirely in his power.'

'And suppose he'd told you, while that man was lying unconscious on the floor, to ... to gouge out his eyes. Would you have done that?'

'Oh, for heaven's sake,' Anna snapped. 'Why must you always think of such horrible things? Cleiner is teaching us to be young ladies who can defend ourselves if any of the men we're going to date try to come on too heavy. That's all. Gouging out eyes! Yuk.'

'This,' Dr Cleiner said, 'is a Walther personal

pistol. You'll see...' He held up the little auto-matic. 'It is very small. It fits into the palm of my hand, just about. It is sometimes called the ladies' pistol, because it is so light and small, and thus can be carried in a Frau's ordinary evening handbag and because it is so easy to fire. The trigger pressure is very light and there is virtually no recoil; also it makes very little noise.' He removed the magazine and gave the pistol to Karen. 'Doesn't that feel good?'

Karen took the gun, slid her hands round it, grasped the butt, curled her finger round the trigger, and pointed it at Blassermann, who was, as usual, sitting to one side of the room. 'Bang!' she said, as the trigger clicked.

'I can see you are a natural,' Cleiner remark-ed. 'Anna.'

Karen held out the gun, reluctantly, and Anna took it, cautiously. She had never held a gun before in her life. To her surprise, she did find it both comfortable and exciting.

Cleiner was as always watching her closely. 'You must get to like it, Anna. Not only will it be a part of your equipment, as it were, but it may one day save your life far more efficiently than any unarmed skill can do. Now...' He held up the magazine and extracted a little cartridge from it. 'It is a small gun, so it fires small bullets. This is a six millimetre. Don't get any wrong ideas; this will kill, if you hit your target in the right place. But as I say, this is a small weapon, and does not have the velocity of a rifle or even a high-calibre pistol. Even if you are an expert shot, you won't do much damage at anything above fifty metres. Twenty-five metres, now, that is a different matter. And twenty-five metres is about three times the width of this room, so there is no need to get right up against your adversary. So let's see what you can do.'

He led the way outside, followed as usual by Blassermann, past several interested squads of soldiers, and to one of the ranges that dotted the camp. This was small, no more than fifty metres long, and was entirely surrounded by head-high sandbags, which effectively shut it off from the rest of the camp, although it had four entrances, one at each corner. A target had already been set up, and beside it waited a soldier. Another waited at the top right-hand corner, behind the target.

'Now,' Cleiner said. 'We will start with single shots. Karen, put the bullet through that bull's eye. Remember, line up the sights, and then squeeze the trigger. Do not pull it, or the gun will move and you will miss. You must close the whole hand in one movement. I would stand aside, soldier.'

The soldier hastily moved well away from the target. Karen took the gun and levelled it, her tongue escaping between her teeth. The noise really was quite muted, and the soldier moved forward to examine the cardboard, and indicate where the bullet had struck. It had actually just nicked the cardboard, perhaps ten centimetres from the bull's eye.

'Excellent,' Cleiner said. 'You have a good eye. Now, Anna.'

Anna took the gun, lined it up, took several deep breaths, and squeezed the trigger. Again the soldier stepped forward to indicate the result.

'But that is brilliant,' Cleiner said. 'You have just nicked the black. Do you not think that is brilliant, Captain?'

'Indeed, Herr Doctor,' Blassermann said. 'I think we may proceed without any further delay. I would like Anna, at any rate, back in Berlin tomorrow.'

'Very good. Well then, ladies, you heard the captain. This is to be a concentrated course. Now, you have both revealed that you have a steady hand and a good eye. But you have been firing at a stationary target. This is very un-likely to be the situation if you ever have to shoot in earnest. In reality, a single shot will very seldom hit, or in any event, hit in any vital or even crippling place, and you need to remember that your target will very likely be shooting back at you. Thus there are two rules you must always follow. When you shoot at a man, or a woman for that matter, you shoot to kill. No foolishness about trying to scare them by just missing, or about trying to bring them down by aiming at their legs. My business is to teach you how to survive, not how to get your-self killed. So you aim at the head or the torso. And you keep on shooting until he – or she – is dead, even if that means emptying your entire magazine. More agents get themselves killed by bringing down an enemy with a single shot and then advancing to inspect their handiwork, than in any other way. If you wish to stay alive, you keep firing until there is no possibility of him, or her, still being alive.'

He paused for breath, and the two girls looked at each other. Then Karen asked, 'You used the word "agents", Herr Doctor. Are we to be agents?'

For the first time Cleiner looked embarrassed, and glanced at Blassermann for assistance. 'Certainly, you are agents,' the captain said, smoothly. 'Anyone who works for the Reich, in whatever capacity, is an agent of the Reich. You may proceed, Herr Doctor.'

'Now we wish to see how you will handle the more realistic situation.' Cleiner pointed at the top right-hand break in the sandbags. 'Come.' He led them forward to stand beside the original target. 'You are now twenty-five metres from those sandbags. Your target is going to emerge through that top right-hand opening, and run as quickly as he can across to the left-hand exit. The distance is about forty metres. As he is not an athlete, this should take him between six and ten seconds. That is ample time for you to fire all five shots in your magazine. Of course, if you manage to hit him with your first shot, that will slow him up and you should find it easy to finish the job, but I would like to think that at least one of your shots will strike home. Karen?' He fitted a fresh magazine into the Walther.

Karen was staring at him as if she were a rabbit and he a king cobra, a fairly apt simile, Anna thought. Now she said, her voice trembling, 'Excuse me, Herr Doctor, did you say "he"?'

'It is a man, yes. As I have said, your targets are most likely to be men.'

Karen licked her lips. 'You wish me to shoot at a man? A living man?'

'My dear girl, there would be little point in requiring you to shoot at a dead man. For one thing, he would be unable to move, eh? Much less run. Ha, ha. Now then.'

He held out the gun and Karen slowly took it. 'This man...?'

'Do not worry about him. He is another condemned criminal. He is due to be hanged. To be killed by a bullet is an infinitely preferable fate. But we have promised him that if he can survive, his sentence will be commuted to life imprisonment. So he will be trying his hardest. Now, are you ready?'

Karen stared at him, then looked at Anna, and then hastily looked away again.

'Very good,' Cleiner said. 'Stand by,' he called to the waiting soldier, who was obviously only one of several just beyond the opening. 'Go!'

The soldier stepped aside, and a man was pushed into the arena. Like the man who had been used as a guinea pig for their unarmed combat, he wore a shirt and pants and nothing

84

else, and was shivering with apprehension. He cast a hasty glance around him, getting his bearings, and then began to run, not very fast and continually tripping.

'Come along,' Cleiner commanded.

Karen raised the gun, and then lowered it again. 'I can't,' she gasped. 'I can't just kill a man.'

'Fraulein,' Cleiner said. 'I have given you an order, and I have explained to you what disobeying an order will involve.'

Tears began to dribble down Karen's cheeks. 'You can't order me to kill a man, Herr Doctor. You can't.'

'Listen to me very carefully, Karen. I am a soft-hearted man, and therefore I am going to give you another chance. I am also going to repeat that if you fail to carry out any order given you by a superior in the SD, then you are of no more use to us, or to anyone. Do you understand this?'

Karen's head bobbed up and down.

'That's a good girl. Again,' he called.

There was a brief hesitation, then the prisoner reappeared. Now he knew the set-up, and immediately began running as hard as he could. Karen raised the pistol and fired again and again and again. Sand spurted from punctured bags, and the man reached the other entrance and disappeared. 'Oh, gosh!' Karen said, lowering the empty gun.

The brief echoes of the reports died away, and for a moment there was silence. 'I think I need more practise,' Karen said.

'Do you take us for fools?' Cleiner inquired.

'I missed,' Karen insisted. 'I'll do better next time.'

'There is not going to be a next time,' Cleiner said. 'You have deliberately disobeyed my command. Well, you were warned. Take her out of here,' he said. 'Strip her naked, tie her to the triangle, and give her twenty lashes. Make sure they are on the buttocks. Then, while she is still hanging there, let a dozen of your men have her, one after the other. Then send her back to Berlin. They will know what to do with her there.'

All the blood had drained from Karen's face. 'No,' she whispered. 'No! No!' she begged, as two of the soldiers grasped her arms. 'No!' she screamed. 'You can't! Give me another chance! One more chance. I'll kill him. I swear I'll kill him!'

'You had your second chance,' Cleiner said. 'Get her out of here.'

'No!' Karen screamed, as she was half marched, half dragged to the rear entrance. 'Please! Help me! Somebody help me! Anna!'

'And shut her up,' Cleiner called.

Karen gasped as one of her escorts hit her in the stomach and took away her breath.

'Well, Anna,' Cleiner said. 'It is your turn, or are you going to defy me as well?'

Anna stared at him. She felt as if she were not really present, but was hovering above the camp, watching, but not understanding. Yet she understood clearly enough. She knew she would die if she were to be publicly flogged and then sent to a brothel. And if that happened, her parents and her sister would also die, perhaps more quickly, but probably even more excruciatingly. The choice was a simple one. Live, at the expense of another life, and perhaps prosper, or...

Cleiner had loaded the pistol, and now he held it out.

Three

The Temptress

'My word,' Ballantine said. 'Have you ever seen a more gorgeous creature?'

Clive Bartley turned his head, trying to focus in the glare given off by the huge chandeliers, only slightly alleviated by the flags draped around the chamber, themselves garish in their red, white, and black, or by the splendid uniforms with which the two Englishmen were surrounded, not to mention the bare shoulders and glittering jewellery of the women. Up to this moment he had found the whole thing inexpressibly vulgar. But ... 'Yes, sir,' he agreed with his superior. 'Worth a second look.'

Or a third, or a fourth, or even a hundredth, he

decided. The young woman, he didn't think she was more than a girl, had just entered the ballroom on the arm of a man wearing the black uniform of the SS. He was a handsome enough fellow, and his uniform was immaculate, but he was utterly insignificant beside his companion. The girl was tall, matching her escort for height, and moved with an almost regal grace. Her face was utterly beautiful, at once in its look of serene confidence as in the perfectly chiselled, slightly aquiline features, the wide mouth, the firm but not obtrusive chin. At this distance he could not see her eyes, but he had no doubt they were either blue or green. She wore a pale-blue off-the-shoulder sheath evening gown, which clung to her body like a second skin, indicating her long legs, delineating her slim hips, and suggesting that the two thin straps over her shoulders were utterly unnecessary, at least for holding the dress up. A diamond-encrusted pendant was suspended on a gold chain, nestling into her décolletage, and she had a pair of matching pendant earrings. But her crowning glory was her hair, which in total contrast to the bobbed curls so prevalent in Britain, was worn long, and lay in straight golden magnificence below her shoulder blades.

'I have got to meet her,' Ballantine declared.

'Ah ... she appears to have an escort, sir.'

'Is that important? Didn't that fellow Hammerbach say that I could have anything I wanted while I am in Berlin? Well, I want her. I mean,' he corrected himself, 'I want to meet her.'

Clive sighed. Having got to know his charge during the several times he had been required to act as his escort, he suspected that the slip was nearer the truth. 'I merely meant to point out, sir, that the gentleman with her is a member of the SS. That would seem to indicate that her political point of view may be different from yours.'

'Oh, really, Clive, you Secret Service wallahs are all alike, seeing sedition under every bush. My dear fellow, half the women I take out in London are dedicated Socialists, or at least determined to oppose the Government wherever possible. They grow out of it. In any event, can you really suppose that such a beautiful, and clearly innocent, young girl could be the slightest bit interested in politics? Now, this is an order. I wish to meet this young lady. Kindly arrange it. And while you are doing that, you can find out if she has any sort of permanent attachment, and if she speaks English.'

Clive could do nothing but suppress another sigh and say, 'As you wish, sir.'

He regarded the Honourable Ballantine Bordman as a pain in the neck, and he suspected there were quite a few people who considered him a pain in other places as well. He was not even very prepossessing, physically. Forty years old, he had thinning hair and a growing paunch, between which was a rather bland face. But, Clive suspected, principally because of his family connections, he was regarded as one of the Foreign Office's most promising diplomats, while he regarded himself as God's gift to the female sex, both reasons why he had to be protected when travelling in an official capacity. But to have to act as his pimp as well...

Colonel Hammerbach was actually standing quite close, apparently in conversation with two other German officers, but as his English was excellent, Clive had no doubt that he had been listening to what they had been saying. Now he inclined his head courteously as Clive stood beside him. He made a glittering figure in his pale-blue tunic, bespangled with gold braid, over his dark-blue trousers with their yellow stripe down each leg. Beside him, Clive, if taller and with a fuller figure, looked positively dowdy in his dinner jacket and black tie.

'Sorry to butt in,' Clive said, 'but my principal would like an introduction to the Fraulein who has just arrived. I assume that she is a Fraulein?'

'You mean the Countess von Widerstand?'

'Ah ... did you say Widerstand?'

'Yes. Do you know the family?'

'No. No, I don't think so. But ... countess? You mean that she is married.'

'No, no. She is the countess because she is the only child and sole heiress to Count von Widerstand. His wife is dead.'

'I see,' Clive said. 'And the young gentleman with whom she is presently dancing?'

'Her cousin. He usually escorts her to functions like this.'

'And do you think she would care to meet Mr Bordman?'

'I am sure of it. As soon as the music stops. Excuse me, Herr Bartley.'

Clive watched him move away and stand on the edge of the floor, alongside another uniformed officer, this one, like the countess's partner, wearing the black of the SS. The two men greeted each other and then conversed briefly. Clive rejoined Ballantine. 'She's on her way.'

'Oh, well done, Clive. Just watching her dance ... Look at the way that lout is holding her, pressing her against him. It makes the blood boil.'

'It doesn't seem to be bothering her. I believe he is supposed to be her cousin. However, I think there is something you should know, Mr Bordman.'

'Don't tell me she's married.'

'No, she's not married. She is, at least according to Hammerbach, an heiress, by name of von Widerstand.'

'An heiress! That sounds brilliant.'

'Yes, sir. However, the name...' He checked what he was going to say as the music stopped and Hammerbach approached, leading the countess by the hand; her partner had disappeared into the throng leaving the floor.

Breathing slightly heavily from her exertions, cheeks a little pink, the girl was more beautiful than ever. 'Countess, may I present the Honourable Ballantine Bordman.' Hammerbach spoke English. 'Mr Bordman is in the British Government. Mr Bordman, I would like you to meet Countess Anna von Widerstand.'

'It's the Foreign Office, actually,' Ballantine said, and bent over her hand. 'But this is a very great pleasure, Countess.'

'And for me, Mr Bordman,' Anna replied, also in English, actually allowing his lips to touch her white-gloved knuckles. Her voice was low and husky, and entirely in keeping with the rest of her. 'And this gentleman?'

'Mr Clive Bartley,' Hammerbach said, somewhat disparagingly. 'He is Mr Bordman's ... How do you say, Mr Bartley?'

'I am Mr Bordman's travelling private secretary,' Clive said, staring at her. She returned his gaze without expression except for a slight flicker of her eyes, and he realized that she would have preferred him to be the principal.

'Would you care to dance, Countess?' Ballantine asked as the music started again.

Anna glanced at Hammerbach. Or was it Hammerbach, Clive wondered, for the colonel continued to smile benevolently, his expression never changing. And behind him, a few feet further away, there stood the SS colonel. Clive was sure that he had given a slight nod. 'I shall be delighted, Mr Bordman,' she said.

'I should like a brandy,' Anna said, slumping into an armchair, kicking off her shoes, and stripping off her gloves.

'Of course,' Elsa said, pouring. 'Who was it tonight?'

Anna sipped, then bent over to inspect her feet. 'I may be crippled for life. He was an overweight, pompous and lecherous Englishman. He called himself an "honourable". What does that mean? I didn't see anything honourable about him.'

'It's an English title,' Elsa explained. 'It means he is the son of a lord.'

'You mean his father is a duke or something?'

'No, no. His father is a peer. That can be hereditary or it can be a reward for services to the country. If this man is the eldest son, he will be a lord himself, when his father dies.'

'Well,' Anna said. 'You'd think he'd be able to have his son taught how to dance. The only way he knew how to dance was on my toes, and his hands ... Shit! I thought he was going to tear my dress to get at my backside. And do you know, Elsa, that swine Glauber made no attempt to rescue me. He let that bastard monopolize me for the entire evening. Last week, when that Frenchman got amorous, we were immediately separated. Tonight I was left to stew in my own juice.'

'Well, then, he must be someone important. Did he say anything interesting?'

'Not really. Only, over and over again, that he is somebody big in the British Foreign Office.'

'And Prime Minister Chamberlain arrives next week for a meeting with the Fuehrer,' Elsa

93

said thoughtfully.

'Oh, yes. He told me that too, over and over again. He is here to make sure everything goes smoothly.' She gave a little sigh. 'Now, that secretary of his ... I thought I would be allowed one dance with him.'

'Handsome, was he?'

'Oh, yes, he was, in that peculiarly British fashion. But more importantly, he's young, and he's fit and, well...' She finished her brandy and stood up. 'I'm for bed. Oh, damn it!' The doorbell was ringing. 'I really don't want to see anyone else tonight, Elsa.'

'It may be important.' Elsa opened the door. 'Why, Herr Colonel! It is good to see you.'

'Good evening, Elsa.' Glauber looked at his watch. 'Or I suppose I should say, good morning. Anna, you looked exceptionally beautiful tonight. And you look exceptionally beautiful now, in a ruffled sort of way. I like that better. It is more, well, intimate. Come and sit down.' He sat himself on the settee, patted the space beside him.

Anna suppressed another sigh and joined him.

'Brandy, Herr Colonel?' Elsa inquired. 'Schnapps?'

'This is business,' Glauber said. 'You did very well tonight, Anna. That Englander was completely bewitched. That was obvious to everyone.'

'Yes, sir. He wants to see me again.'

'And so he shall. Yes, indeed.'

'Sir?'

'This is the most important moment of your life, Anna. This far, at any rate. All those other men were nonentities, trial runs. This is the business you were trained for, and the reason your training was rushed through in time for tonight. Bordman is a Principal Secretary at the Foreign Office, entrusted with making the final arrangements for Prime Minister Chamberlain's visit next week.'

'Yes, sir. He told me this.'

'Did he also tell you why the British prime minister is coming to Germany?'

'No, sir.'

'It is because of this Czech business. You know of that?'

'I know there is some trouble there.'

'Some trouble? There is a large minority in the north of the country, the Sudetenland, which is of German descent and heritage, carelessly awarded to this manufactured state by the Allies after the war, and the dissolution of the Austro-Hungarian Empire. We have watched the plight of our blood brothers ever since we came to power. Now their ill treatment by the Czechs has become intolerable. We have protested, and our protests have been ignored. It is incumbent upon a great nation to protect its people and not to submit to insults by inferior people. So we have retaliated by threatening to occupy the Sudetenland by force, and suddenly we find all Europe against us, calling us aggressors. However, these democracies, and even the Communists, find it very difficult to take such a big step as military action. They could have done so when the Fuehrer reinstated conscription, three years ago. But they rattled their sabres, and did nothing. They could have done so when the Reich reunited ourselves with Austria, this spring. But again, they rattled their sabres and did nothing.'

Oh, if only they had done something, Anna thought.

'This time it is more serious,' Glauber went on. 'Because Russia is involved. They are claiming that the Slavs are their blood brothers, and they will not see them crushed. Now, Czechoslovakia is saying that if we attempt to take over the Sudetenland they will fight. They are relying on the fact that they have a mutual defence treaty with France. Russia is saying that they will fight with the Czechs, if France also does. And the French are saying that they will fight with the Czechs, and thus the Russians, if Great Britain also comes in. You'll remember I told you at our first meeting that Britain was our ultimate enemy, simply because she is afraid of our growing strength. Now Chamberlain says he wishes to have another meeting with the Fuehrer, face to face, to resolve the crisis. It is not possible for us, at this time, to take on all those four powers together. We need a few more years to bring our armed forces up to the required strength to challenge all Europe. So, as I am sure you have already grasped, the key to the situation is Britain. The Czechs cannot fight us on their own. Russia says she will support them, if France will also. But France will only come in if with the backing of Britain. We have to know, before he arrives, if Chamberlain is coming with an ultimatum, or if he is coming to make peace. We have to know in what circumstances Britain will go to war.'

'And you think this Bordman will know this?'

'We think he must. Now, tomorrow evening you will have a soiree here.'

'Me? Here? But...'

'It is all arranged. The caterers will move in tomorrow morning, and the waiters and waitresses tomorrow afternoon.'

'But the guests...'

'Have all been notified. Save one. It is a small and intimate soiree, the sort of thing you are throwing all the time, eh? Now, you write to Bordman, inviting him to your party. Do it now.'

Anna went to the desk against the wall and sat down.

'Dear Mr Bordman,' Glauber dictated, standing above her. 'I so enjoyed this evening. I wished it never to end. I am therefore writing to invite you to visit me tomorrow at six. I am having a small party, just close friends, and I would so like to include you. Do not bother to reply, just come yourself and make me happy, all over again. Yours always, Anna von Widerstand.'

Anna finished the letter and signed it. 'Am I allowed to say "yuk"?'

'You can say anything you like, as long as you do not say it to him.'

'I mean, he may not be very bright, but this is pure treacle. Isn't he going to be suspicious?'

'Anna, let me tell you, a man whose greatest ambition is to get between the legs of a beautiful woman only believes what he wants to believe, principally that she feels the same way about him. This letter will convince him of that.'

I would need my head examined, Anna thought. But ... 'Did you say "get between my legs", sir?'

'I repeat, Anna, this could be a matter of life or death for the Reich. You are permitted – in fact, you are commanded – to give Bordman anything he desires, anything, to find out the intentions of the British Government. Do you understand me?'

Shit! She thought. If she had always known this moment had to come, she had always hoped, and even dreamed, that it might be someone handsome, or at least attractive ... like the secretary. She clutched at straws. 'Suppose he doesn't know anything to tell me?'

'I have already said, we believe he does. Anyway, you are required to try, to the limit of your ability. That is a direct order from Colonel Heydrich.'

'Yes, sir. What about the secretary? We have not invited him.'

'I do not think that is the least necessary. The fellow is clearly of lower class. I should think

98

Bordman will be happy to be rid of him for one evening.' He folded the letter into an envelope. 'Now, write on this, "The Honourable Ballantine Bordman, by hand". Very good. This will be delivered to his hotel first thing tomorrow morning. Now, tomorrow evening, you will be charming, but discreet, and discreetly invite Bordman to remain after the other guests have gone, to have what I think the English call a bite of supper. Then you will take it from there. You must invite him into your bedroom; our people will install a microphone and tape recorder in there. Have him spend the night, if necessary. But make him tell you what we want to know.' He squeezed her hands. 'I look forward to hearing of your adventure.'

Elsa closed the door behind him. 'Are you afraid?'

'I don't know.'

'You look afraid.'

Anna went into her bedroom. 'Will it hurt?'

Elsa followed her with the pills and a glass of water. 'Yes. How much it hurts will depend on whether he is gentle or vigorous. Or even brutal. Some men are brutal. But after the first, or perhaps the second time, it stops hurting.'

'You mean he may want to do it more than once?'

'With you? He will wish to do it all night, if he can. But listen, see if he will let you suck him early on. Most men like that. And he may run out of steam.'

Anna shuddered.

'Take your pill.'

Anna placed the tranquillizer on her tongue, gulped the water, made a face. 'How long do I have to go on with these things?'

'Until you stop having nightmares. You are still having nightmares?'

'I suppose so. But maybe tonight I've had enough to drink.'

'The pill is better,' Elsa said. 'Come along now.' She helped Anna out of her gown – she wore nothing underneath – and escorted her into the bathroom to have her make-up removed. 'Now, sleep well,' she recommended. 'Tomorrow night you may not sleep at all.'

Anna slid beneath the sheets and closed her eyes. As a rule, she had no problem controlling her waking thoughts; her new life was too full. But when she nodded off, the nightmares were always the same. One was of Karen's naked body dangling from the triangle, blood dribbling down her legs. She always looked unconscious, but as Anna was about to wake up, she would open her eyes, her face a tortured mask, and scream, 'I hate you! May you rot in hell!'

Why? Anna would think, even when asleep. I did what I had to do.

But the other nightmare was far worse, as the man ran across the range, body jumping and spurting blood, as each bullet slammed into it, until he fell to his knees, as he had done on that terrible day, and still she had fired, her last bullet, to hit him again. He had been already dead, but not in her nightmare. As with Karen, just as she was about to wake up, he would raise his head, and look at her, and ask, 'Why?'

He spoke in a normal voice, and yet the word went winging through her brain like a scream, over and over again. 'Because I had to,' she would scream back, in her sleep. 'Because I must. Because my masters make me.' As they were now making her give her body, that so precious, so private body, to a man for whom she could feel nothing but contempt. As they would go on requiring her to do until they had no more use for her, when they would send her to join Karen in a state brothel.

She wondered how long she would last. But, as with her unhappy victim, as it had to be done, it would be done, to the very best of her ability.

'I hope you slept well, sir,' Clive asked while Bowen the valet poured coffee.

Ballantine, wrapped in a multi-coloured, striped dressing-gown, gulped greedily. 'I have a head.'

'The things one does for England. But I agree; it was rather poor champagne.'

'But it was worth it. That girl ... Clive, I must see her again.'

'I'm not sure that would be a good idea, sir.'

Ballantine buttered toast. 'I suggested it, and she seemed to like the idea, but what with one thing and another she forgot to give me either her address or her telephone number. Still, Countess von Widerstand ... she must be in the telephone book, or the embassy will know where she lives. Be a good chap and find out for me, would you?'

'I don't think the embassy will be able to help, sir. And I doubt she'll be in the book.'

'What do you mean?'

'Simply that everything she may have told you about herself, or Hammerbach told you about her, was a lie.'

'My dear fellow...'

'Do you know what the word *Widerstand* means, in English, sir?'

'How am I supposed to know that? I imagine it's her family seat.'

'It means *resistance*.'

'What?'

'Have you ever heard of anyone known as the Count, or Countess, of Resistance?'

'No, I haven't. But it is rather romantic, what? And she is the most gorgeous creature. I would say she's entitled to a lie or two. There's someone at the door.'

Bowen, who was fully dressed, opened the door. 'For The Honourable Ballantine Bordman, by hand,' the bellhop said.

'Thank you.' Bowen tipped him, took the envelope to the table. 'Perfumed, sir.'

'Well...' Ballantine slit the envelope with his thumb. 'My word! This is my lucky day. Read that.' He handed the note to Clive.

'As you say, sir, my word. She is a persistent young lady. Would you like me to reply for you?'

'She says not to reply, just to go.'

'Yes, but as you won't be going, it would be polite to decline rather than just not turn up.'

'Decline? Not turn up? After an invitation like that? For God's sake...'

'I have just established that she's a fake.'

'You have established that you *think* she is a fake. If you wish, I will ask her about her name this evening. But I don't think she's a fake. I mean, look at this crested notepaper.'

'Any printer could create that for her. Or her employers.'

Ballantine stared at him. 'What do you mean?'

'Simply that, apart from her name, she attended a government-sponsored ball last night, in the company of an SS officer...'

'Her cousin.'

Clive sighed. 'That is what we were told, yes.'

'And what about that gown? That jewellery? That necklace she was wearing was worth ten thousand pounds if it was worth a penny.'

'We don't know it was hers.'

'Clive, you are starting to really upset me. But you are a good fellow, and I know you feel you are just doing your job. So I'll tell you what we'll do. I will attend this soiree with my eyes wide open and my ears as well, and I will find out the truth about this young lady, and then we'll know where we stand.'

Clive looked at the note again. 'I see that I am

not invited.'

'No, you're not,' Ballantine said happily.

Anna accepted a last embrace and kiss on the cheek, returned to the drawing room. 'The trouble with these parties is that people never know when to go home.'

'Well...' Ballantine looked at his watch. 'Good heavens! Nine o'clock! I should be going as well.'

'But I would like you to stay. I think you have been bored with all this Berlin chatter. Let us sit down together.'

Ballantine drew a deep breath. He actually had found the conversation boring; most of it, when addressed to him, had been in almost indecipherable broken English. But the evening had not been boring, as he had spent his time looking at his hostess. Tonight she was wearing a deep blue – obviously her favourite colour – calf-length cocktail dress which indicated that her legs were at least as good as the rest of her, and if she had discarded her necklace, the huge sapphire ring, matching her eyes, on her left forefinger was hardly less valuable. The only disappointment was that she was wearing a cloche, and had tucked her hair out of sight, although the exposed face only doubled in beauty. But now to his delight she removed the hat, tossing it across the room, and shook her head to let the golden tresses come tumbling down. The movement, and the result, was at once entrancing and intimate, almost as if they were old friends, or even more than that. His heart began to pound as he suddenly realized that it might be going to happen. But that had to be impossible at only his second meeting with a girl of noble birth. On the other hand, she did seem terribly attracted to him.

The thought reminded him that he had promised Bartley to find out the truth about her.

'Would you like another glass of champagne?' she asked.

'Ah ... I think I've had enough, thank you.'

'That is very good. Very wise. So many of my friends think of nothing but to drink themselves insensible. But you will stay and have, how do you say in England, a bite of supper?'

'Oh, I say, that would be awfully nice of you. But are you sure?'

'Of course. As I have said, you are such a change from all these people with their *Heil Hitlers* and their Nazi salutes. I should like to get to know you better. Elsa!' The woman, who Ballantine had gathered was her maid, appeared in the doorway. 'Mr Bordman will be staying for supper.'

'Of course, Fraulein.' Elsa withdrew.

'Did I gather from what you just said that you are not a supporter of the regime?' Ballantine asked, again hardly able to believe his ears.

'Well, of course I am not. The Nazis are a bunch of lower-class thugs who are determined to ruin our country.'

She was so vehement he could have no doubt she was telling the truth, as she saw it. 'But should you be saying something like that in public?'

'I am not in public. I am alone with you.'

'Yes, but that woman, your servant...'

'Elsa? Elsa is absolutely faithful to me. She has been with me for years. She was my nurse when I was a baby.'

'This would have been at Widerstand.'

Anna gave a delightful tinkle of laughter. 'Widerstand is not a place, Mr Bordman, or may I call you Ballantine?'

'Oh, please do.'

'And you must call me Anna. As I was saying, my father has a *schloss* not far from Munich. It is very lovely down there. You must visit with us and see it.'

'I should like to do that. But...'

'The name. People always ask me about that. Well, you see, over a hundred years ago, during the Napoleonic Wars, the French just about conquered Germany. Well, not all of our people wished to accept this, and my great-great-great-grandfather was one of those. In fact, he led one of the groups who continued to fight, and he became known as Lord of the Resistance. He was only a colonel in the army then, but when we regained our sovereignty he was presented to King Frederick William who ennobled him, and gave him the title as his name. That is what Widerstand means – resistance.'

'I say, what an incredibly romantic story. You must be very proud of your ancestor.'

'Oh, I am. I think Elsa is ready for us.'

'Tell me what you do,' Anna asked as they ate their cold meat and salad and Elsa refilled their wine glasses. 'I mean, I know you are a diplomat, but I have never been sure what diplomats do. I have met Ribbentrop several times, but he never seems to do anything, except leer at me.'

'A detestable fellow,' Ballantine agreed, happy to fit in with his hostess's mood. 'I'm in the Foreign Office. You know, looking after our relationships with other countries.'

'And now you are looking after England's relationship with Germany?'

He smiled. 'Sadly, I'm not that important. I'm here to make sure everything is ready for the visit of our prime minister to your Fuehrer next week.'

'Your prime minister is coming here? To Berlin? Why is he doing that?'

'Oh, there's some problem with Czechoslovakia. As to whether he is actually coming to Berlin, that hasn't been decided yet. The meeting will take place where the Fuehrer chooses. My business is arranging the agenda.'

'But your prime minister is coming here to see the Fuehrer? To tell him where to get off? Oh, that will be fantastic. Someone should have done that long ago.'

'Ah, well ... Good lord, look at the time. Eleven o'clock! I really must be going.'

'You have somewhere to go?'

'Well, no, but...'

'I would like you to stay with me. To be nice

107

to me. And then, I will be nice to you.' She put her arms round his neck and kissed him on the lips.

The body moved beneath him, slowly, sensuously. He had never known such a body, perhaps never truly believed it could exist. Ballantine did not know a great deal about women's bodies. Although well-known as a ladies' man in London, in the upper-class society in which he existed, sex was a matter of lips and hands, and the occasional fumble. He well knew that adultery was supposed to be rampant amongst his peers, but the opportunity to indulge in it had never been his luck; most women seemed to regard him as rather a joke. While no virginal young woman in the marriage market would ever permit any activity below her waist, or dream of taking off her clothes in front of a man before her marriage – if then. As for those times when the requirements of the flesh had become overwhelming, he had invariably been accompanied to the brothel by some of his friends, for him at least an occasion of continued embarrassment, nor had the 'girls' been either beautiful or inclined to remove more clothing than absolutely necessary.

The image of this magnificent creature slowly removing her clothes while facing him – not that she had been wearing many clothes – would remain in his memory for the rest of his life; he only wished he had not had that wine with dinner. And then, to have her submit so utterly, as she was submitting now, seeming to both groan and whimper as her body continued to move. And he was there!

He gasped, and relaxed, and lay still. She continued to move for a few seconds, then also subsided. But she was still panting. 'I can't breathe.'

'Oh, I'm sorry.' He rolled off her, lay beside her, tentatively slid his hand over her breasts. She made no objection. 'That was the best I've ever had,' he said.

'Yes,' she agreed.

'Was it for you, too?'

'It was the first.'

'What?' he almost screamed, sitting up. They had not switched off the light, and now he saw that there was blood on his drooping penis. He looked down at her thighs, and saw more blood. 'Oh, my God!'

'It wasn't that bad,' Anna said. 'Elsa told me it would be worse. When it happened.'

'But, I've ruined your life. Why? I mean, why did you let me?'

Her eyes had been half shut. Now they opened wide. 'Because ... Do you believe in love at first sight?'

'Well ... it's not happened to me.'

'I thought you were attracted to me when we met last night.'

'Well, I was. You're the most beautiful woman I have ever seen. But you don't mean you were equally attracted to me? I mean...'

'You're too modest. Too shy. You know,

109

since, what do you English say? Since I came out, eh, men have been constantly proposition-ing me.'

'I can believe that.'

'And I have refused them all. A girl must always wait for the right man. And then last night, when I saw you, I realized that here was the man I had been waiting for, the man to whom I could yield.' She put her arms round his waist, first to nuzzle him, and then to bring him down on top of her again.

'Oh, I say. But what are we going to do?'

'Can we not do it again? Would you like me on my face? I have been told that some men like to have women from behind.'

'My darling girl, that would be heavenly. But what about you? Your husband?'

'I do not have a husband.'

'Yes, but when you marry...'

'I do not think it will be possible for me to marry, now.' She gazed at him, her big, soft blue eyes again wide. 'You think I have been very foolish. I suppose I have. But what was I to do? I fell in love at first sight, and I knew you were not going to be here very long. Now I must pay for my moment of madness. But it was not madness. It was the most glorious moment of my life.'

He gazed at her for several seconds. But could any man ask, or expect, more from life than this so vulnerable girl? He squared his shoulders. 'Of course you're not going to pay for it for the rest of your life. You're going to marry me.'

'What? I cannot marry you.'

'Why not? I may not be a count, but the pater is a wealthy man. He'll love you.'

'Bally,' she said. 'I cannot marry you because our countries will be at war before the end of this year.'

'Eh?'

'Is not your Mr Chamberlain coming to Germany to tell Hitler than he must stop meddling in Czechoslovakia? The Fuehrer will defy him. He is mad, drunk on power. When he reintroduced conscription, everyone said the Allies will never let you get away with it. But the Allies did nothing. When he reoccupied the Saarland, everyone said the Allies will never let you get away with it. And the Allies did nothing. When he occupied Austria, everyone said now, certainly you have gone too far. And now Czechoslovakia ... Everyone is saying that Chamberlain is coming here with an ultimatum, and will declare war on Germany if Hitler persists in this madness. But Hitler will, I am sure of it.'

Ballantine kissed her. 'My dear, delightful darling, you have got hold of entirely the wrong end of the stick.'

'What do you mean?'

'Our Neville will never go to war, with anyone. He is a businessman, not a soldier. He believes in peace, mutual understanding, mutual prosperity. So Britain and Germany are having a little bit of a misunderstanding at the moment, and he is coming here to resolve it. By talking.

Believe me.'

'How can you be sure of that? Suppose Hitler point-blank refuses to give up his claims to the Sudetenland? Is not Great Britain bound by treaty to defend Czechoslovakian integrity?'

'No, no. We are bound by treaty to support France if they decide to defend Czechoslovakia. But if we say that is not practical, then the French will not do so. And it is not practical, you know. Great Britain's strength lies with its navy. How can our navy defend a totally land-locked country like Czechoslovakia? In any event, the country would never go for it. I bet that if there were a nation-wide poll tomorrow, ninety per cent of the British population will not even know where Czechoslovakia is. As for shedding our wealth and our blood to defend it, Chamberlain would be out on his ear tomorrow if he were to propose it.'

Anna wriggled her body under his. 'You are certain of this?'

'Absolutely. Anyway, you know, my darling, between you, me, and that wall over there, we have nothing to defend Czechoslovakia with. We may have a navy, but we don't have an army capable of fighting a European campaign, and we certainly do not have an air force capable of defending Britain.'

'So if Hitler is intransigent...?'

'Neville will have to find some face-saving device, probably something like having the Czechs accepting German inspectors to prove the Sudeten Germans aren't being ill treated after all, and perhaps give up a border post or two. Something acceptable to both sides.'

Anna gave a great sigh, inflating her breasts against his. 'You have made me so happy.'

'So will you marry me?'

'Of course I want to marry you, Bally. But I must ask my Papa.'

'Oh, yes. When will you be able to do that? I leave in two days' time.'

'I will try to go down tomorrow. But it is a long journey, and I cannot go and come back in two days. But it does not matter. I am sure he will agree when I tell him about you, and then I will write to you, and we will arrange our wedding.'

'That sounds tremendous. I only wish I could come with you. But if you're sure he'll say yes...'

'I am certain of it.'

'Well, then ... I say, my boy is ready again. Can you feel him?'

'It is entrancing,' Anna said. 'But, Bally, I am so tired. I had virtually no sleep last night, and now it is past midnight, and I need to take that long journey tomorrow ... Do you think you could leave me now, to get some sleep?'

'Oh. Yes, of course. But ... Will I see you again before I go?'

Not if I can help it, she thought. 'I'm afraid not, my darling, if you are leaving the day after tomorrow. But we have all of our lives together, have we not?' She kissed him.

Four

The Bride

The tape clicked to a stop, and for a moment the large office was absolutely silent. Anna, seated before the huge desk, found that she was holding her breath as she stared, not at the full-length portrait of Hitler that hung on the wall behind the desk, but at the man seated at it. She had never even seen Heinrich Himmler in the flesh before today, much less spoken with him. But she knew that he held her life, as perhaps he held the lives of everyone in this room, in the palm of his hand.

Everything about him was immaculate. His black uniform was neatly pressed and fitted at every joint; his black boots, which she could see beneath the desk, as well as his black belts, were polished to a high sheen. His slightly thinning hair was brushed straight back on his head and his rimless glasses sat on the centre of the bridge of his nose. The reflecting light made it difficult to see his eyes, but perhaps the most disturbing thing about him was the utter lack of expression in his rather plain face. His voice was equally lacking in character.

'That is remarkable,' he said. 'If it is true. Heydrich?'

'I believe it is true, Herr General,' the handsome colonel said. 'Our estimation of this man is that he is a pompous fool.'

'Well, he must be, seeing that Widerstand first of all tells him she did not know that Chamberlain is coming here, and then proceeds to tell him exactly why we suppose he is making the visit. That was careless of you, Fraulein.'

'I understand that, Herr General. The heat of the moment...'

'For which reason you got away with it. There is no fool like an old fool, eh? Or even a reasonably young fool, when he is in love. I congratulate you. I was told that you revealed exceptional promise, and this estimation has been proved to be correct.'

'Thank you, Herr General.'

'There is just one thing you need to be careful of. You went rather overboard in your denunciation of the Reich and the Fuehrer.' He held up his finger, as she would have spoken. 'I understand that you must have considered this necessary to win the confidence of your subject, but you should know that I intend to play this tape to the Fuehrer, as it will supply him with the knowledge he needs to conduct a successful negotiation. I cannot say what his reaction to your remarks may be, although I do promise that I will do my best to protect you.' He smiled. 'In any event, you will be out of the country by then, and I am sure you will find sufficient information for us over the next few years to earn his forgiveness.'

Anna had been breathing very deeply to stop herself from openly panting. Now she swallowed. 'You are sending me away, Herr General?'

'Of course. You are going to England, are you not? As the Honourable Mrs Bordman.'

Anna gulped, and looked at Glauber, who was also present. He gave her an encouraging smile.

Himmler was addressing Heydrich. 'How long will your people require to complete her training?'

'It should not take more than a week, Herr General. It is simply a matter of teaching her to use the micro-camera and to memorize a few things.'

'Excuse me, Herr General,' Anna said. 'Are you saying I am to marry this Englander?'

'That is what you are going to do, yes.'

'But...'

'I am giving you the assignment of your career. Of any woman's career. This man is wealthy and well known, and high up in the British Government. He refers to Chamberlain as Neville. He is also desperately in love with you. You will be at the very centre of the English establishment. You will meet important people, you will talk with them, you will bewitch them, and you will listen to them. In England you can be as anti-Nazi as you wish. You will also encourage your husband to bring important documents home from the office, and these you will photograph with the camera you

116

will be taught how to use. You will be given a contact to whom you will deliver your information. It will be ... What do the English say? A piece of cake.'

'But...' I don't want to marry that tub of lard, she wanted to shout. Having sex with him was repulsive. To have to do it every night for ... My God!

Himmler might have been able to read her mind. 'Now, Anna, I would be very disappointed if you were to come over all feminine and start talking about love, or the lack of love. We don't expect you to love him: he is an enemy of the Reich. But you are an agent of the Reich, and there can be no higher calling. We expect you to please this man, and use him. Understood?'

'Yes, Herr General,' Anna said faintly. 'For how long...?'

'For as long as your relationship is productive. When we feel that it has ceased to be so, you will divorce him, and return to Germany.'

'Suppose he finds out what I am doing?'

'Then he will divorce you, I would say. But, Anna, we would prefer it if he did not find out. We would look unfavourably on that.'

'Yes, sir. Suppose I get pregnant? He will hardly wear protection when in bed with his wife.' He didn't last night, she remembered ruefully. 'Nor will he expect me to.'

'Well then, you will bring the baby, or the babies, back to Germany with you.'

Oh, my God, she thought. Babies!

'Now,' Himmler hurried on. 'We have a lot to do. You told him that you are going down to Bavaria to see your father. But he is leaving tomorrow. We want this thing sewn up before he leaves, just in case he goes off the boil, eh? So you will telephone him and say that just as you were about to leave, who should turn up at your apartment but your father, thus saving you the journey. You would like him to meet your father, and formally obtain his permission for the marriage, therefore you would like him to come to lunch today. There you will arrange the marriage. I would suggest a civil ceremony here in Berlin.'

'Just like that? I have only known him two days.'

'Love at first sight, my dear. On both sides, as it says on the tape. However, should there be any difficulty, your father will remind the gallant Englishman that he has virtually raped you, an innocent young virgin. On the other hand, again judging by the tape, I do not think that will be necessary. But of course you will have to make it clear that it will be impossible for you to accompany your husband back to England immediately, as you have to pack things up here.'

'But my father...'

'You go on home now to make that phone call. Your father will join you very shortly so that you can get acquainted. Well, I think that covers everything. I imagine the Englander will wish to see as much of you as possible before

118

he leaves, so you will accommodate him in this, and report to Colonel Heydrich the moment he departs. Are there any more questions?'

Anna drew a deep breath. You have just delineated my life for the foreseeable future, she thought. A future in which I am to have no say, in which I am required to submit entirely to the whims and desires of a man I do not like and hold in the most utter contempt, but who I am also required to betray at every possible opportunity. But there can be no questions, because it is for the Reich. Yet she could, perhaps, slightly mitigate her position. 'Am I allowed to take Elsa with me?'

Himmler looked at Heydrich. 'Of course,' the colonel said. 'That is imperative. Frau Mayers is your senior officer and will be your controller.'

'But if Mr Bordman...'

'He cannot possibly object,' Himmler said. 'A countess should have her own maid.'

Anna wondered what Elsa would make of England.

'If you'll forgive me, sir,' Clive said, 'you look as if you had a heavy night.'

It was eleven o'clock, and Ballantine had just emerged from his bedroom into the suite's sitting room, still wearing his dressing gown and looking distinctly bleary-eyed. 'Heavy night,' he grunted, sinking into a chair. 'By golly!'

Clive hastily poured both coffee and juice, and presented them. 'The party went on rather late, then? But you must have enjoyed it.'

Ballantine drank juice and coffee in rapid succession. 'Enjoyed it? I'm getting married!'

Clive, who had finished his breakfast but had poured himself another cup of coffee, spilt some on the tablecloth. 'Would you repeat that, sir?'

'She is the most marvellous girl in the world,' Ballantine said dreamily. 'But you know that.'

Clive drank the last of his coffee. 'You wish to marry that woman we met at the ball?'

'I do not wish to do so, Clive. I am going to do so. As soon as she has spoken to her father.'

Clive's brain was doing handsprings; his charge had obviously flipped his lid. 'Forgive me for appearing obtuse, sir. But if I may just get my facts straight: you attended a party thrown by a woman you had met just once before, and during the course of the evening you proposed marriage? And she accepted? It must have been some party. Would you like me to telephone her and explain that it was all a joke? Or at least a mistake?'

'What on earth are you jabbering about? It wasn't like that at all. She asked me to stay on after the party and have supper with her. It was just her and me, and we got talking, and one thing led to another, and then she sent her maid home, and, well...' He gazed at Clive, eyebrows arched.

'Oh my God! You mean you went to bed with her?'

'A gentleman does not talk about these

120

things,' Ballantine said pompously. 'We talked, and we discovered that we loved each other.'

'She told you this, did she?'

'Well, she confessed that she had fallen in love with me at first sight, at the ball.' He buttered toast. 'She calls me Bally,' he said dreamily.

She got the initial wrong, Clive thought absently; she meant *Wally.* 'You do realize, sir...'

'No, no, Clive. *You* must realize that everything you have said, or are about to say, is slander against a beautiful and virtuous young woman who I have grievously wronged.'

Clive scratched his head.

'I even,' Ballantine went on, 'took your strictures so much to heart that I asked her about her unusual name, and she told me the whole story.'

Clive poured more coffee as he listened.

'And then,' Ballantine said, flushing as he contradicted his own ethical declaration, 'one thing led to another, and, well, Clive, I know you think she is some kind of a tart. But she was a virgin.'

Once again the tablecloth suffered.

'I thought that would shake you up,' Ballantine said triumphantly. 'So there we were. I couldn't let her down after that, even had I wanted to. But I didn't want to. I'm the happiest man in the world. Now come, Clive. Be a man and apologize.'

'It certainly seems that I was wrong, sir. May I ask what happens now?'

121

'Well, she obviously has to obtain her father's permission, and that means a trip down to Bavaria to see him. She can't possibly be back for a couple of days...'

'By which time you'll be back in England,' Clive said with great relief.

'Oh, she is quite sure her father will go for it. As soon as he gives his formal permission, she'll come over and join me. I intend to arrange all that and get her visa as soon as we're home. Now, what's the programme for today?'

'Ah ... there's a meeting at the embassy this afternoon, and a reception at the Wilhelm-strasse tonight.'

'What a bore. Still, I suppose duty calls.'

The telephone jangled.

'Maybe something is being cancelled.'

Clive was on his feet to pick up the receiver. 'Mr Bordman's suite.'

'Bally?'

'Ah, no, Fraulein. This is Clive Bartley. Would this be the Countess von Widerstand?'

'Give me that!' Ballantine took the receiver from Clive's hand.

Oh, pray to God she's about to give him the brush-off, Clive thought.

'My darling! How wonderful to hear your voice. But I thought you were on the way to Munich ... What? Oh, good heavens, how splendid ... Oh, yes. Twelve o'clock? I'll be there. My dearest girl, I can hardly wait.' He hung up. 'Her father's turned up in Berlin. He wants to meet me. Today. I feel like a small boy again.'

Did you ever stop being a small boy? Clive wondered. 'There's the meeting at the embassy at three, sir.'

'Oh, bugger the meeting. I'll be there if I can. If I can't, you'll have to make my excuses. Tell the ambassador I have a chill or something. Now, I'm off to have a bath.'

'Yes, sir. Would you mind if I stepped out for a while?'

'Of course I don't mind, my boy. Enjoy yourself.' He burst into song as he entered the bathroom.

'Von Widerstand? You're pulling my leg.' Gottfried Friedemann had managed the library of the Berlin Embassy for years, and was their acknowledged expert on German history; a short man who wore a goatee beard and horn-rimmed spectacles, his thick black hair somewhat carelessly brushed, he was the picture of a savant.

'Let me tell you a story,' Clive said, and did so.

Gottfried burst out laughing. 'The young Fraulein is having you on.'

'Are you sure?'

'As sure as can be. The period is very well documented, and I can assure you that there was no army colonel made Count of Resistance. That is the dream of a romantic novelist.'

'I would like you to put that in writing.'

Gottfried stroked his beard. 'You think this

girl is a fortune hunter?'

'No, I do not. I think she is a plant.'

Gottfried frowned. 'I do not understand.'

'I think – I am certain – that she is an agent for the German Government, meant to seduce visiting diplomats or military experts and see what she can find out, who just happens to have sunk her claws into Bordman. I mean, Gottfried, be reasonable, can you imagine any young woman, much less a real beauty, going for someone like Bordman? He's old enough to be her father, and he has the charisma of a frog.'

Gottfried gave a brief smile. 'I think you fancy this girl yourself.'

'Well...' Clive could not suppress a flush. 'As I said, she is very good-looking. But I'm a one-woman man, and I happen to have a woman. In any event, I'm not susceptible to a come-on quite this heavy, and blatant.'

'Do you think she has got anything worth-while out of Bordman?'

Clive merely nodded.

'My God! You mean he does have knowledge which could be of use to a foreign power? This power? And she got it out of him in two days? She must indeed be a remarkable young Fraulein. Couldn't you warn him?'

'He's not susceptible to warnings, certainly not when there's the best pair of legs he has ever seen on offer.'

'You are making me wish to see this prodigy for myself. But it would appear that the damage is done. And if you are taking him back to

England tomorrow...'

'You haven't got the picture, old boy. He has asked her to marry him, and needless to say, she has said yes.'

Gottfried whistled. 'She is a fast worker.'

'So she is going to be at the very centre of our establishment. And with her looks and charisma she is going to be the sensation of the season. He has got to be stopped from committing virtual suicide. And the only way I can stop him is by providing written proof that she is a fake. So...'

'You wish me to provide that proof. I do not think I can do that, Clive.'

'What?'

'Clive, if I were to come to you, as a friend, and ask you to discredit a British agent here in Berlin, would you do it?'

Clive stared at him.

'There is another point,' Gottfried went on. 'If, as you say, she is working for the Reich, then it has to be for one of our secret services. It does not matter whether it is the Abwehr, or the SS, or even the Gestapo – my own bet would be the SD – these gentlemen all have very long arms and fingers which can get into every household. Even this embassy. If I gave you a signed document proving that this woman is not what she is pretending to be, my life would not be worth a *pfennig*.'

Clive continued to regard him for several seconds. Then he said, 'We would, of course, look after you.'

125

'How would you do that?'

'Well, we'd get you a job in England.'

'Do you not suppose the SD could reach me there as easily as here? And what about my wife? My son? My mother and father? Besides, you are asking me to betray my country. I cannot do this.' He glanced across his desk. 'We have been friends for a long time. I have served your embassy for a long time; I hope to go on doing so. For a long time to come. You came here to ask for information on German history. I have given you that information. You will do with it as you think best. But I can do no more than that, and you have no right to ask me.'

Clive nodded, and stood up. 'I was out of line. Thanks anyway.' He held out his hand. 'No hard feelings, I hope.'

Gottfried squeezed his fingers. But Clive knew he had lost a friend.

Ballantine had not returned by two, but Clive had not expected him to. He could only wait, but when his charge did not come in by three o'clock, he had to telephone the embassy and tell them that the Honourable Mr Bordman was indisposed. The ambassador was not amused, as this meeting was to be the final determination of the agenda for the prime minister's visit. However, as all Ballantine had to do was agree to what the ambassador and Foreign Minister Ribbentrop had hammered out, Clive suggested the itinerary be sent to the hotel and assured them that Ballantine would read it and initial it the moment he felt better.

'You're sure he's taking this thing seriously?' the ambassador inquired, somewhat acidly.

'Oh, indeed, sir. Very seriously,' Clive assured him.

The afternoon drifted by, and the evening began to close in. Clive dressed for dinner, but still Ballantine did not return. He cancelled their appearance at the reception, again to a rather chilly response, and then decided there was nothing for it, no matter how annoyed his boss might be, and telephoned the number on the invitation notepaper.

'Yes?' asked the woman's voice.

This was not the same voice as that morning. But it had to be the right address. 'Would I be speaking with the Countess von Widerstand?'

'No, sir. I am the countess's maid.'

'Ah. Well, can you tell me if Mr Bordman is there?'

'May I ask who is calling, please?'

'Mr Bordman's private secretary.'

'Ah. One moment, sir.'

Clive could hear voices in the background, and laughter, and a moment later Ballantine was on the phone. 'Clive, my dear fellow. Is there something wrong? I did tell you I'd be out for lunch.'

'Yes, sir. And dinner?'

'Ah. Well, yes, I am also out to dinner.'

'Yes, sir. I have made our apologies for not attending the reception. I also made our apolo-

127

gies to the ambassador for your missing the meeting at the embassy, sir.'

'Oh, good fellow. Just one moment.' A woman's voice could be heard in the near background. 'Of course, my dear. That's very decent of you. Clive, my dear fellow, we've been neglecting you. My wife would like you to have dinner with us.'

For a moment Clive thought he had lost the power of speech.

'Are you still there?'

'Yes, sir. Forgive me, but did you say *wife*?'

'Yes. We were married this afternoon.'

'Wasn't that rather sudden?'

'Not here. When these people want to get something done, they get it done. Gunther, that's my father-in-law, thought that in all the circumstances, well ... in all the circumstances, yes, that we should get married as soon as possible, especially seeing that I am due back in London tomorrow. So he made a couple of telephone calls, and the licence was delivered, by the magistrate himself, would you believe it?'

'I do believe it,' Clive said grimly.

'As I say, when these people decide to do something, they do it. It was a civil ceremony, of course.'

'Of course, sir.'

'So put on a dinner jacket and hurry along and have some champagne, and I'll even let you kiss the bride. Oh, and would you bring my toothbrush and shaving gear? I'll be spending

128

the night here. Honeymooning, what?'

Clive replaced the receiver, but remained staring at it for several seconds. For one of the very few times in his adult life he had absolutely no idea what to do. He had assumed that he had time, time in which to regain control of the situation, either by presenting the evidence supplied by Gottfried and persuading Ballantine that it was true, or, once they were back in England, having pressure brought – whether by Ballantine's superiors in the Foreign Office, or his own superiors in MI6, or even Ballantine's widowed father – to have the love-sick oaf repudiate the girl, even if that made him appear the most utter cad.

But now ... Ballantine was forty years old. There were absolutely no grounds for annulling his marriage. And if this woman had indeed been a virgin, there were no grounds for divorce. He could not see any judge accepting a plea with the reason given as 'suspicion that the Honourable Mrs Bordman is a German spy'.

He packed the toiletries and called down for a taxi.

'I have a feeling,' Anna said, 'that you do not like me.'

They sat together on a settee while her 'father' and Ballantine drank brandy and discussed politics rather loudly, as neither spoke the other's language very well.

'I would have to be blind, ma'am, not to consider you the most beautiful woman I have ever seen,' Clive said, stating the exact truth. Tonight she wore a white evening gown. He might consider that an incongruous choice of colour in view of what he knew of her, but that it was immensely flattering could not be argued, just as her deep décolletage promised every delight known to man. He had never seen her legs, but he did not doubt they were as splendid as the rest of her; the height of her hips certainly indicated that they were long. Her hair was loose, her only jewellery, apart from a no-doubt hastily bought gold wedding band, was a pearl choker which enhanced the glowing flesh of her neck and shoulders and breasts. If, as a professional diplomat and self-proclaimed man of the world, Ballantine was behaving like an idiot, as a man he had every reason to do so. The thought of him holding this goddess naked in his arms was quite nauseating.

'Why, that is charming,' she said. 'But admiration is not necessarily liking.'

'I do not think whether I like you or not need be of the slightest interest to you.'

'But will we not have to see a lot of each other if you are Bally's private secretary?'

He decided to take a stab in the dark: the situation required desperate measures. 'Well, no. I'm not really Mr Bordman's private secretary. I was just lent to him for this visit.'

Her eyes became enormous, but he did not suppose it was an inadvertent reaction. 'Aha,' she said. 'You are a detective. You are his bodyguard.'

'I suppose you could put it that way.'

Anna glanced at the two men, who were still engaged in animated conversation. 'Do you mean that his life is in danger?'

'I don't think so. It's routine. He's an important man.'

'I understand. But then ... do you carry a gun?'

'That is a professional secret, Mrs Bordman.'

'Good heavens! And I suppose you can kill a man with your bare hands.' She smiled. 'Or a woman.'

'I could have a pretty good go, I suppose.'

'Have you ever killed a man, Mr Bartley?'

'I think that, too, should be a professional secret, Mrs Bordman.'

Her tongue came out from between her teeth, just for an instant, and was then withdrawn again. 'What does it feel like? What did you feel, when you did it? Or didn't you feel anything?'

'I think that your husband and father would like us to join them,' Clive said.

'As I told you on the phone, I shall, of course, be spending the night here,' Ballantine said when they had finished their brandies. 'Honeymooning, what? You and Bowen can do the packing, and I'll meet you at the airport. What time is the flight?'

'If you can be there by ten o'clock, sir.'

'Ten. Hmm.' He glanced at his wife.

'I will see that he is there, Mr Bartley. In fact,

I will bring him myself. Have you no kiss for the bride?'

It was Clive's turn to glance at Ballantine.

'Oh, go ahead, old boy. Just this once, mind.'

Clive kissed her on the cheek, and she whispered in his ear, 'I look forward to continuing our discussion.'

'You never told me that Mr Bartley is a detective,' Anna said, when she had managed to move Ballantine off her and get her breath back.

Ballantine was still panting. 'A detective? Good lord! Did he tell you that?'

'Yes, he did. Do you mean you didn't know? Or was he lying to me?'

'Well, I suppose he is sort of a detective.' Ballantine's breathing returned to normal and he rolled on his side to face her and play with her nipple. 'He works for the SIS.'

Anna rolled on her side as well, both to make it easier for him to reach her and also to look at him. 'What is the SIS?'

'The Secret Intelligence Service. It has several branches. Bartley works for Military Intelligence Number 6. They deal with overseas security.'

Anna rose on her elbow, and his fingers slipped away. 'You mean he is a spy?'

'Oh, good lord, no. I mean, well ... I suppose he has been trained to be an agent. But his job right now is protecting me. You are married to an important man, you know, my darling,'

Ballantine said importantly.

Anna kissed him on the nose. 'I knew you were important. But not *how* important. Do you mean your life is in danger?'

He got hold of her again, this time pulling her against him. 'Important men's lives are always in danger.'

'Then my life is in danger too.'

'The risk is very small. We are protected all the time.'

'By Mr Bartley?'

'No, no. I told you, he deals with external security. Inside England we are protected by the Special Branch of Scotland Yard.'

'So we will not have anything more to do with Mr Bartley?'

'I shouldn't think so.'

She snuggled against him. 'I'm glad of that. I don't think he likes me.'

'You see, Mr Bartley,' Anna said. 'One minute to ten. I am always early.'

She was even more beautiful than usual in a sable coat. Clive bowed over her gloved hand. 'I can see that you are going to do Mr Bordman a world of good, Mrs Bordman.'

'And this gentleman is?'

'Bowen, ma'am. I am Mr Bordman's valet.'

'Ah. Then I am leaving you in good hands, Bally. Have a good journey.'

Clive and Bowen exchanged raised eyebrows as she kissed her husband goodbye.

'And you'll be with me a week today,' Ballantine reminded her.

'Of course.'

The Englishmen shook hands with her 'father' and went off to the VIP lounge. Anna led the way back to the taxi rank.

'I think that went off very well,' Gunther remarked.

Anna settled herself on the cushions. 'Ballantine is very easy to get on with. He only wants one thing.'

'I could see that. Does he do anything for you?'

Anna's gaze could be very cold. 'Isn't that my business?'

'I am your father, my dear.'

Anna blew a raspberry.

'Very well,' he agreed. 'That is over now. But tell me this...' He picked up her hand and stroked it. 'Were you really a virgin when he got to you?'

'That is also my business.'

'And the business of the SD, no doubt. But now, as they say, it is done and dusted. And I would hate to think of your bed being lonely for the next week. Do you not think, as your father, I should keep you company?'

'I can think of nothing I would like less.' She tapped on the glass. 'Stop here.'

The driver obligingly pulled in to the kerb.

'This gentleman is getting out here,' Anna told him. 'I have somewhere to go, Gunther, so I shall not be seeing you again. Kindly be removed from my apartment by lunch time.'

He glared at her. 'Do you think you can order me around like a messenger boy?'

'That is what I am doing, yes.' She stared into his eyes. 'And if you attempt to lay a finger on me, I will break your arm.'

A last glare, then he got out of the car. The driver, who had been listening to the exchange as he watched them in his rear-view mirror, gave a sigh of relief.

'I wish to go to Gestapo Headquarters,' Anna said.

Now he gulped. People, and especially un-attached young women, did not usually ask to be taken to Gestapo Headquarters. 'Yes, Fraulein.' As she was wearing gloves he had not observed her wedding ring.

Fifteen minutes later she was in Heydrich's office.

'Anna!' He came round his desk to squeeze her hands and kiss her on each cheek. 'How well you look. Married life agrees with you.'

'You mean, Herr Colonel, that it stretches in front of me like an immense black cloud.'

'Aptly put. But you are serving the Reich, remember. And it will not be for so very long. How old are you? Eighteen? You will have your whole life in front of you when you come home.' He helped her out of her coat, and hand-ed it to the waiting secretary. 'Now, we have a lot to do. Klaus is waiting for you. The camera itself is very easy to handle; once you have persuaded your husband to bring some of his work home – so that you can spend more time together, you understand – it will be very simple. It is the procedure of passing on the film, and all other information you will gather, that you have to learn very carefully, as you must carry it all in your head, eh? And a mistake could be fatal. Thus you must learn the procedure and follow the rules exactly at all times. You must remember this. However, Elsa will be there. You should bear in mind that she is your superior officer in the SD, and she also must be obeyed at all times. I have instructed her to set up the information transfer system with your local contact. As I have said, it is important to use this channel and none other. We would regard it as a serious matter if any of the information you are sending back should go astray or fall into the wrong hands.'

Anna sat down and stripped off her gloves. 'I will obey the rules, Herr Colonel.' That is all my life consists of, she thought: obeying rules. 'However, there are problems.'

Heydrich returned behind his desk 'What problems?'

'Gunther seems to think he has rights.'

'Such as?'

'He wishes to have sex with me.'

'That is not a problem. Where is he now?'

'I sent him back to the apartment and told him to pack up and go. But I do not know if he will do so.'

Heydrich nodded. 'My people will attend to it. He will not be there when you get home.'

'I would not like him to be badly hurt. He

played his part very well, for the Englanders.'

'I am delighted to hear that. And I am certain that he will suffer no pain at all. At least, this is what I am told by those who should know. You can put him out of your mind.'

Anna swallowed. 'I did not mean that I wanted him killed. He is basically a harmless little man. I just don't want him making himself a nuisance.'

'My dear girl, it is what the Reich wants that matters. This man knows your secret, and therefore he is a danger both to you and to the Reich.'

'Oh my God,' Anna muttered.

'Why, Anna, I cannot believe the removal of a potential enemy can possibly disturb you.'

'But will not my husband expect to see my father again, from time to time?'

'Your father will die of a heart attack some time in the next six months. That he needs to be disposed of immediately is not relevant. That is when the news will be released. You will be properly distressed. In fact, I think you should return to Germany for the funeral. Then we can have a get-together and discuss how things are going. You said there was more than one problem?'

Anna licked her lips. Although Clive Bartley disturbed her, he really was a most attractive man; she did not wish him to wind up with a bullet in the base of his skull. Then she remembered that if she failed to carry out her mission to the best of her ability, or wound up in a British gaol, or even was deported back to Germany, the fate of her family would be sealed. No doubt the order for their execution would be signed by this same handsome, smiling demon who was now waiting for her to speak.

'Yes,' she said. 'The man Bartley.'

'Bartley? I do not know this name.'

'He came to Germany as my husband's private secretary. But actually, he was his bodyguard.'

'That is not unusual, and certainly not to be concerned about. Important men are always provided with bodyguards, and Bordman is regarded as an important man, at least by the British Government.'

'So he keeps reminding me,' Anna agreed. 'But I have learned that this man is not merely a policeman. He works for an organization that is called Military Intelligence Number 6. Do you know of this, Herr Colonel?'

'Now, that is interesting,' Heydrich agreed. 'MI6. Yes. It is the overseas counter-espionage section of the British Secret Service. And you say he was Bordman's bodyguard? The British Government must think the fellow is *very* important.'

'He is a spy.'

'Perhaps. But I do not see what he hoped to discover following Bordman around.'

'He suspects the truth about me.'

Heydrich frowned. 'You know this? You have proof?'

'Well, no. It is the way he looks at me.'

Heydrich smiled. 'You mean he cannot suppress his admiration for a beautiful woman. You are nervous, Anna. I do not blame you. You are very young for such an important assignment. But think of this: your Mr Bartley arrived in Berlin already installed in his position as Bordman's bodyguard. Therefore the decision to appoint him must have been taken several weeks ago, when this visit was first arranged. At that time, and indeed up to the night of the ball, just seventy-two hours ago, neither he nor Bordman had ever heard of you, or had any idea that you even existed. Therefore he cannot possibly have been appointed to investigate you.'

'Oh,' Anna said. 'I did not think of that.'

'So, you see, there is nothing for you to worry about. It is perfectly natural for this man, having been appointed Bordman's minder, to be perturbed at his charge's sudden marriage. But now that he is married, there is nothing he can do about it.' He stood up. 'Now, let us see what Klaus has for us.' He turned his head as there was a tap on the door. 'Yes?'

His secretary stood to attention. 'There is a gentleman asking to see you, Herr Colonel.'

'Me?' Heydrich sounded as surprised as Anna's taxi driver; very few people outside the SD ever asked to see him.

'He says it is very urgent, sir.'

'Concerning what?'

'He would only tell me that it was to do with

the Countess von Widerstand.'

Anna caught her breath, and Heydrich glanced at her. 'Then I think you should show the gentleman in, Fraulein.'

Anna stood up.

'No, no,' Heydrich said. 'Stay. This concerns you as much as anyone.'

Anna sank back into her seat.

The secretary opened the door wide. 'Herr Gottfried Friedemann, sir.'

Gottfried was wearing a well-cut and pressed suit, a quiet tie, polished shoes, and an air of self-confident importance. If he also looked a little tense, Anna did not suppose that was to be surprised at, in these surroundings. She liked the look of him.

He saluted. 'Heil Hitler! Colonel Heydrich?'

'I am he. Have we met?'

'No, sir. I...' He stared at Anna.

'The Honourable Mrs Bordman.'

'Of course,' Gottfried said, clicking his heels and bowing. 'Your servant, ma'am. I did not know ... well ... I did not expect ... well...'

'You know this woman?'

'Oh, no, sir. We have never met.'

'But you have something to tell us about the Countess von Widerstand. Have a seat.' Heydrich sat down himself, behind the desk.

Gottfried took the chair beside Anna. Now he was definitely nervous. 'I am chief librarian at the British Embassy.'

'Yes?'

Gottfried licked his lips. 'I was approached,

140

yesterday morning, by a man called Bartley.'

Again, Anna caught her breath, and Heydrich gave her one of his quick, commanding glances. 'Go on.'

'Please forgive me, sir, ma'am, but the man Bartley, who I have known for some time...'

'How have you known him for some time?'

'Well, he uses the embassy when he is in Berlin.'

'You mean he is often in Berlin?'

'Oh, indeed, sir. He works for the British Government.'

'In what capacity?'

'He has never told me. I would say that he is some kind of agent.'

'Of whom you have known for some time. But you have never reported it before?'

'Well, Herr Colonel, the embassy is full of agents, whether they call themselves secretaries, attachés, or just clerks. I could not report them all. Nor was there any reason for it. They are mostly entirely harmless.'

'I see. But now you have decided that this man Bartley could be harmful, is that it?'

'I don't really know, sir. I do know that he was in Berlin on this occasion as some kind of aide to the Honourable Mr Bordman, and he came to see me because he was perturbed at Mr Bordman's desire to marry ... ah ... well, a woman he described as the Countess von Widerstand, and he wanted to know if I could tell him anything of the family background. Well...' He gave Anna an anxious glance. 'At

141

that time I had no idea what he was talking about. So I laughed, and told him it had to be a joke.'

'Go on,' Heydrich said.

Gottfried looked at his expression, and swallowed. 'He told me that there was no joke. He asked if there was any possibility that there could be a family called Widerstand, and I had to say no. He then asked me to put that in writing for him. But I refused.'

'That was very wise of you. Why did you refuse?'

'Well, I had to presume that if there was someone going around calling herself the Countess von Widerstand with government support ... He told me that he had met her at an SS ball ... Well, it was not a matter in which I wished to become involved.'

'Again, a wise decision. What did he do then?'

'Well, he was clearly very disappointed. He just left.'

'This was...?'

'Yesterday morning.'

'And you have only just come to us?'

'As I said, sir, I did not wish to become involved, and I did not know how much of what he told me was the truth. Frankly, if you will forgive me, Fraulein, I could not believe that a visiting British diplomat could wish to, well...'

'Marry some itinerant German girl with a false name?' Heydrich suggested.

'Well, yes, sir. Of course, now I have seen

142

you, Fraulein ... er...'

'You may call her Anna,' Heydrich said kindly.

'Thank you, sir. As I was saying, now that I have seen Fraulein Anna, I entirely understand. And when I read in the newspaper this morning that the Honourable Mr Ballantine Bordman had married a Countess von Widerstand, well, I felt I should report the whole thing. I did not expect the Fraulein to be here.'

'Of course. I think you have acted in a very proper manner, Herr Friedemann. As a true servant of the Reich. Be sure that you will be rewarded. There is just one more thing I need to know. Have you told anyone else about this incident?'

'Oh, no, sir.'

'Are you married?'

'Yes, sir. I have a son.' His tone was proud.

'Again, I congratulate you. And you have not told your wife?'

'I never discuss business matters with my wife, sir.'

'You are indeed a wise man. Thank you, Herr Friedemann. Now, I spoke of a reward. It will, of course, take a tangible form. But for the moment, why do you not take Mrs Bordman out to lunch?'

Anna turned her head sharply, and Heydrich smiled at her. 'On second thoughts, I think it would be better if Mrs Bordman were to take you out to lunch. I'm sure you would like to do that, Frau?'

'Of course,' Anna agreed in a low voice.

'Excellent. Now, if you will excuse us, Herr Friedemann, Mrs Bordman and I have a few small remaining matters to discuss. She will be with you in ten minutes.'

Gottfried stood up. 'Ma'am! Herr Colonel! Heil Hitler!' He left the room, and the waiting secretary closed the door.

'Now you see what I meant,' Anna remarked.

'I do indeed. And I apologize for not believing you.'

'What are we to do?'

'About Bartley? I will have to consider that. He is back in England, where disposition is not so simple. Did he make any attempt to interfere with the wedding?'

'Well, no. By the time he got around to wondering where Bally was, we were already married.'

'And he said nothing. So he has obviously decided that his next step needs thinking about. That gives us time, and in any event he has nothing but suspicions, which can only come down to your being an adventuress who has wormed her way into the highest circles. I am sure Bordman will defend your honour and your reputation to the utmost. No, we must deal with the immediate threat first.'

'Is that man a threat?'

'Of course he is, my dear girl. Don't you realize that this mission of yours is top secret? There are only six people in the Reich, including you and me, who know what you are about.

144

Your exposure, apart from being highly dangerous for you, could bring down our entire diplomatic corps in London. And now this lout
knows all about it.'

Anna sighed. 'He seems such a nice little
man.'

'Nice little men are the worst. They have
consciences and they think too much. Now,
there is no time to be lost. Klaus will have to
wait until tomorrow. You say you sent Peltzer
back to the flat, and told him to pack and get
out?'

'Ye-es,' Anna said cautiously.

'He may still be there. I will have him picked
up immediately. My people know nothing of
what is going on; he is a known subversive and
was offered this job in exchange for the charges
being dropped. Even if he has left the flat, they
will soon find him.'

'And ... dispose of him?'

'Well, of course. But they may need a little
time. I think you should take Friedemann to the
Albert. My secretary will book you a table. It is
an expensive place and he will be impressed.
Wine him and dine him to the maximum, be as
charming and sexy as you know how. And after
lunch invite him back to your apartment. By
then he will have his tongue hanging out.'

'And your people will be waiting for him?'

'No, no. I told you this must be kept secret. A
known criminal is one thing. The head librarian
at the British Embassy is another. He must just
disappear.'

'You wish me to...' She bit her lip.

'Please don't play the little innocent with me, Anna. I have your record. You are equipped with a Walther automatic, are you not?'

Anna nodded slowly.

'That means there should be very little mess, if you act promptly. The moment you leave here, I will telephone Fraulein Mayers and tell her to prepare. You will take Friedemann home, after lunch, be nice to him, have sex with him if you wish, then while Mayers distracts him, put the pistol to the back of his head and do the job. As I say, there should not be very much blood. Mayers will help you put the body in a bag, and clean up the mess. My men will be along later this afternoon to remove the bag.'

Anna licked her lips. 'Won't they know what's in it?'

'Oh, they will know that it is a body. But they won't know *whose* body. You are an SD agent, and they will be SD operatives. And Herr Friedemann will simply have disappeared.'

'The police will be able to trace our movements after we leave the Albert. Our taxi driver will remember us, for a start.' She forced a smile. 'I am not easily forgotten.'

'Anna, I control the police. Their investigation will lead them nowhere. Now off you go, have a good lunch, do what you have to do, and report here tomorrow morning for your session with Klaus.'

146

Five

Crisis

'I am so nervous,' Anna whispered into Ballantine's ear as they embraced on the tarmac at Croydon airport. 'All of these people.'

'They have come to see you.'

'But how do they know who I am?'

'I have told them. I want all England to know of you. I am the proudest man in the world.' He held her hand to lead her towards the waiting cameras and reporters.

She had not expected this reception, and looked at Elsa, who merely smiled. Elsa was wearing a frock and a new coat and had had her hair done, although it was lost beneath her hat. Anna wore her sable and a matching fur hat. Now she braced herself as the cameras started to flash in front of her.

'Over here, Mrs Bordman.'

'A quick smile, Mrs Bordman.'

A man, supported by two more carrying various pieces of equipment, thrust a microphone at her. 'Will you say a few words for the BBC, Mrs Bordman?'

Anna looked at Ballantine. 'Oh, yes, please,'

he agreed.

Anna drew a deep breath. 'I am so happy to be in England to join my husband. I so wish you to like me.'

This seemed to surprise them, but also to delight them. They applauded, while more flash bulbs went off. Ballantine held her arm to escort her through the throng.

'My luggage,' she said.

'It will be delivered,' he assured her.

'But do I not have to go through customs?'

'Of course you do not. You are my wife. Mrs Bordman. Coming into England as my wife you are immune from mundane regulations.'

Anna glanced at Elsa, who winked.

'Good heavens!' Anna exclaimed as she got out of the Rolls. 'Is this our house?'

She had not been impressed with the drive in from Croydon, through extremely dilapidated-looking streets. Even the river could not compare with the Danube. North of the Thames the general appearance of the city had improved, but she was still taken aback by the size of the building in front of which the car had stopped.

'Well, not all of it,' Ballantine explained. 'We have the top two floors. What they call a maisonette. I do intend to find us a house, perhaps in Epsom or somewhere like that, but it is necessary for me to have a base in town, don't you know. Business, what?'

'I think it is charming,' Anna said as he

148

escorted her into the lobby. 'I just know I am going to love it. Where is the elevator?'

'Ah ... the lift? I'm afraid there isn't one. This is rather an old building. But we are only two floors up.'

'And I am young and strong,' Anna commented, and looked at Elsa, who, from her expression, shared her consternation.

'Of course, my darling,' Ballantine said, and led her to the stairs. 'Now, there is something I must tell you.'

Anna, already started on the climb, stopped and turned her head. What now? she wondered.

'The pater will be here.'

'The what?'

'The pater. My father. He is waiting to meet you.'

'Oh, Lord! Oh, forgive me, Bally, I had not expected...'

'I know, my darling. It is an imposition. But he does want to meet you, and, well, he is a little long in the tooth. We must humour him.'

'Because you are his only son,' Anna suggested hopefully. She remembered what Elsa had told her; if that were true she could wind up as Lady Bordman. That sounded rather attractive.

'Why, yes,' Ballantine agreed. 'The last of the Bordmans, what? Until we have a son.'

'Oh. Yes. Is your mother here as well?'

'The mater is dead, poor old soul.'

'Oh, I am sorry.'

'Well, it means I am in the same position as

149

you: half an orphan. Actually, I sometimes wonder if the mater was ever fully alive.'

Which might explain a lot, Anna thought.

'Here we are.'

He unlocked a somewhat ornate front door, while Anna got her breathing back under control after the somewhat steep climb. But the moment she entered the lobby she was totally reassured. Here was every evidence of considerable wealth. Another door led into a large drawing room, a place of Persian carpets, leather upholstery, occasional tables covered with obviously expensive objets d'art, and along one entire wall stood a vast, high bookcase.

Unfortunately, it also contained a very old, decrepit, white-haired man, who was slowly rising from one of the armchairs with the aid of a stick. He looked Anna up and down.

'What a beauty! Well done, my boy. Well done. She's a damned pretty gel.'

Anna had a distinct feeling that she was not actually there.

But Ballantine was clearly delighted. 'I knew you'd be pleased, Father. Give him a kiss, Anna.'

Anna cautiously advanced, to be seized and embraced, while to her alarm, Lord Bordman's free hand immediately slipped down her back to grasp her buttock; fortunately, he could make no progress through the sable. Even more to her alarm, while doing this, he appeared to fall over, his face bumping into her bodice – she

150

was several inches the taller.

She got him upright again, while he prodded the floor with his stick.

'Now, Father,' Ballantine remonstrated. 'You know the quack said that you must not get excited.'

Between them, they got his lordship on to a settee, while a man, dressed in a morning coat, who Anna remembered as Bowen the valet, arrived with a glass of brandy. He relieved Anna of her coat, and she found herself seated beside her father-in-law.

Having laid down his stick, he held her hand and at the same time rested his other hand on her knee. 'You must come and see me,' he announced. 'Often. Every week.'

Shit! Anna thought, and wondered if Himmler had had any idea what he was letting her in for.

However, Lord Bordman was eventually removed, thanks to the combined efforts of Bowen and his chauffeur, to get him down the stairs.

Anna's mood improved considerably when she was shown the rest of the maisonette. There was a dining room, which matched the drawing room – the mahogany table could seat twelve – and beyond was a kitchen and pantry, and then sleeping accommodation for Bowen who, she gathered, doubled as a butler. There were two other servants: a cook named Mrs Sloan, and a maid, Nellie. Upstairs, there were three bedrooms. The master was delightfully large, with a breakfast area and an en-suite bathroom. The guest room was only slightly smaller, and the third room was to be used by Elsa; these two rooms shared another bathroom. The furniture and fittings were all top quality.

'But this is superb,' Anna said.

Ballantine was clearly pleased. 'I know, of course, it can't possibly compare with your castle in Bavaria, but you will find it very convenient for shops and restaurants. I'm sorry Father mauled you like that; it's so long since he got his hands on any woman, much less a beauty like you, I wouldn't be surprised if he had a heart attack.'

'I didn't mind, really,' Anna lied. 'But ... I don't really have to visit him every week, do I?'

'No no, we'll sort something out. But now, let me tell you that I have organized a cocktail party for Friday night. Everyone who matters, what? I am going to make London sit up and take notice. And welcome you, of course.'

Anna thought she might survive after all.

Baxter turned over the sheets of paper, then picked up the photograph and studied it again. 'I must say, the *Times* didn't do her justice. She really is a looker.' Baxter smoked a pipe and his waistcoat was invariably sprinkled with tobacco; together with his pince-nez and his shabby clothes he suggested a down-at-heel schoolmaster. But Clive, seated before the desk, knew that his boss – because of both his acute brain and the ruthless determination that it governed

152

– was probably the best spymaster in the world.

'I have a feeling,' he said, 'that her looks are not even her most potent weapon.'

Baxter proceeded to fill his pipe, slowly and messily, as he always did when he wanted to think. 'I have a feeling that you have something going for this woman.'

'She's a difficult woman to meet and not have a few lascivious thoughts about, I'll grant you that.'

'Even if you think she's a tramp?'

'I never said she was a tramp, Billy. I said she's a fake.'

'So she claims to be something she's not. She also claims to be a damned beautiful woman, and there's nothing fake about that. Come now, Clive, if Bordman had taken up with a chorus girl, would you be so agitated? It's his bed, so he's entitled to decide who he puts in it. It certainly isn't our business. I understand that you feel maybe you failed in your job, by allowing him to sneak off and get married without your knowing anything about it and thus while you weren't standing behind him. And maybe you're right and she's just after his money, but your business was to protect his person, not his pocket book. You can't seriously suppose that a girl who looks like a cross between Greta Garbo and the Venus de Milo, and who has a face like an angel, is going to be physically dangerous to anyone, much less her husband.'

'I sincerely hope you're right. However, may

153

I just point out that the Venus de Milo, Greta Garbo, and the most itinerant of chorus girls all have traceable backgrounds. This doll has no background at all. She just appeared out of the wall, like a wraith. A better analogy would be Athena, but I don't think that Mrs Bordman sprang from the head of any god.'

Baxter slapped the papers on his desk. 'But it says here that Bordman met with the Count von Widerstand to get his consent to the marriage. You met him too.'

'We met a man who called himself Count von Widerstand. No such man exists. No such family exists or has ever existed. I checked with Gottfried Friedemann, who must know as much about German history as any man alive. As for being Mrs Bordman's father, there is not the slightest resemblance between them in looks, speech or demeanour. He is about five foot six; she is pushing six feet. He looks and moves like a spiv; she looks and moves like a goddess. He speaks with a Bavarian accent. I can't place hers, but it certainly isn't Bavarian. I'm not even sure that it's actually German. Her English comes across more naturally.'

Baxter at last lit his pipe. 'All right,' he conceded, 'you've convinced me that there could be some gigantic confidence trick going on. But really, old boy, it isn't our pigeon. We are responsible for the security of our people outside of the UK. And even if we tried to involve MI5, I imagine they'd laugh at us. I mean, if the Secret Service and Special Branch had to do something about every British aristocrat who makes an unwise marriage, we'd never have time to do anything else. And to interfere in this case, with a woman who is presently taking London society by storm ... there could well be questions in the House, especially with the PM apparently so determined to play footsie with the Nazis no matter where Hitler puts his foot. Bordman is a grown man. If he's picked up some pretty floozie who means to take him for everything she can get, well, it won't be the first time that's happened, and it won't be the last. Maybe he'll be a wiser man at the end of it. I'm sorry, Clive, but this file is closed. Take a week's leave, and then Athens is expecting you.'

'There is just one more point I would like to make.'

'I said, the file is closed.'

'You also said that I have convinced you that this woman is probably a fake. So tell me why she was introduced to us, as the Countess von Widerstand, by a colonel in the SS. Are you suggesting that she has managed to fool the SS as well? The SS?'

Baxter slowly laid down his pipe. 'No,' he said. 'I do not believe that anyone, certainly any German citizen, could fool the SS for more than ten minutes. You know, of course, that Bordman has requested British citizenship for his wife? And that it will be granted as a matter of course?'

'Isn't that all to the good? Our good? It means

that when she's found out she will be subject to our laws, not merely a deportation order.'

'When she's found out. There can't be any slip-ups, Clive. Everything we have got so far is circumstantial. When we prick her balloon we have to have facts. So, first thing, go back to Friedemann and ask him to reconsider his attitude. Do it by letter, and we'll send it in the diplomatic bag. That way there is no risk of the SS getting hold of it. Tell him to reply by letter to me, again using the diplomatic bag; we'll square it with the ambassador.'

'I'm not sure he'll go for it. He was pretty definite when I saw him.'

'So you may have to be heavy. That's a good job he has there, isn't it? Well paid?'

'Very well paid.'

'And he has a wife and family, and also, I believe, supports his parents.'

'Ye-s,' Clive said hesitantly.

'Well, tell him that if he cannot do this little job for us we will have to advise the ambassador that he is a security risk and will have to be let go.'

'That is very nasty. He's a decent fellow.'

'Anything to do with the SS is, by definition, nasty. Do it. Meanwhile, I will take what you have told me to the boss and see if he will let us put Mrs Bordman under twenty-four-hour surveillance. There is no possibility of getting a phone tap, and I'm not at all sure he'll go for surveillance on what we presently have. That's where whatever you can get out of Friedemann

156

will come in handy.'

Clive sighed, but nodded. And then snapped his fingers. 'The maid!'

'What maid?'

'Mrs Bordman has a German maid, who she brought with her to England. Her name is Elsa. I don't know her last name. But she certainly knows who and what her mistress actually is, and who she is working for.'

'I hope you're not suggesting we pick her up and beat the truth out of her.'

Clive grinned. 'I'd rather have a go at her mistress. But I have an idea: Belinda.'

'Oh, come now, Clive.'

'Hear me out. I'm damned sure these people are smart enough to spot one of our females a mile off. But they can't spot anything about Belinda, because she isn't one of us. On the other hand, she's a natural for this job. She's fashion editor of the *Pictorial*. And here we have a glamorous newcomer on the social scene, who wears her hair differently from any-one else save Veronica Lake, whose clothes are out of this world, who is, at this moment, the talk of London ... Any fashion editor would give her eyeteeth for an interview either with her or about her, maybe get a peek into her wardrobe, talk about her likes and dislikes...'

'I'm sure you're right. But the word is that she doesn't give interviews.'

'That's where our friend Elsa comes in. Butter her up instead of beat her up.'

'You think Belinda would go for it?'

'Belinda will go for anything I ask her to. Certainly if there's a fashion story at the end of it.'

'You'd have to tell her what we're after.'

'Just enough.'

Baxter considered for a moment. Then he said, 'Give it a whirl. But get that letter off to Friedemann. And enjoy Athens.'

'What's it like out there?' Belinda Hoskin asked as she opened the door of her flat.

'It's snowing.' Clive said, reaching for her.

Belinda was always someone worth reaching for. She was a small woman, only just over five feet tall, with a slender figure, and straight black hair which she wore short, cut just above her shoulders. Her features were piquant, in keeping with the rest of her. No stronger contrast with Anna Bordman could be imagined. But while Anna, at least from Clive's point of view – and looked at as a female object rather than a potential enemy – remained the ultimate unattainable and unapproachable love goddess, Belinda was a woman one wanted to hold and protect and cherish, even if he knew that she would deeply resent any suggestion that she needed protecting from anything.

Now she skipped away from his grasp. 'You'll have to take something off. You're sopping.'

Clive removed his coat and soft hat and hung them on the stand while taking her in: she was wearing a house robe and slippers, and he

158

estimated that she had just got out of her bath. 'And the shoes,' she insisted. 'And socks,' she added, going into the bedroom to fetch the slippers he left there.

'Shouldn't I go the whole way?' he asked.

'After dinner. Eating with naked men gives me indigestion.' She knelt before him to fit the slippers on his feet. 'There we go. What are you drinking?'

'I think scotch on a night like this.'

She went to the sideboard, poured, then held out one of the glasses. Clive had followed her across the room. Now he placed his glass beside hers and took her in his arms for a long, slow kiss, while he slid his hands across her shoulder blades and down the curve of her back to find her buttocks. As he had surmised, she was wearing nothing under the robe.

'Hello,' she remarked. 'Have you spent the day torturing some beautiful female spy?'

'Chance would be a fine thing. Come and sit down.' He picked up the drinks and led her to the settee.

'But something has turned you on,' she insisted. 'The weather out there would freeze the balls off a brass monkey, and certainly keep them in their proper place.'

'You don't think it could be the sight of a lovely woman in extreme deshabille welcoming me in from the cold?'

'If it were the first time, I might say possibly. But I consider myself, as regards you, worn goods.'

159

'Now who's the one in a funny mood? Why don't you just say yes and marry me?'

'Our lifestyles would clash too much. Certainly our work styles. Now tell me what's up, apart from your principal attribute.'

'I sometimes think that you should be the spy catcher and me the one who wanders around peering at beautiful women.'

'You would spend your life falling in love with your subjects. And your business would be their clothes. Not what might be in them. I'm waiting.'

'What do you think of Mrs Bordman?'

'Aha! As you were in Germany with the ghastly Ballantine, I assume you have met the countess.'

'Yes, I have.'

'And, like everyone else, fell madly in love with her?'

'I did not fall madly in love with her,' Clive snapped, his vehemence giving him away. 'And has everyone fallen madly in love with her?'

'I would say so, yes. Ballantine is both the most popular and the most envied man in London at this moment.'

'So what is your opinion?'

'I haven't actually met her yet, worse luck. But she is certainly stunning. And her clothes are out of this world.'

'I would like you to interview her, at her home.'

'Pffft!'

'I'm serious.'

'So am I. Don't you think we – and every editor of a glossy in London, not to mention most of the dailies – have been after an exclusive, or even some kind of press conference, ever since she arrived? The answer is "nein". Mrs Bordman does not give interviews to the press. Anyway, what's your interest? I mean, apart from her hair and her eyes and her mouth and her tits and her bum and her legs and everything else?'

'We need to know more about her.'

'We? You mean the department? But she's not your field.'

'She was when she started out.'

'You mean she could be a spy?'

'We prefer not to speculate. And we would prefer you not to, either. What we know is that she is not what she pretends to be – that is, a German aristocrat. So we need to find out just what she is.'

'For Bordman's sake?'

'Partly.'

'Working for MI6! That's exciting. But I don't see what I can do if she won't give me an interview.'

'Can't you be a very pushy, aggressive reporter? Foot in the door type thing?'

'They'd very likely throw me out.'

'If they do, I'll make it up to you.'

'I don't see how you will be able to do that, if my special assets are covered in bruises. All right, I'll give it a whirl. On one condition.'

'Name it.'

'That you won't be thinking of her when you're shagging me, after dinner.'

'You have my word.'

'And how long have I got you for?'

'All night, tonight.'

'I meant, when are you off again?'

'Well, actually, next week.'

'What did you say?'

'Seems there's something going on in Athens. I shouldn't be too long, maybe a couple of months.'

'Months!' she shouted. 'Well in that case, we'll skip dinner.'

Anna took off her gloves, threw her sable on to a chair, and kicked off her shoes.

'Your bath is ready,' Elsa said, helping to remove the rest of her clothes. When they were alone together they spoke German. 'It has not been a good day?' She piled Anna's hair on the top of her head and secured it with a ribbon.

Anna sank into the hot foam. 'Every time I have to attend one of these tea parties I think I am going to go mad. The inanity of these people! And do you know what Bally told me at lunch? Next month we have to go to some place called Cheltenham to watch some horse racing. Apparently it is absolutely de rigueur. Horse racing! What can possibly be interesting about that?'

'It is the betting.' Elsa knelt beside her to soap her back. 'The English are a nation of gamblers. Now, I have something to tell you.'

'Yes?'

'That woman was here again today.'

'What woman?'

'That fashion editor. I told you she came twice before Christmas, and she has been back every couple of weeks since. She wishes to interview you. She is very pushy.'

'Oh, yes, I remember. Is she genuine?'

'Every time she comes she leaves her card.' Elsa held it out; Anna flicked foam from her hand and studied it.

'Belinda Hoskin, Fashion Editor, the *Pictorial*,' she read aloud. 'Isn't that one of the magazines that has been telephoning us all winter?'

'Yes it is,' Elsa said.

'Well, they are persistent.'

'Very persistent. She actually tried to force her way in today. But when I called Bowen she desisted.'

'But she will presumably call again.' Anna laid the card on the table beside the bath.

'Do you not think it strange that an editor, having been turned down when she made a formal approach, should attempt to push her way in? Is fashion that important?'

'It is to some people, I suppose.' Anna soaped her breasts and stomach, slowly and sensuously. If she continued to find Ballantine an utterly unattractive man, his constant desire to hold her and stroke her and fondle her had awakened sensations and desires she had not known she possessed, and kept her in a constantly aroused state, which he naturally assumed was because of her adoration of him. 'You think she is suspicious?'

'I think anyone who shows too much interest in you is suspicious.'

Anna smiled. 'That covers half the male population of London. I do not see what this woman can know about me to make her so interested. But, if it bothers you, when next do you see Schmidt?'

'The day after tomorrow. Do you wish her eliminated?'

The SD's answer to everything, Anna thought. If the memory of the desperately running convict at the training camp was just beginning to fade, she could still feel Gottfried Friedemann against her. He had so enjoyed that lunch – had, like all her victims, living or dead, been unable to believe that so beautiful, sophisticated, and obviously wealthy a woman should be attracted to a humble librarian. He had accompanied her back to her flat in a state of euphoria, and when she had sat beside him on the settee and put her arm round his shoulders, she had thought he might be about to burst into song.

She had been kissing him when Elsa had entered the room. Elsa had walked behind the settee, her feet making no sound on the carpet, and had placed the pistol on the table, again noiselessly. Friedemann had only realized she was in the room when she had emerged in front of him to ask him if he would like something to drink. He had released Anna, turned away from her, and looked up in dismay at having his idyll interrupted. In that moment, her arm still round his shoulders, Anna had extended her hand, picked up the pistol, placed the muzzle against the nape of his neck, pointing upwards in line with his head, and squeezed the trigger.

How easy it was to kill a man. But when he is actually in your arms ... She had been unable to suppress a shriek as blood had spurted over her hand and on to the cushions. She had fled to the bathroom while Elsa had laid the body flat, still on the cushions, so that not a trace of blood had fallen on the carpet. By the time Anna had returned, Elsa had wrapped the dead man's head in a towel, by no means to conceal the features but to sop up the blood. 'I think he died happy,' she had remarked.

Anna wondered how many more people were going to have to die happy before her blood-stained course was done. But she certainly did not want the number to include some innocent woman who was only doing her job, if perhaps a little over-zealously.

'I think that would be a mistake at this time,' she said. 'We do not have Scotland Yard working for us as the SD had the police in Germany. Get Schmidt to find out something about her.'

'You do understand the consequences if anyone discovers the truth about you?'

'No one can possibly do that as long as Bally is protecting me. But if this woman is in any way likely to be a problem, then we will deal with it.'

'Very well. But Schmidt is also getting anxious about something to show Berlin. At present all they are getting is photographs in the newspapers of you living the high life.'

'That's what they sent me here to do, isn't it? Don't worry, I am working on it. I should have something for him within a fortnight.'

'I think you're enjoying yourself too much, being the toast of London, living in this splendid ... what do they call it in England?'

'It is a maisonette. And why should I not enjoy it? It just about makes up for Bally. Besides, I've never lived anywhere quite as nice as this.'

Elsa snorted. But even she had to agree that Ballantine's home was even more luxurious than the Berlin apartment. The whole ambience was one of an upper-crust society to which Anna had never belonged, but which she intended to enjoy for as long as possible.

But that did depend upon doing her job.

'So there it is,' Baxter said. 'Absolutely no surveillance. Political dynamite, blah, blah, blah. Has your girlfriend had any joy?'

'I'm afraid not,' Clive admitted. 'Belinda isn't really the forceful type. I mean, she's brilliant at her job. What she doesn't know about women's clothes and fashion wouldn't cover the back of a postage stamp. But she's strictly on the up and up. She's tried to gain access to the Bordmans several times and been rejected. She's not used

166

to that, and frankly she's fed up. And with me away, I'm afraid she lost interest. I think that the written evidence provided by Friedemann remains our best bet. Have you shown it to the boss?'

'There isn't going to be any written evidence,' Baxter said.

'Say again? You mean Friedemann is still refusing to co-operate?'

'Friedemann has quit his job.'

'Good God! You mean he quit because we wanted that information?'

'No, no. At least, he didn't quit because of your letter. He actually left his job the very day you and Bordman returned from Berlin. The bastard didn't even have the courtesy to resign. Just walked out and didn't go back. The embassy didn't even realize he'd quit for several days.'

'That's incredible. And impossible. Something has happened to him.'

'Now Clive, don't go tilting at windmills. Nothing has happened to him. The embassy received a letter written by his wife informing them that her husband had suffered a nervous breakdown and would be unable to return to work.'

'And they believed that?'

'The letter was supported by another,' Baxter continued patiently, 'from a psychiatrist, stating that Herr Friedemann is suffering from clinical depression, and has to be kept under constant supervision to prevent the risk of his harming himself.'

'And they believe that?'

'Clive, this fellow is one of the most eminent men in his field in Germany. You cannot possibly suppose that he would supply a false diagnosis.'

Clive sighed. 'What you, and it seems everyone else in this country, don't understand, is that to be eminent in Germany today you have to be a member of the Nazi Party. And once you are a member of the Nazi Party, you do, and say, and write what the Party tells you to, without question.'

'Clive, I would hate to think that you are becoming paranoid.'

'I would like your permission to return to Berlin.'

'To do what, precisely?'

'Just to go to Friedemann's house and talk with him.'

'The psychiatrist's letter rather suggests he may be in hospital.'

'I would say he's in prison.'

'In prison?'

'Well, obviously someone found out that he had given me that information, even if he refused to put it in writing.'

'I think you're making a large number of rather prejudiced presumptions. Anyway, if, as you say, he's in prison, how do you propose to get to see him?'

'Getting to see his wife could be equally important.'

Baxter considered for a moment. Then he nodded. 'All right. We'll fix you up with a cover and a visa. It'll take a couple of weeks.'

'A couple of weeks?'

'Every i has to be dotted and every t crossed. Anyway, what's the rush? He quit his job six months ago. So if you can find him now, good luck. But, Clive...' He pointed. 'We want no international incidents.'

Clive grinned.

'Oh, my darling,' Anna murmured, nestling against Ballantine's shoulder as she sat beside him on the settee, legs curled beneath her. 'This is so good. We simply have to cut back on all these parties and receptions, and spend more time together.'

His arm went round her. 'Unfortunately, the parties go with the job.'

'And then all this working late at the office...'

'There happens to be a bit of a flap on.'

'There is always a flap on. And your part in it can't go on so late in the evenings...'

'There are all these papers to be read. I have to study them, and then pick out the salient points and précis them, ready for the Foreign Secretary to have available before he goes to the House the next day.'

'Can't you do that here just as well as at the office?'

He looked down at her. 'You mean you would not object? I have to concentrate, you know.'

'I understand that, and I would not interfere

169

with your concentration, believe me. It's just to have you here. And then, you know, the hour it always seems to take for you to be driven home from the office – well, you'd already be here. A whole extra hour!'

'I'd still have to be driven home at some time, you know.'

'Yes, but if you were driven home at five o'clock, well, no one really makes love at five o'clock in the afternoon, do they? But if you were home from then on, we'd have that hour whenever we wanted it. To make love.'

He kissed the top of her head and slipped his hand inside her dressing gown to fondle her breasts. 'Did anyone ever tell you that you have got to be every man's dream of how a woman should be, and act, and look? You should give lessons.'

'I only want to look, and be, and act for you, Bally. Say you'll spend more time at home. Please.'

'Well ... it's irregular, you know, to bring FO papers home. But I don't see any harm in it; we're perfectly secure up here, and they can go in my safe overnight. All right.'

'Oh, my darling! Didn't anyone ever tell you that you are a dream husband? But of course no one has. I am the only wife you've had. Now, tell me about this flap. Or is it top secret?'

'It'll be in all the papers tomorrow. Hitler is occupying the rest of Czechoslovakia.'

Anna sat up straight, so suddenly she gave a grunt of pain as his fingers dragged across her nipples. 'But...'

'I know. After all the assurances he gave the PM back in November.'

'I told you he was a treacherous bastard.'

'Yes, you did. Now we have egg all over our faces. And you know what is really making the PM see red? It's the way Hitler is assuming that no matter what he does, we won't respond. Well, I suspect he is going to get a very big surprise.'

'You mean ... Oh, my God! But you said we couldn't go to war because we weren't strong enough.'

'I said we couldn't go to war because we weren't *ready*. But that was six months ago.'

'And we are ready now?'

'Ready enough. With the French, of course. They have the best army in Europe; we have the best navy. Don't get me wrong. We don't want to have to fight anybody, but we will if we have to, and Hitler has got to be told that if he tries any more of these territorial grabs we are going to stop him. By force, if necessary.'

'There is mail for you, ma'am,' Elsa said, serving breakfast.

'From Germany,' Ballantine said, picking up the envelope. 'Must be from your father; I was wondering why he never wrote you.'

Anna slit the envelope. 'Oh!'

'Not bad news, I hope, my darling?'

'He's dead! Daddy's dead!'

'Good lord! Just like that? Oh, my darling,

I'm so terribly sorry. What did he die of?'
'Beckman says it was a heart attack.'
'Who is Beckman?'
'Our doctor. The family doctor. He says
Daddy has had trouble for some time. And he
never told me. Bally, I must go to the funeral.'
'Of course you must, my dear. It's just that it's
such a damned awkward time, with this Czech
crisis blowing up all over again...'
'You don't think the FO would approve of
your paying a private visit to Germany?'
'Well, it could be dashed awkward, don't
you know? If the situation were to seriously
worsen...'
Anna rested her hand on his. 'I entirely
understand. But they can't object to my going,
surely. He is my father.'
'Of course no one is going to object to your
attending your father's funeral. I only wish I
could come with you.'
She squeezed his fingers. 'I know you do, my
darling. I wish you could come too. But it'll
only be for a few days.'
'A few days?'
'Well, I imagine there will be some legal
matters to be sorted out – Daddy's Will, things
like that. Certainly it can't take more than a
fortnight.'
'A fortnight,' he muttered. 'We haven't spent
a single night apart since our marriage.'
'I know. I hate the idea of sleeping alone more
than you do. But when I come back...'
'When you come back,' he said dreamily.

'When do you want to go?'

'It should be tomorrow. As soon as I can arrange a passage.'

'I'll do that for you.' He finished his coffee, got up, and leaned over to kiss her. 'I must rush. A fortnight!' He hurried from the room.

Anna finished her own coffee while she waited for the front door to slam. Then she said, 'Thank God for that. I wouldn't have liked to confide that information to Schmidt.'

'You told Himmler that England would not fight,' Elsa said.

'And he made the assumption that their attitude would not change.'

'He won't be happy.'

'That's why I have to explain it to him in person. He'll understand that it is his mistake, not mine.'

Elsa looked doubtful. 'I hope you're right. Talking about Schmidt, he has reported on that woman.'

'The so-called fashion editor? What has he got?'

'That she is an absolutely bone fide fashion editor, very well known in England.'

'Well then, that's something we can stop worrying about.'

Elsa started to clear the breakfast dishes. 'You have to admit Schmidt is very efficient. He has her home address, the make of car she drives ... he even has the name of her lover.'

'Who I suppose is some English aristocrat.' Anna got up and went into the bedroom to run a bath.

'No, no. Schmidt hasn't yet found out exactly what this man does, but he is definitely not an aristocrat. His name is ... ah ... Bartley.'

Having turned on the taps, Anna had thrown her dressing gown across the bed. Now she reappeared in the doorway. 'What did you say?' she asked very slowly.

'I said the name of this man was Bartley. Don't tell me you know him?' Elsa turned her head to look at her mistress, and gave a little gasp. 'Anna? Are you all right? You look quite pale.' She dropped the handful of cutlery she was holding with a clang.

Anna had advanced into the bedroom. Now she collapsed into a chair, knees drawn up tight against her breasts. 'Bartley was the name of the man who was posing as Bally's private secretary in Berlin last year. He is actually an agent for MI6. Heydrich told me that is virtually the English equivalent of the SD.'

'Shit!' Elsa commented. 'What a coincidence.'

Anna raised her head. 'There is no coincidence about it.'

'Now, we don't know that, Anna. This woman is a fashion editor, and right now you are news. Your clothes are news, what you do ... Everyone wants to interview you.'

'So they telephone for an appointment, or they send a reporter with a photographer. And when we tell them we are not interested, they go away again. The editors never come themselves. This woman came herself, time and again, and she came alone. I've always thought that was strange. She didn't have a photographer with her, did she?'

'No,' Elsa said, frowning.

'But she was trying to gain access to this house. She was sent, Elsa. She has to have been sent. By Bartley.'

'Shit!' Elsa said again. 'It was all going so well. What must we do? I am sure Schmidt could take her out for us.'

'Elsa, she is the mistress of a very high-powered secret policeman. Were anything criminal to happen to her, we would have the entire resources of Scotland Yard turned loose on us. If Bartley sent her to see what she could find out about me, he will know that I had something to do with her murder.'

'But if he sent her in the first place, it means that he suspects you.'

'I have an idea he suspected me from the beginning. But he's never been able to prove anything about me. Using his girlfriend to try to get in here shows that he's clutching at straws. If he had anything – anything at all concrete against me – he would simply have obtained a search warrant.'

'But if we know he's working on you, he will turn up something eventually.'

'I think it is something on which we should take advice. We'll be in Germany the day after tomorrow. We'll ask Heydrich what we should do.'

'Why, Anna.' Reinhardt Heydrich held her hands to draw her forward for a kiss on the cheek. 'How good you look. High society agrees with you. As for that black dress...'

'Thank you, Herr Colonel.'

'Sit down.' He returned behind his own desk. 'London seems to agree with you so much that you have forgotten our existence.'

'How could I do that, Herr Colonel? But it has taken time to set things up, and also there have been problems. However,' she hurried on, watching his expression, 'it is all in place now. In fact, I have brought some photographs with me.' She opened her handbag.

Heydrich frowned. 'These are sensitive subjects?'

'I would say so. Bordman brought them home to read, and then he locked them in his safe.'

'To which you have access?'

'I have obtained the combination, yes,' Anna said proudly, and took out the roll of film.

'And you've brought that with you, in your handbag, just like that. Do you realize what would have happened had you been stopped and searched?'

'With respect, Herr Colonel, no one is going to stop and search the Honourable Mrs Bordman. At least in England. They do not do that sort of thing over there.'

'What they do, or do not do, in England is not relevant. The Reich has spent a great deal of time, and money, making you what you are.

176

Tell me what was the most important thing you were taught.'

Anna drew a deep breath. 'To obey any order immediately and without question.'

'That also means following procedural rules to the letter, as I remember explaining to you before you began this assignment. It is neither your duty nor your prerogative to change the rules to please yourself. Why did you not use Schmidt as you were instructed to do?'

Anna licked her lips; this was the first time she had encountered any hostility from her employers since leaving training school. 'I knew I was coming here personally in a couple of days.'

Heydrich gazed at her for several seconds. 'You said you had a problem.'

Anna sighed with relief; the crisis seemed to be over. 'It's to do with the man Bartley. I spoke to you of him.'

'So you did. And?'

Anna outlined what had happened.

'And you still think he is after you?'

'Yes, I do.'

'You flatter yourself. As a matter of fact, he is in Berlin at this moment.'

'Well, then...'

'He arrived here two days ago, Anna. Was your intended visit published in the Court Circular?'

Anna flushed.

'Yet you think his visit could be to do with you,' Heydrich went on, 'even if he doesn't know it. He is trying to find his old friend Gott-fried Friedemann.'

Anna clasped both hands to her neck. 'Oh my God!'

'Absolutely. A gentleman into whose head, as I recall, you expertly introduced a bullet last October.'

'And he has tracked me here? But as he is here...'

'No, no, Anna. He is staying at the embassy and is operating under their auspices. He cannot be tampered with. In any event, as I keep telling you, he is not after you. He is looking for his old friend, and he is not going to find him, or his family, who are safely in Dachau. He will only know that Friedemann has left the embassy and disappeared. He can only learn the truth if someone were to tell him the truth, and I cannot imagine who might do that. Can you?'

Anna swallowed at the implied threat.

'So all we really have to consider,' Heydrich said genially, 'is your ignoring of regulations and your undisciplined behaviour.'

'I...'

Heydrich raised a finger. 'I know you are going to say that no harm has been done. This time. But put yourself in the position of a com-manding general, who issues his plans for a campaign and then discovers that one of his subordinates has completely ignored those plans and followed his own ideas, and claims that he should not be punished because he was not defeated. That subordinate would be shot.'

Anna swallowed. 'I understand, Herr Colonel. It will not happen again.'

'It *must* not happen again. It *cannot* happen again. Perhaps you have forgotten that when you agreed to work for us – ' Anna stared at him in amazement – 'you were given a set of rules that had to be obeyed, and informed of the consequences if any of those rules were disobeyed in the slightest degree.'

Anna gasped. At the training camp she had carefully avoided breaking any rules, save for perhaps over-reacting to Gerda's advances. Now the situation had to be retrieved, and immediately. 'I understand what you are saying, Herr Colonel. And I have promised that it will not happen again. I think my judgement was distorted because I recently came into possession of the most important news, which I felt it was necessary to tell you personally.'

'What news?'

'It is that the British are determined to go to war.'

Heydrich stared at her for several seconds. 'Over Czechoslovakia? You said they would not.'

'That was in October. And I was proved right, was I not? But the English believed what the Fuehrer told them, that he had no more territorial ambitions in Europe. Now they feel betrayed.'

'Are you calling the Fuehrer a liar?'

'Of course I am not, Herr Colonel. I am reporting what the British are saying, as you are employing me to do. Herr Chamberlain especially feels betrayed. I do not believe that he is going to go to war over Czechoslovakia, but my husband says that he is going to issue a public statement that any further German aggression – that is his word – will be a casus belli.'

Again Heydrich considered this for several seconds. 'We moved into Czechoslovakia over a week ago. But you are only telling me this now.'

'I only learned of it two days ago, Herr Colonel. And as, by then, I knew I was coming to Berlin in any event, I thought it best to bring the news myself, with everything else I had for you.'

'You thought it best!' Heydrich scoffed. 'When I wish you to think, I will inform you. I think being married to an English aristocrat has gone to your head. You need to remember that being Mrs Bordman is a façade, a cover story. You are employed by the Reich.'

'I have said I will not forget that again, sir.' Anna could not prevent her voice from rising an octave as she realized that she might have dug herself a deeper hole than the one she had previously been in.

'Oh, I intend to make sure of that, Anna.' He pressed his intercom. 'Is Captain Blaner in the building?'

'Yes, sir,' the woman's voice said. 'He is with Commandant Gehrig.'

'Is she in Berlin? Excellent. Ask them both to come in, please.'

Anna drew a deep breath. 'What ... I mean...'

'You see, Anna, when a young girl wishes to remember something, she ties a knot in her handkerchief, does she not? We are going to tie a knot in your brain, to make sure that you never again forget who you are working for, and the rules you have to follow.'

Anna gasped. 'My family...'

'Ah, yes, your family. That is an interesting point. Would you rather your family was punished for your errors? Or would you prefer to suffer that punishment yourself?'

Another deep breath. But she still had a weapon left. 'I would prefer you to punish me.'

'Oh, good. I had intended to do that anyway, but it makes it so much simpler if you are in agreement.'

Anna licked her lips. 'My husband is expecting me back at the end of next week.'

'And we mustn't alarm the good fellow, must we? I would expect you will go back, Anna, a wiser and more compliant woman. Come.'

The doors were opened, and the two people came in. Both wore uniform, and both stood to attention, arms outstretched. 'Heil Hitler!'

'Heil! Gehrig, you remember Anna Fehrbach?'

Frau Gehrig looked at Anna. 'I do, Herr Colonel. She is looking well.'

'Well, we don't want to interfere with that, do we? She seems to have a loving husband. However, she also seems to have forgotten who and what she really is, and must be reminded of

181

this. I would like you to assist Blaner in this duty, as you know the girl already.'

'Of course, Herr Colonel. I shall enjoy that.'

Anna tried to catch her eye; this woman had almost been a friend when last she had seen her.

'May I ask exactly what you have in mind, Herr Colonel?' Blaner enquired.

'She is to be punished for disobeying orders,' Heydrich said. 'It is neither necessary nor desirable for you to know what those orders were. However, it is necessary, as I have said, that she should suffer no permanent injury, or that any mark be left on her body that will not fade within forty-eight hours. For this reason she should be caned, not whipped, and the blows should be strictly on her buttocks.'

Anna's head jerked. My God! she thought. He is talking about me! She remembered Karen screaming for mercy. Am I going to scream for mercy? Never. But she could not stop herself saying, in a voice she hardly recognized as her own, 'I have done everything you required of me, Herr Colonel. I have committed...'

Heydrich laid his finger on his lips. 'No secrets, Anna. The betrayal of State secrets is a very serious breach of rules, and your punishment will be at least doubled.'

Anna found that she was panting.

'Apart from the caning, Herr Colonel,' Blaner said, 'what else is to be done to her?'

'Anything you like, within the parameters I have outlined. Your business is to make her feel pain to the extent that she will never wish to suffer such a punishment again. What did you have in mind?'

'He is going to rape me,' Anna muttered.

Heydrich looked at Blaner.

'Well, sir, it would seem a pity to...'

'Pass up the opportunity to have sex with a beautiful woman? I have said that you may do what you wish, as long as she finds it unpleasant and is not marked.'

These people are talking about me, Anna thought again. And it is going to happen! Now she did have an urgent desire to scream. She had only had sex with one man in her life – her husband – and while Bally was an absolute gentleman in everything he did, she had still never enjoyed it. To be at the mercy of this lout...

But Blaner was still speaking. 'I was wondering, sir, if we might try out the new method on her.'

'What new method?'

'It is the use of electricity, developed by our scientists.'

'I do no wish her electrocuted.'

'No, no, sir. The emissions are strictly controlled. But attached to certain selected parts of the body, they are supposed to inflict exquisite pain. The technique is being suggested for interrogation, but of course it can be used for other purposes as well. The important point is that, however severe the pain, no mark is left upon the body.'

Oh my God! Anna thought. Oh, my God! But

God could not possibly come to her rescue; she had forsaken God when she had shot that desperately running convict. Was that not yet a year ago?

'That sounds very interesting,' Heydrich said. 'Call me when you are ready to proceed, and I will come down and see how it works. Off you go, now, Anna. We will talk again later.'

Six

Revenge

'Come along, Anna,' Frau Gehrig said kindly.

Anna stood up, but her knees gave way and she sat down again.

'You don't really want to be carried downstairs, do you?' Frau Gehrig asked.

Anna held the arms of her chair and pushed herself up. Blaner was actually holding the door for her. This can't be happening, she told herself. I am the Honourable Mrs Bordman. I am the darling of London society. But no doubt Karen had also told herself that this couldn't be happening as she was strapped to the triangle all those months ago.

Frau Gehrig walked beside her on the stairs, holding her arm against a stumble, as she did from time to time.

'I thought you were my friend,' Anna muttered.

'We are all your friends, Anna,' Gehrig said. 'That is proved by the fact that you are not to be permanently harmed and that Colonel Heydrich wishes to give you a second chance.'

'But you intend to torture me first.'

'We intend to punish you, and there can be no punishment without pain.'

They had reached the lower floor. Clerks and secretaries looked at them curiously, and then hastily looked away again. And in front of her was another flight of steps, these also leading down. She shuddered; she had been here before, even if not in this building. And the cell level was surprisingly similar to that in Vienna, save that there were no barred cells, merely closed doors, although they all had their sliding inspection hatch.

But the room at the end of the corridor was different, and again Anna's knees threatened to give way, so that Gehrig's grip tightened and jerked her upright.

'Listen,' she said in a low voice, 'let me give you some advice. Do not attempt to resist them. Submit to everything without a word. But when they hurt you, forget your pride and scream as loudly as you can. This will please them. But if they feel you are defying them, even in your mind, they will wish to hurt you more than ever.'

'But are you not one of them? Will you not be hurting me as well?'

'Yes, I will be hurting you, and I will enjoy doing so, because it is always enjoyable to hurt a beautiful, wilful woman, but that does not mean I wish you to be destroyed.'

Because you are hoping to have the opportunity to work me over again sometime, Anna thought.

Blaner was holding the door for her again, most politely, but inside the room there waited two men. Both were large, and both were in their shirt sleeves. Both had been looking rather bored, but their eyes brightened at the sight of Anna.

She entered the room, and the heavily padded door clicked shut behind her. She waited, keeping absolutely still, trying to convince herself that this was going to be nothing worse than a visit to the dentist.

'Would you undress, please,' Blaner asked courteously.

Anna looked at Gehrig. 'You would not like that lovely dress to be torn, now would you?' Gehrig asked. 'I will help you.' She released the buttons at the back of the dress, her fingers nimble. Anna drew a deep breath and shrugged the dress from her shoulders, allowed it to slide down the petticoat and gather round her ankles. 'I will hang it up for you,' Gehrig offered again.

Anna stepped out of the dress. Gehrig picked it up, shook out the creases, and took one of the hangers from the hook on the door, replacing the dress beside the two men's tunics. Anna waited. 'Now come along, Anna,' Gehrig said.

'The petticoat. The sooner we get it done the sooner it will be over.'

Anna took off her cloche hat and her hair tumbled down. The two men's eyes gleamed some more, as did Blaner's. Then she lifted the petticoat over her head and handed it to Gehrig, just as if the commandant were her maid.

'Continue,' Gehrig said.

'You mean you wish everything?'

'We wish you naked, yes.'

Anna opened her mouth. The only men, apart from Bally, before whom she had previously appeared naked had been Cleiner and Blassermann, and that had been in the quick act of changing from her uniform into her gym clothes. More importantly, neither of them had revealed the slightest sexual interest in her, while when she had been receiving instructions in male desires the man had fondled her through, or beneath her clothing – and he also had been merely doing a job of work. But these men reeked of sexual desire, and if they too would be doing a job of work, they clearly intended to enjoy it.

She closed her mouth again without speaking; to protest would be a waste of time, and might merely make things worse.

'Do not make them think you are resisting them,' Gehrig had said. She removed her cami-knickers, and Gehrig took them from her hand while Anna endeavoured not to meet anyone's eye. 'And the shoes and stockings,' Gehrig said. 'You may use that chair.'

187

There was a straight chair beside the desk. This was the most humiliating moment of the morning so far as, having released her suspender belt, she had to sit facing the men to roll down her stockings. Then the cold of the stone floor struck upwards through her body and she could feel her nipples hardening. Don't think, she told herself. Don't think.

'Now use the toilet,' Gehrig commanded.

Anna looked from her to the open toilet against the far wall in consternation. She had never done that before another person in her life, not even Elsa.

'We don't want a mess, do we?' Gehrig asked.

Anna stood up uncertainly, crossed the floor, and obeyed her; it actually was very necessary and a considerable relief.

'Now stand against the bar,' Gehrig commanded.

Anna had not noticed the bar before; she had been too busy trying not to look at any of her surroundings. The bar, a rounded steel tube, was situated to one side of the room, raised horizontally some three feet from the floor on two other rounded steel tubes. These had grooves into which the parallel bar fitted, and handles by which it could be raised and lowered as required. She drew a deep breath, then stood up and slowly crossed the floor. Her knees felt weak and she almost fell. This time no one assisted her. But she had no doubt that if she did fall she would be dragged to her feet, and the thought of them touching her was unbearable.

She reached the bar and stood against it; the steel pressed against her thighs.

'Now bend over,' Gehrig said.

Anna obeyed, bending from the waist, every muscle tensed, because now she knew she was going to be touched, as intimately and indecently as it was possible to imagine.

One of the men came into view as he stood in front of her, grasped her right arm, and pulled it down, so that she all but toppled over, prevented from actually falling by the bar. Then she saw the handcuffs attached to a ring in the floor. He did the same to her left wrist. Before he had finished she felt other hands on her legs, as they were pulled apart and each ankle in turn attached to another pair of handcuffs.

'Make her tight,' Gehrig instructed. 'She must not be able to move.'

The men cranked the handles, and the bar came up until it fitted into her groin, stretching her away from her wrists and ankles, leaving her both helpless and utterly exposed, buttocks highest.

Gehrig stood in front of her. 'If one is allowed to move when being caned,' she said, 'one runs the risk of suffering serious harm, or permanent scarring. And we wouldn't want that, would we? You are such a beautiful creature.' She reached under Anna's arms and gently caressed her breasts. 'There is no aspect of you that is not superb.' Anna stared at her legs, feeling tears running down her cheeks and hearing them plop on the floor. Was there perhaps a glimmer of hope? But now Gehrig said, 'You may commence, Captain. The cane, remember. Not the whip.'

'Ahem,' said one of the men.

'What is it?'

'We have our perks, Frau Commandant.'

Gehrig looked at Blaner.

'That is correct, Frau Commandant. It is boring work being confined down here, and there is so seldom anything ... shall I say ... worth handling.'

They are talking about me as if I were a piece of furniture, Anna thought as she desperately tried to raise her head far enough to catch Gehrig's eye. And in fact the commandant did return her desperate gaze. But she merely shrugged.

'If that is the custom, I will allow one touch each. Colonel Heydrich is waiting to be called.'

Anna closed her eyes and felt hands on her buttocks. Then other hands passed between her spread legs to close on her groin.

'I suppose you are included?' Gehrig suggested.

'Well,' Blaner said, 'I like to know what I am about.'

Anna felt his hands on her buttocks, kneading the flesh, which she tried to keep as tensed as possible – a difficult task when she had been so tightened as to be standing on tiptoe.

Gehrig picked up the phone on the desk. 'Colonel Heydrich,' she said.

Anna felt the hands move, and heard a swish-

190

ing sound. She turned her head, and one of the men grinned at her.

'Herr Colonel?' Gehrig asked. 'We are about to commence the punishment. Very good, sir.' She replaced the receiver. 'He is on his way, but he says to continue. It is the electrical treatment he is interested in. Remember, she is to be struck only there.' She touched Anna's buttocks herself.

Anna drew a deep breath. The commandant had said not to attempt to defy them, to scream as loudly as she could. But she *wanted* to defy them. They could not destroy her. She was the Honourable Mrs Bordman. More important, far more important, she was Annaliese Fehrbach, and she was a woman who had been trained to fight, and to kill, and to survive. Perhaps these morons had forgotten that, or considered her no more than a lump of meat, to be chewed up and then spat out, when they were tired of the taste of her. But one day, she told herself, one day...

It seemed as if a knife blade had been drawn across her flesh. She gasped, and her mouth sagged open, even as her body drooped, to be held only by the bar pressing into her groin, still stretched taut so that she could not twist.

Before she could draw a breath, she was struck a second time, making her body stiff again. There seemed to be no air in her lungs, and she thought she was choking. But when the third blow came she involuntarily sucked at the air. At the fourth blow she couldn't control a whimper, and her eyes were burning as the tears

191

started again. Now her whole body seemed to be in pain, which was even penetrating her brain, and she hardly felt the last two blows, but between them – and even above the drumming in her ears – she heard the door opening and closing and realized that Heydrich had joined them.

The blows ceased, and she hung across the bar, feeling her cheeks suffuse as the blood rushed into them. The room was rotating about her, but she refused to open her eyes. I did not scream, she told herself. They could not make me scream.

'Is she all right?' Heydrich asked.

Gehrig stooped beside her, held her wrist and felt her pulse. 'She is all right. But perhaps we should wait a few minutes...'

'I am a busy man,' Heydrich pointed out. 'And I wish to see this new method. Show us, Blaner. And explain it.'

'Of course, Herr Colonel.'

Heydrich was apparently peering at her bottom. 'You are sure there will be no permanent marks?'

'None,' Gehrig assured him. 'That is the beauty of the cane. Those marks will fade within forty-eight hours. But she will remember the beating.'

'She will remember this more,' Blaner said enthusiastically. 'Now, sir, you see this box. It is the generator, which is activated simply by turning the handle. The faster it is turned, the more current is delivered, so that the interrogator can control the strength of the charge according to the mental and physical strength of the subject. Now, these two wires, each ending in an alligator clip, are attached to whatever part of the subject's body the interrogator wishes to use. One is negative and the other is positive. The charge will flow from one to the other, causing the severest discomfort to the part of the subject's body through which it travels. Favourite places are the big toe, on each foot – so that the current passes up one leg, across the groin, and down the other – or the ears, in which case the current passes through the head. But I would not recommend that in this case, if it is your wish that the subject be, shall I say, preserved intact. The current passing through the brain can induce permanent damage. However, there are other useful places. The nipples, for example. This is especially useful for women, who – if you will forgive me, Frau Gehrig – have more ... how shall I put it ... flesh for the interrogator to play with. But of course the most efficacious of all are the genitals. One of these clips inserted into the anus, and the other clipped to the male penis can rob a man of any ability to resist further. A woman of course is even more susceptible, as she possesses two orifices, the invasion of which by steel and then electricity is both humiliating and agonizing.'

'But you say it does no permanent damage?' Heydrich asked.

'None at all, Herr Colonel. We coat the clips

in grease, you see, to ease the entry. This in no way interferes with the flow of current. But it does prevent any tissue damage, or even permanent marking. Once the current is switched off, the pain soon subsides. There is continuing discomfort for a few hours, but then that too wears off, and the subject is, shall I say as good as new. Although the memory remains, to be sure.'

'Then that is the method we wish to see,' Heydrich said.

'Very good, Herr Colonel. Now, the first thing to do is pull her apertures wide apart, like this.'

Anna screamed.

Elsa opened the apartment door.

'What...?' She stepped back as the two men entered the lobby, Anna between them. She was fully if untidily dressed, wearing her hat and her sable, and her clothes did not look terribly crushed, but she did not seem able to walk very well, and the men were holding her arms to keep her up. Now they half dragged her into the lounge and laid her on the settee, where she remained on her side.

'Thank you,' Gehrig said, having followed them. 'That will be all.'

'Heil Hitler!' they said as they left.

Elsa closed the door behind them. 'What in the name of God...? There's been an accident? Is she badly hurt?'

'I am assured that she is not hurt at all. Her feathers have been ruffled, that is all.'

'But what happened?'

194

'She has been a naughty girl, and has been disciplined. It had to happen some time. She has always had a tendency to do things her way instead of by the book. Well, hopefully, she will now be over that.'

'She has been beaten?'

'Only spanked a little.'

'But ... she looks unconscious.' Elsa bent to peer into Anna's face. 'Although her eyes are open.'

'She is perfectly conscious,' Gehrig assured her. 'She is just not in the mood to communicate. They used electricity.'

'I don't understand.'

'My dear Elsa, they fucked her with an electric current.'

Elsa clasped both hands to her neck. 'That is barbaric.'

'We live in a barbaric age. But it was very ... interesting to watch. I feel quite...' She regarded Elsa speculatively.

But Elsa had other things on her mind. 'We are supposed to return to England in just over a week's time. What are we going to tell her husband?'

'She will be perfectly fit to travel by then. In fact, she will be perfectly fit tomorrow, although she may be in an odd frame of mind. But that too should wear off. Do you know, I feel like a drink? Do you have alcohol?'

'Yes,' Elsa said absently.

'Then I will have schnapps. And pour one for yourself. You are too tense.'

'And Anna? She looks as if she needs one more than either of us.'

'I think it would be better to leave her there until she feels like moving.' Gehrig took the small glass, drained it, held it out for a refill, and sat at the dining table. 'Sit down, here, beside me.'

Slowly Elsa lowered herself into the chair next to the commandant.

'Is this apartment bugged?' Gehrig asked.

'It is. But it is not turned on. It is only used for special guests.'

Gehrig nodded. 'One cannot be too careful. I am telling you this because we have known each other a long time. But you also need to look to yourself.'

'Me?'

'You are her minder. Therefore you are responsible for what she does, or does not do. Your name has been raised.'

Elsa's hand was trembling as she drank; the glass clattered against her teeth.

'Because I trained you – because you are my friend – I interceded for you. I hammered the point that Anna is, or was, a most wilful girl, and that you undoubtedly found it difficult, if not impossible, to control her without endangering the entire mission. So they do not intend to proceed against you at this time. But it must not happen again, or you may also have an interesting encounter with an electric current. Or worse. Anna, you see, has established herself in a position of great importance to the

196

Reich, and, at least for the time being, needs to be maintained in that position. So while she cannot be allowed to run wild, she equally cannot just disappear, certainly without careful preparation. But as far as the world is concerned, you are merely a lady's maid. And in England you are an alien lady's maid. If you were simply not to return from a visit to Germany, and were replaced by someone else, no one in England would give a damn.'

Elsa's hands moved back to her throat.

'You should remember that. You need to get closer to her. Have you ever had sex with her?'

'There is no chance of that.'

'Nonsense. Every woman is a lesbian at heart, because men are so unpleasant.'

'It is a point of view. But Anna is not every woman. She is not interested in sex.'

Gehrig turned her head to look at the settee and, as she did so, Anna suddenly got up. Her shoes had come off and she walked, a little uncertainly, to the corridor leading to the bedrooms, still without saying a word.

'Do you think she heard what we were saying?' Elsa asked.

'If she did, I don't think it matters; she is not fully compos mentis at this moment. What do you mean, she is not interested in sex? She is a married woman.'

'The two things are not necessarily synonymous. She submits to her husband because it is her job to do so, but I can tell you that she hates it, the more so because he is insatiable, and is always at her whenever he is home. It is quite disgusting. But she never shows any emotion. Her heart is as cold as ice.'

Gehrig nodded, thoughtfully. 'Yes, I do remember her from the training school. She nearly killed that girl Gerda.'

'I have read the file.'

'And as you say, she revealed absolutely no emotion except for a determination not to be interfered with. Dr Cleiner reported that she was ice cold emotionally, and was a born killer. I always supposed he was referring entirely to her emotional state. Well, perhaps he was. But you, Elsa, you are not frigid.'

Elsa pulled a face. 'In this present assignment I have not much chance to be anything else.'

'Well, you must somehow get through to her. It is necessary for both of you. However, as you are here, and I am here, I think I should refresh your memory. Do you not agree?'

Anna closed the bedroom door. For a moment she stood absolutely still. Then she moved forward, still uncertainly. It was not that her feet hurt, or that she was dizzy; it was simply a reluctance to feel her legs move, against each other.

When she reached the bed, she fell across it, and then rolled into the centre, feeling the sable gathering beneath her. She lay on her back, legs pressed together. She wanted to keep them like that for the rest of her life. But she would not be able to. Her masters required her to return to

198

London and resume being pawed by that tub of lard. She felt that if any man were ever to touch her below the waist again she would go mad. Actually, she remembered, Bally very seldom touched her below the waist with his hands. He was too much of an old-fashioned gentleman, too easily embarrassed by anything too overtly intimate. But he would certainly wish to enter her. As he wished to enter her every night. And, as always, she would have to make appreciative noises.

She was amazed, and even a little disturbed, at the clarity of her thoughts. But then, her eyes were open as she stared at the ceiling above the bed. When her eyes were open, she could think. The moment they closed, she could only feel, and the feeling was not merely the piercing, humiliating agony that seemed to be splitting her in half – that lurked all the time. But now it was combined with a no-less consuming hatred of the men and woman who'd been standing around her, of the whole SD, the Reich, Germany itself – perhaps the whole world.

That hatred – that burning anger at her fate – had, she knew, begun that March day the previous year when her family had been so brutally torn apart. It had existed throughout the training school, rising to a climax the day she had shot that helplessly doomed man, but had then gradually been sublimated beneath her role as Countess von Widerstand, beneath the beautiful clothes, the expensive jewellery, the sumptuous lifestyle. Above all, the privacy.

And if she had been aghast at being commanded to marry Ballantine, she had always known that she would have to have sex with *someone* – as one always knew that one day one would have to go to the dentist – and marriage to an English aristocrat had at least promised the continuation of the lifestyle to which she had become accustomed. She had hated again when she had been ordered to kill Friedemann, but that hatred had been directed at herself. And after that she had allowed herself to drift into a world where she was *somebody*. Where she mattered. Of course it was a fake world, which would one day – perhaps quite soon – have to end. But she had felt, however much she had hated them and everything they represented, that she was of value to her masters, and that they would always seek to protect and nurture her.

That misguided belief had ended today. She was their slave, and had been treated as a slave, and would be treated as a slave for the rest of her life. She did not know if she would ever be able to look any of them in the eye again. But she did know that if she'd had her pistol she would have shot them all, even if she had herself been killed while doing so. And if it had also meant the deaths of her mother and father and Katerina? That was the stone wall against which she found herself whenever she attempted to run.

In any event, it was academic. Her pistol was in England, Elsa having considered it too risky to cross several borders with a gun in their baggage – she had been sufficiently agitated on their outward journey.

The door opened. 'How are you feeling?'

Anna turned her head, opened her mouth, and realized that her throat was sore. There were so many parts of her body that were sore she had not noticed it before. But she had spent several minutes screaming her lungs dry. She licked her lips.

'You need something to drink,' Elsa said. She left the room and came back a few moments later with a glass of water, which she held to Anna's lips, raising her head from the bed. 'You need to rest, but you are still fully dressed. Let me help you.'

'If you lay a finger on me,' Anna said, 'I will kill you.'

Elsa regarded her for several seconds. 'You haven't eaten anything since breakfast,' she said, 'and it is now five. Would you like an early supper?'

'No.'

'You must eat something.'

'I will eat tomorrow. Just bring me a glass of brandy, and two of those sleeping pills.'

Elsa considered this, then nodded. 'Perhaps that would be best. Things will look better tomorrow.'

Elsa was right. Anna's bottom was still sore when she awoke, and there was still some discomfort in her genital area, but she did feel

201

much better, even if her brain still seethed with angry indignation.

Elsa was solicitous. 'Would you like me to put some cream on your ass?'

'How does it look?'

'Roll over.'

Anna had slept naked, as she always did. Now she lay on her stomach and Elsa pulled back the sheet. 'There are still marks.' She touched the reddened flesh. 'Is it very sore?'

'Yes.'

'Cream will help. I will fetch it.'

'Will the cream make the marks fade more quickly?'

'Well, no. But it will alleviate the discomfort.'

Anna pulled up the sheet. 'I do not wish to be touched.'

Elsa seemed inclined to press the point, but changed her mind as she gazed into Anna's eyes. 'But you will eat something? You must.'

'I will have breakfast. I am hungry.'

Anna spent the day in bed. She understood very well that she was having a form of breakdown. But there were so many things to think about, of which the only important one was herself. Not merely what she was, what she was being required to do, or even the punishment she had received, as such. It was about what the punishment had done to her, to her essentially private persona, and perhaps even to her character.

To have to strip naked in front of those men – and Gehrig. To be touched by them, and beaten

202

by them, and then to feel their fingers, followed by those dreadful clips ... She shuddered. Even now that the discomfort had almost entirely faded, she could still feel the clip being closed on her clitoris, still feel ... She found that she was holding herself, and could not let herself go. She gasped, and shuddered, and was exhausted. Had she climaxed when they had been torturing her? She couldn't believe that was possible. But she didn't know.

So what was Bally going to be met with when she returned to England next week? Someone who would scream in horror when he tried to enter her? Or someone who would reveal a voracious appetite, a screaming desire to be satisfied, when she could never be satisfied again? She did not know, just as she did not know whether this frightening mood was to be with her for the rest of her life, or was merely a temporary result of her ordeal.

By next morning the discomfort was almost entirely gone. She peered at herself in the mirror. There were still marks, but she knew they would be gone in another couple of days. In any event, Bally was not a bottom man. She remembered how embarrassed he had been on the night she had seduced him, when, as instructed, she had suggested he might like to come in from behind.

She had a bath, washed her hair, and dressed herself in her black outfit. Elsa had breakfast waiting for her, and she beamed benevolently as she watched Anna eat.

'Now you are looking fine again. Are we going somewhere?'

'I'm going for a walk.'

'That is an excellent idea. I'll just get my hat and coat.'

'I wish to walk by myself.' Anna fitted her still-wet hair into her cloche and put on her sable.

Elsa frowned. 'By yourself? I don't think I can permit that.'

'I wish to be by myself, in the midst of other people. I think this is necessary therapy. Do not be frightened, Elsa. I am not going to throw myself under a bus. I have too much to do.' She went to the door. 'I won't be long.'

She went down in the lift, which was fortunately empty. The concierge had of course seen her being brought in two days before, and he looked apprehensive at the sight of her, but she gave him a bright smile, put on her dark glasses, drew a deep breath, and pushed the revolving doors.

It was a bright spring morning, and still at the height of the rush hour. People hurried to and fro, and car horns blared. There was a distinct air of crisis, with men standing on street corners, muttering over their newspapers, but she got the impression it was less in apprehension of what might be about to happen, than in slight shock at what had already happened. At the Fuehrer's latest brilliant coup. He seemed to be able to get anything he wanted without

204

shedding a drop of blood.

Quite a few heads turned to look at her as she walked by, but none knew who or what she was. They were simply admiring a beautiful woman wearing beautiful clothes, noting her poise and allure.

She felt like going to church. Did she dare? She did not have to confess; just to sit there in the quiet solitude would be so nice. She decided she would do that, turned to cross the street, and was taken utterly by surprise by a voice at her shoulder.

'Mrs Bordman?'

She turned back in a jumble of chaotic emotions, and gazed at Clive Bartley.

'I'm terribly sorry,' he said. 'I didn't mean to startle you. I suppose you don't remember me. Clive Bartley.'

Anna realized her mouth was open. Hastily she closed it, and then opened it again. 'I remember you very well, Mr Bartley. But what are you doing here?' As if she didn't know what he was doing, at least what he was doing in Berlin. But here, on the street outside her apartment? 'Were you coming to call on me?'

Even as she spoke, her brain was spinning in several different directions at the same time. He was her enemy, and the enemy of her people. But they were not *her* people; they were her masters, brutal and unprincipled. Could he possibly be a weapon to use against them? That was absurd; it would be far too dangerous. If

Heydrich were ever to find out she had even thought of betraying the Reich, she would probably be skinned alive. While if this so attractive man were ever to find out that she had two murders to her credit, he would place her under arrest the moment she again set foot in England.

But not even Heydrich had been able to find out just what this so attractive man was after, or how much he knew about her, about her mission. And she would never have a better opportunity to do that than here in Berlin – and, in fact, in her own apartment. She should even be commended for her initiative. More importantly, this so attractive man might be able to teach her something about herself, about where she had been, and where she was going as a woman. Where she *wanted* to go. She remembered when, six months ago, she had been told to have sex with Bally, she had thought how preferable it would have been to seduce this so attractive man. And what did she have to lose now?

He was looking embarrassed. 'I was toying with the idea of seeing if anyone was there. I mean, I didn't know that you were in Berlin. But...' He looked her up and down.

'Yes, I am in mourning,' she agreed. 'I am here for the funeral of my father.'

'Ah ... the Count.'

'That is correct. But as I am here, and you were hoping to find me here ... That is what you were hoping, was it not?'

'Well, actually, I wasn't. Coming here was

pure speculation.'

'Speculation about what?'

'Ah...' People were constantly passing them on either side. 'I'd love to talk with you, Mrs Bordman. Is there somewhere we could have a coffee?'

'Of course. My apartment.'

Now he looked startled. 'Your apartment?'

'Why not? You were thinking of calling there, on the off-chance someone might be there. Now you know someone is there: me. And we will be able to talk in complete privacy.'

'Well, that would be awfully decent of you.'

She could tell that he was also making some furious calculations, wondering how much he could get out of her. If he had any idea of how much she was prepared to give...

'It will be my pleasure. I was lonely.' She led him back to the apartment building, past the concierge, and into the lift. They faced each other as it went up. 'So who are you protecting today?' she asked.

'I'm actually on a private visit, trying to look up an old friend.'

'Trying?' The lift stopped and she led him across the lobby and opened the door.

'He seems to have disappeared. Given up his job. I have a home address, but he's not there either. Neither is his family. The whole lot seem to have left Berlin, but nobody knows why or where they went.'

'How frustrating for you.' She led him into the lounge, closed the door, and turned to face him. 'Would you prefer coffee, or a drink?'

'It's a little early for a drink. I suppose there's no chance you might have heard of this fellow? Name of Gottfried Friedemann.'

Anna knew her eyes had flickered, and that he had seen it. 'Why should I have heard of him?' she asked, and looked past him at Elsa, who was just emerging from the bedroom corridor.

'That was a quick—' Elsa hastily checked herself, glanced at Clive, and then looked again, her jaw also dropping. 'Excuse me, ma'am, I did not know you had company.'

'We would like some coffee.'

'Of course, ma'am. But may I have a word?'

'Excuse me,' Anna told Bartley. 'But do, please, sit down.' She followed Elsa into the kitchen and closed the door.

'Are you mad?' Elsa demanded. 'Don't you remember who that is?'

'I remember him very well. That is why I have brought him here.'

'I do not understand you at all. Well, Colonel Heydrich must be informed.'

'Colonel Heydrich knows that Bartley is in Berlin, and why. He is looking for the man Friedemann. But as he will not find him, the colonel has decided he will not be interfered with. He told me this himself.'

'But, if he is here...'

'Exactly. I think it is my business to find out why he is here, how much he knows. Then we can inform the colonel. Now make the coffee.'

Elsa looked doubtful, but she put the kettle

on. Anna returned to the lounge. Clive had seated himself exactly where Friedemann had been sitting when he had been shot; the cushions had been replaced. But that had to be coincidence. Anna sat beside him. 'Nothing wrong, I hope?' he asked.

'A small domestic matter. Now, Mr Bartley ... or may I call you Clive?'

'I should like that.'

'Because we have known each other for some time, have we not? And you must call me Anna.'

'Well...'

'At least when we are alone together.'

'All right. If that is what you wish. I very much doubt we will ever be alone together again.'

Anna stared into his eyes. 'Do you not like being alone with me?'

'Well ... look, Mrs Bordman ... I mean, Anna...'

'Ah, coffee,' Anna said, as Elsa placed the tray on the low table before them. 'I shall not need you again today, Elsa. I think you should visit your mother. She is unwell, is she not? I am sure she would like to see you.'

Elsa stared at her with her mouth open.

'Take the rest of the day off,' Anna said. 'I will prepare my own lunch.'

Still Elsa stared at her.

'I said take the rest of the day off.' Anna spoke very deliberately.

'As you say, ma'am.' Elsa went to her bedroom.

'She will be gone in a minute,' Anna said. 'And then we can ... talk.'

'I really don't think...'

'You mean you want to leave? Because you do not like me? Yet you were standing outside my apartment wondering if I might be here.'

'Well, I saw the lights in the windows.'

'But you came here, in the first place. I think you need to explain that. As you do not like me.'

'I will say good-morning, ma'am.' Elsa was wearing her hat and coat. 'Sir.'

'Good morning, Elsa,' Anna acknowledged. 'Have a nice day.'

The front door closed, and Anna got up and checked the latch. 'We have so much to talk about.' She sat beside him again, drank some coffee. 'You have not answered any of my questions.'

Clive's brain was settling down. She was such an overwhelming woman, both in her looks and her personality, that she took a man's breath away when she decided to turn on the charm – and when she indicated so brazenly that she wanted to be alone with him ... clearly she wanted something from him. Equally clearly, he had to find out exactly what that was, however many ideas he might already have on the subject. But most clearly of all, he would have to proceed very cautiously, if there was even the slightest chance she was any of the things he thought she might be.

'I have never disliked you,' he said now.

'Oh, come now, Clive. Did you not attempt to put Bally off me? Why did you wish to do that?'

'I suppose because there were too many things about you that did not fit the character you were portraying.'

'Of course. You are a detective. Tell me about these things.' She finished her coffee and leaned against the settee cushions, her arm along the back, half turned towards him, one leg draped across the other. Her skirt had ridden up above her knees, and she straightened it, but did not pull it down.

Clive also leaned back, turned to face her. 'I may have to be indelicate.'

'You may be as indelicate as you wish.' Her tongue came out for a moment as she smiled. 'A man and a woman, alone together, should always be indelicate.'

Clive realized that she might be playing an even deeper game than he had first supposed. But ... in for a penny, in for a pound, especially when the pound was the closest earthly representative of the goddess Aphrodite he could possibly imagine.

'In the first place, I found it difficult to understand why a young woman with your looks and elegance and obvious connections should throw herself at a man like Ballantine. With respect.'

'Do you not suppose a man like Ballantine could appeal to a woman?'

'Perhaps. But not to a woman like you. I mean, sexually.'

'Ah.'

'You said I could be indelicate.'

'Of course I did. Go on.'

'And then, that cock and bull story about your background...'

Anna raised her eyebrows.

'Well,' he said, 'you must admit it was a bit fanciful.'

Anna kicked off her shoes and curled he legs beneath her. Now her skirt rode up to her thighs, revealing an expanse of black silk stockings. 'Did not Bally tell you how I, my family, came by our name?'

'He did. At least, he repeated to me what you had told him. But when I had the matter investigated, I discovered that there was not a word of truth in your story. I'm sorry.'

'Why should you be sorry? You were doing your job. You say you had me investigated ... here in Germany?'

'Yes.'

'Ah. Would that have been the man Friedemann you spoke of?'

'As a matter of fact, yes.'

'I can understand why you wished to see him again. And now he has gone off. How very inconvenient. So what have you done with this knowledge?'

He shrugged. 'I have not been able to do anything with it. I have no proof. Everyone else accepts you as what you claim to be...'

'But if you have returned to Berlin to find your friend again, you are still seeking proof.

Tell me what you suspect of me? Or me of?'

'Are you sure you want me to do that?'

'Of course. I wish us to be friends. I am in very deep trouble.' It was Clive's turn to raise his eyebrows. 'It is the truth, and I will tell you the truth, if you will tell me what you know. Or think you know. Or even suspect.'

Once again she gazed into his eyes. That gaze, he thought, could dissolve a granite rock. But, as he was a believer in yin and yang, he had to suppose that it could also become as hard as granite itself. But if she was really in trouble ... 'There are two possible scenarios,' he said. 'One is that you are the most consummate gold-digger I have ever encountered.'

'And the other?'

'That you are working for the German Government. As we met you at an SS ball, that seems the most likely.'

Anna uncoiled her legs, stood up, and went to the sideboard. 'Don't you think,' she said over her shoulder, 'that if that were true, you are taking an inordinate risk in saying it to me, in my apartment, when we are alone together?'

'I can't envisage you committing murder, Anna.'

How innocent you are, she thought, and turned to face him. 'In that case, may I offer you a drink? You may pour it for yourself. And pour one for me as well.'

He got up and stood beside her. 'What would you like?'

'Oh, schnapps, at this hour.'

He filled two small glasses, and she raised hers. 'Here's to friendship. Do you really think I am an SS spy?'

'I would be over the moon if you were to prove to me that you are not.'

Their faces were very close together; he could feel her breath on his cheek. She could tell that he had completely fallen under her spell. Was it possible to use that to her advantage, to turn her world and the world of the SD and Heydrich upside down ... and survive? Did she dare take such a risk? But would she ever have such an opportunity again? As he had said, once he left this apartment, they were very unlikely ever to be alone together again unless, before he left it, she had made him hers. And it was just a matter of mixing fact with fiction, of telling him just enough to make him believe. She drew a deep breath. 'Will you excuse me a moment?' She went into the bedroom and, as she had suspected, found that the tape recorder had been switched on. She doubted it would have picked up more than a background mumble of what had been said in the lounge, but she couldn't chance it, and she was already anticipating being back in this room very soon. She switched the set off and returned to the lounge.

'Suppose I were to tell you that both your theories are very close to being correct?'

He frowned at her. 'I hope you are not serious?'

'I am a serious person. Come and sit down.' She held his hand and led him back to the settee. 'I admit I set my cap at Bally. I could see that he was attracted to me and I thought I might make a profit out of it. It never occurred to me that he would propose marriage. But how could someone in my position refuse an offer like that?'

'Your position?'

'My real name is Annaliese Fehrbach. I come from Vienna. My father is – was – a newspaper editor. I was given a good education, but I hated it there, especially after the Nazi occupation. I have always hated the Nazis. My family accepted it, and became Nazis themselves. So I hated them as well. I ran away from home, took various jobs, and then decided to reinvent myself. I knew I was very good-looking. That is enough for most men. So I dreamed up an entirely new background for myself.'

'And you were accepted?'

'By the Nazis, yes. They are very ignorant people. Don't you believe me?'

Not a word of it, he thought. She had made no attempt to explain how she had obtained the financing for her clothes and jewellery, not to mention this apartment. Although ... 'What about your "father"?'

'He, of course, was not really my father. He was my financier. My partner in crime.'

'Who is now dead. That must be very convenient for you. As you no longer need him.'

'Absolutely. But I hope you are not supposing that I killed him? I thought we had agreed that it is not my style. Anyway, I was in London when he died.'

'Yes,' Clive said thoughtfully. 'I suppose he was also your lover?'

'Certainly not. It was his idea that I should marry well, and that meant I had to be a virgin on my wedding night.' She gave a little giggle. 'I didn't make it. But Bally is still the only man I have ever had sex with.'

'Now that I can believe. He may not be very bright, but Ballantine knew you were a virgin when he had you.'

'I know that. That is why he married me. He thought he had ruined my life.'

'So it all worked out exactly as planned. What I don't understand is why you are telling me all this. What is to stop me repeating it all to Ballantine when I get back to London?'

'There are three reasons, Clive. The first is that I do not believe you would do such a thing. The second is that I would simply deny that I ever told you anything like that, or indeed, that we ever met on this trip. You have no witnesses; I have my maid, who will support any story I care to tell. You have already accused me of being what you now know I am, and no one has believed you. Why should they believe you now?'

'You said there were three reasons.'

'The third reason is the reason I am telling you all this: your theory that I am an agent employed by the SS.'

'You mean you are prepared to admit to that as well?'

She got up again and took their glasses to the sideboard. 'Another?'

'All right.' As far as he was concerned, the morning was quite out of control.

Anna poured, handed him his glass. 'Two days ago I was raped. Quite savagely.'

Clive nearly dropped the glass. 'You were ... *what*?'

'I was strapped across a bar, beaten with a cane, and then raped.'

He looked her up and down.

'You don't believe me.'

'Well ... you just said that you had never had sex with any man save Ballantine.'

'This was not a man. It was an electrical current, which was forced into my vagina and my anus at the same time.'

'Jesus Christ!' He spluttered into his drink.

'It was very painful,' she agreed. 'But, in retrospect, more humiliating. On the other hand, it actually wasn't as humiliating as being bent over the bar to be caned.'

'You're not making this up?'

Anna reached behind herself to unbutton her dress, and let it slide from her shoulders.

'Just what are you doing?' Clive asked.

'Proving that I am telling you the truth. Are you afraid to look at a naked woman?'

Clive gulped as she very rapidly removed the rest of her clothes, down to her suspender belt and stockings. To think that that fat toad had all of this at his disposal every night. Then he frowned. 'My God!'

She had bent over, her back to him. She had also removed her hat, and her hair tumbled down to brush the floor. 'Come and look. The marks are fading now, of course. But they are still visible.'

Cautiously Clive went towards her and bent slightly himself. 'Shit!' he muttered. 'Have the police got the people who did this?'

Anna straightened and turned to face him, taking his breath away all over again. 'It was the police who did it.'

His head jerked upwards.

'Well,' she said, 'the secret police.'

'The Gestapo did that?'

'The SD. They are superior to the Gestapo.'

'But why? I mean, *how*...?'

Anna returned to her seat, glass in hand, draping one knee over the other. 'I told you that you were close in your estimation of the situation. As part of my climb up the social ladder, I accumulated a boyfriend, an officer in the SS. In Germany today it is necessary to have friends in high places. So he squired me, and I was able to attend things like that SS ball, where I met Bally. And you.'

'And this fellow never...'

'I told you that I was a virgin when I met Bally. Hans tried from time to time, but I would permit him only a kiss and a cuddle. I told him he could have me if he would marry me. But I knew he was not senior enough to be able to do that. I do not know if his seniors had any plans for me, although I now suspect that they did.

218

But then I got away from them. Bally and I had our whirlwind courtship and marriage, and then there I was in England. Out of their reach. Or so I supposed.'

Clive gave a low whistle. 'So that's why you were in such a hurry.'

'For the first time in my life, I was free. And then last week I fell into a trap. I received a letter informing me that Gunther was dead, and I foolishly showed it to Bally. Well, he of course said I had to attend my father's funeral. He could not come with me because of this latest crisis. I had to go along with that, otherwise he might have found out the truth about me. But I did not think there would be any risk. I am the Honourable Mrs Bordman. No one would dare interfere with me. I would spend a week or two quietly in this apartment, and then go home. But I reckoned without Heydrich. Do you know this man Heydrich?'

'I have heard of him.'

'Well, I can tell you that he is the devil incarnate. He had me arrested the moment I set foot in Germany, taken to Gestapo Headquarters, where he told me what he wants. He wants me to use my position inside the British Establishment, by being married to an important diplomat, to keep the Reich Government informed of the probable British reaction to any further German moves in Europe.'

'What did you tell him?'

'I refused, of course. I am not a spy.'

'So...'

'He handed me over to his people, to "convince" me.'

Clive sat beside her, trying desperately to keep looking at her face instead of the superb body within touching distance. 'Are you convinced?'

'I could not survive another ordeal like that. But he has other methods. He has also arrested my parents and my sister, and says that if I do not co-operate they will go to a concentration camp, or even be executed. You know about these camps?'

'There are rumours.'

'Well, the rumours bear no relation to the truth. The inmates are flogged daily, fed starvation rations, and forced to work until they drop. I know I quarrelled with my parents, but I cannot expose them to such a fate.' She stared into his eyes. 'Will you help me, Clive? Can you help me?'

She laid her hand on top of his, and was in his arms.

Her flesh was like velvet, her movements like silk. Clive knew he had been bewitched, and tried to convince himself that this could be a necessary part of his investigation of her, and for that reason Belinda would forgive him, while all the time knowing that he was doing what he had dreamed of doing from the moment he had first seen her.

Everything seemed to flow so naturally, but he knew she was in total control. While they kissed, she continued to hold his hand and guide it over her body, from her breasts to between her legs, which parted for him. She seemed to know exactly how much time to allow him, then gave a little sigh, leaned her head on his shoulder for a moment, then stood up, again holding his hand, to lead him into the bedroom.

There she undressed him as quickly and expertly as she had undressed herself, and was naked in his arms. They rolled on the bed, but when he sought an entry she spoke for the first time. 'Behind,' she said. 'Take me from behind. That is how they took me.'

She rolled, still in his arms, and spread her legs. He knelt between them, and she gasped in a mixture of discomfort and ecstasy. But it was what she had wanted, and what she did want. He didn't know if she had climaxed or not, but when he did her knees gave way and she subsided on to her face, yet continued to move beneath him for several seconds. Then they lay still, bodies glued together, and the bedroom door opened.

Seven

Turnabout

Clive rolled off Anna and sat up, as did she, turning on her knees.

'What are you doing here?' Anna demanded. 'I told you to take the day off.'

'You rampant bitch!' Elsa declared. 'That man is a British spy.'

'He is not spying at this moment,' Anna said. 'Anyway, as you're here, you can prepare lunch.'

'I am going to telephone Colonel Heydrich and put him in the picture. Now he will really burn your ass. And this time I am going to watch it.'

'No! Elsa!' Anna got out of bed. 'It is not what you think. I can explain.'

'Explain to the colonel,' Elsa said, and turned back to the door.

Anna acted with amazing speed, crossing the floor in three long but almost noiseless strides. Elsa checked and started to turn back, but Anna was already up to her, and swinging her right arm in a tremendous blow, which started above her head and ended as the edge of her hand

222

crashed into Elsa's shoulder, precisely where it joined her neck. Elsa went down without a sound, save for the thump of her body striking the carpeted floor.

'Holy Jesus Christ!' Clive cried as he too got off the bed.

Anna was panting and rubbing her arm. 'There was an unarmed combat class at school,' she explained, not altogether untruthfully.

'That must have been some school,' he commented, standing beside her. 'You'd better do something about her. She looks done in.'

Anna knelt beside Elsa's body and felt her pulse. 'She is, as you say, done in.'

'What?' He also knelt. 'With one blow? You can't be serious.'

'Feel for yourself.'

There was no question that Elsa was dead. Or that he was kneeling, naked, next to the beautiful naked woman who had just killed her, and with whom he had just had the best sex in his life. He couldn't be sure whether it was a dream or a nightmare, but had to clutch at reality. 'They taught you how to do this at school? A *girl's* school?'

'Our Mother Superior was very big on her senior girls being able to defend themselves.'

'Are you saying this was a convent?'

'Yes, it was. Nuns can be very severe. Mother Superior brought in an instructor from the army. He said that blow would lay anyone out. He did say that if delivered with too much force, it could kill. But he didn't think any of us had that

223

much strength.'

'The idiot hadn't looked too closely at your muscles. Did you mean to hit her that hard?'

'I don't know. It was instinctive. I do know that if she had managed to telephone Heydrich we would both be dead.'

She raised her head to look at him, saw the disbelief in his eyes. 'That is the truth. These people have no regard for human life. This man you're looking for, this Friedemann, they have executed him because he told them of your inquiry into my background.'

'God Almighty! But that was last October.'

'He disappeared last October, when he was arrested. He was killed only when they knew I was returning to Germany and they had determined to make me work for them. Then they could no longer leave him alive, as he would have been able to denounce me.'

Clive scratched his head. He had had to assimilate so much over the past few hours that his brain was now a mass of conflicting ideas, thoughts, knowledge and emotions, all compounded by the proximity of this naked woman. And by the knowledge that she could kill with a single blow of her hand? He needed desperately to think, but he was not about to abandon her to an unacceptable fate – if what she had told him was true. And he had the evidence of her bruised flesh to convince him of that.

So, first things first. 'We have to get out of here. Get dressed.'

'Where do you wish to go?'

'Well, back to London. We can be there before anyone finds out about this.'

'But when they find out, they will send behind me.'

'We'll protect you.'

'Then they will execute my parents.'

'Shit! But aren't they done for anyway?'

'Not if you will allow me to handle it. If you will trust me.'

'How on earth can you handle it?'

'These people want me to work for them. That is all that matters to them. If I tell them that Elsa somehow found out that I was going to be a German agent and threatened to denounce me to the British,' she smiled, 'to you, and therefore I had to kill her, they will accept that. That is how their minds work.'

'But the risk...'

'That is minimal. Believe me.'

He gazed into her eyes and could do nothing else, especially when she held his hand against her breast. 'I would like to work with you, Clive.'

'I'm not sure that's practical.'

'Because I have killed someone? Did you not tell me you had had to kill?'

'I don't remember doing that.'

She inhaled, and swelled into his hand. 'You did not deny it when I asked you.'

'Anyway, that's not the point. If you stay here and try to sort it out with the Gestapo, you will have to work for them. Then I will have to arrest you.'

'Even if I am actually working for you? Telling you what the Nazis want? Perhaps giving them what you would like them to have? Pinpointing their agents in England?'

Clive released her breast, stood up, and went to the bathroom. Anna also got up from beside the body and lay on the bed, while Elsa continued to lie in a crumpled heap on the floor.

'You have some very deep areas in that brain of yours.'

'Should I not? I have an IQ of a hundred and seventy-three.'

He sat beside her, his thigh against hers. 'You're either a gift from the gods, or...' He bit his lip.

Anna smiled. 'Or from the other place. Believe me, I only want to bring the Nazis down, if I can.'

He gazed at her for several seconds, but while he was doing that he found coherent thought next to impossible. 'I cannot do a deal like this on my own authority,' he said. 'I will have to put it to my superiors.'

A faint frown appeared between her eyes. 'Can they be trusted?'

'If they can't, my life wouldn't be worth a red cent.'

'But as you just said, if I am to handle this successfully, I have to agree to work for the SS.'

Clive nodded. 'I understand that.'

'And when I get back to England, I cannot do anything that might endanger my parents.'

226

Again he nodded. 'If it's humanly possible, we'll work something out.'

'And will I be able to see you again? I would like that more than anything else in the world.'

He kissed her. 'That's high on my agenda, too.' He went to her desk and wrote down a number. 'You can get me there when you think it may be possible to arrange a meeting. Now, I think we had better get moving.'

'I know. But, you would not like to...?'

'I would like to, very much. But I don't think I could right now, in view of the company we're keeping. So...' He snapped his fingers. 'The concierge saw me come in with you...'

'I will take care of the concierge.' She smiled at his expression. 'Don't worry. It will not be necessary to kill him.'

She got off the bed, helped him dress, and kissed him at the door. 'I will be in touch as soon as I am back in London.'

She closed and locked the door, and leaned against it for several seconds while she took deep breaths. Then she had a quick bath, dressed herself, and picked up the telephone.

Heydrich himself came, together with Glauber and Gehrig. Anna stood to one side while they wandered around the apartment, carefully stepping over Elsa's body. Her heart was pounding, but she kept her features under control. If this failed, she and her entire family were dead, and she suspected that death, at least for her, would be a long and painful time coming.

Heydrich stood above Elsa's body for a few minutes, then returned to the lounge. 'I think you should sit down, Anna,' he said. 'Before you fall down.'

'It has been quite an experience,' Anna conceded, and sat on the settee.

'I am sure it was.' Heydrich sat beside her. He might never have smiled as he listened to me scream, she thought. 'I think Anna could do with a drink,' he said. 'In fact, we all could. Would you do the honours, please, Gehrig?'

Frau Gehrig went to the bar and poured.

'Now, Anna,' Heydrich said. 'I wish you to repeat what happened, exactly as you said on the phone.'

'Yes, Herr Colonel. I went for a walk, and encountered the man Bartley watching the apartment windows. As he had seen me, I had to greet him. But I also felt that I had to discover what he was after, so I invited him upstairs for a drink.'

'According to the concierge, Elsa was still here at that time.'

'Yes, sir. But I had already given her the morning off, to do some shopping before our return to England. She left immediately after I returned.'

'She was not concerned at leaving you alone with this man?'

'She gave no indication of it. She did not know who he was; she had never seen him before.'

'I see. So you sat and talked with Bartley

for...' He looked at Glauber.

'According to the concierge, it would have been more than two hours. He says Bartley left at a quarter to eleven.'

'Which was soon after Elsa returned. How soon?'

'He can't be sure, sir. As Elsa was a resident, he did not keep a record of the time she left or returned.'

'It would have been about twenty minutes,' Anna said, sipping her schnapps.

'So you sat and talked with Bartley for over two hours. And yet you say you discovered nothing?'

'I discovered nothing of the least importance. He admitted that he was seeking some information about Friedemann, but he accepted that I had never heard of the man.'

'Yet he stayed for two hours.'

'I know. As soon as I realized his visit could not affect my position, in the absence of Friede-mann, I tried to get rid of him. But he wouldn't go. I think he was trying to get some admission out of me to support his theory that I am either a fortune hunter or a German agent, but I told him nothing. And then at last Elsa came home. I was so relieved to see her. Bartley still did not go immediately, but he understood that he was not going to get anything incriminating out of me, especially with Elsa home, so he soon left.'

'Did you notice anything odd about Elsa when she came home?'

'No, sir. But I was concentrating more on

getting rid of Bartley.'

'And the moment he was gone, she attacked you. Had she ever done this before?'

'No, sir.'

'You had not quarrelled?'

'No, sir.'

'Never?'

'Well, we had our differences of opinion, from time to time. But I would not describe those as quarrels.'

'Finish your drink, Anna,' Heydrich recommended. 'And fill her glass, Gehrig.'

Anna frowned as she obeyed. Gehrig took the glass and refilled it.

'Now,' Heydrich said. 'I would like you to tell us the truth.'

Anna could feel her entire body tensing, but she managed to keep her voice low. 'Sir?'

'There is no need to be afraid or embarrassed. Frau Gehrig has explained it to me, because, you see, Mayers had confessed the truth to her.'

Anna drank some schnapps.

'I take full responsibility,' Gehrig said. 'Elsa was very upset when we brought you home on Wednesday; she was afraid you might have been scarred for life. She told me how she had always wanted to make love to you, but had been afraid to make advances because of your reputation. And I stupidly suggested that then, when you were clearly feeling traumatized, might be her best chance of getting close to you. I thought it might be good for you, too.'

Lights were flashing in Anna's brain; they were giving her the most perfect out!

'So tell us the truth, Anna,' Heydrich repeated. 'We are on your side in this matter.'

Anna licked her lips. 'I did not know she ... wanted me. And she did nothing until today. I think perhaps she thought I had been having sex with the Englander, and this excited her. He had barely left when she put her arms round me, and began to touch me. I asked her to stop, but she would not. So we wrestled and I got away. But she came after me again, so ... I hit her. I did not mean to kill her.'

'Of course you did not. You just did not know your own strength. But tell us, Anna, did you have sex with the Englander?'

'How could I do that, Herr Colonel? He is my enemy, and an enemy of the Reich. Besides,' she added coyly, 'I am a married woman.'

'Of course you are,' Heydrich said, somewhat drily. 'The question was indelicate. But now we must press on with our plans. My people will be here in an hour to remove the body. It is very important that you return to England as arranged next week. Things are going to be very tense over the next few weeks. That idiot Chamberlain has actually given guarantees to Poland and Romania, that Great Britain will go to their aid should they be invaded by the Reich. Can you believe it? How on earth could Great Britain hope to aid two such remote countries when we lie between them? But there it is.'

'Is the Reich going to invade Poland, or Romania, Herr Colonel?' Anna asked, with her usual devastating innocence.

'That is not something for you to worry your pretty little head about. What we need you to do is keep us informed about British public opinion on the prospect of a war with Germany, and what is actually being said and planned in the government, as opposed to bombastic statements.'

'I will do that, Herr Colonel.'

'Just remember to use the proper channels. Now, as to this business, you will tell your husband that Elsa has resigned, as she wishes to remain in Germany with her sick mother.'

'Yes, sir. I will have no trouble finding a new maid.'

'In England? Oh, Anna, be sensible! You must always have one of my people at your side, to support you and, frankly, to keep you in order. Frau Gehrig will replace Mayers.'

Anna looked at Gehrig in consternation. 'Commandant? You wish to be my maid?'

'She has volunteered for the post,' Heydrich explained. 'She wishes a spell in the field. And she probably knows you better than anyone else in the world. You will work well together. Will you not, Hannah?'

'I am sure of it,' Gehrig said.

Baxter filled his pipe, slowly. 'Forgive me for wondering if you have completely lost the plot, Clive. Are you actually proposing that we work with a self-confessed German spy?'

'She is not a spy yet,' Clive argued. 'She has been coerced into becoming a spy. Now she is offering us her services. She could be very useful to us.'

'This is assuming that a single word of what she told you was true.'

'She was certainly beaten. I saw the marks.'

'Did you now?'

'Well...' Clive flushed.

'You said she was caned.'

'Well ... yes, I did.'

'If I recall my schooldays correctly, one is generally caned on the backside. Would I therefore be correct in assuming that you have had the great privilege of inspecting Mrs Bordman's bottom? Who said our job has no perks? What else did she remove, apart from her knickers?'

'Oh, all right. We had sex. It was her idea, and she's a difficult woman to resist.'

'Let's stick to essentials. This woman seduced you, and then made some kind of phoney confession, and offered to work for us. And you went along with it. Presumably while her hands were still wrapped round your dick.'

'Look, Billy, I saw her kill that woman. With a single blow.'

'Aren't you capable of doing that?'

'Certainly. But I am six feet two and weigh a hundred and eighty pounds. Anna may be five feet ten, but she can't weigh more than a hundred and forty.'

'It's mass at the moment of delivery that

233

matters. Didn't they call Jimmy Wilde the Ghost with the Hammer in his Hand because, although he weighed just over a hundred pounds, when he punched, his timing was so perfect that he delivered every one of those hundred pounds at the same moment. Anyway, is her ability to despatch people without too much effort or the assistance of a weapon supposed to make me eager to employ her? Don't you think the German authorities have worked out who killed the woman? There'll be an extradition order slapped on her at any moment, and then ... I think I am right in saying that the Nazis use a sword to cut off the heads of their convicted murderers. Now *there* is a vision to stir the imagination.'

'Sometimes you are perfectly nauseating. Anyway, she seemed confident she could sort that out.'

'So she has friends in the Berlin underworld. That doesn't surprise me. It also doesn't make her any the more employable.'

'It confirms my point that she is an absolutely unique human being. Just add it up. She is a genius—'

'Pffft!'

'She has an IQ of a hundred and seventy-three. She can be lethal. She's stunningly beautiful. And she wants to work for us. Tell me, Billy, if someone came into this office and laid a million pounds on your desk and said he, or she, wanted to donate that to our rearmament programme, would you refuse to accept it? This girl could be worth a whole lot more than a million.'

'Or she could be the most consummate femme fatale since Mata Hari. I'm sorry, Clive. You have been utterly and completely seduced. I've never seen the lady in the flesh, but judging by her photographs you can hardly be blamed, certainly if she invited you to get to grips with her vital statistics. However, I think you need to put all further thought of her out of your mind. My advice would be to get Belinda into bed ... Does she know of this fling, by the way?'

'No, she does not.'

'Very wise. I do like my operatives to possess two fully functioning eyes. As I was saying, get her into bed and shag her until that busy fellow of yours feels like dropping off. Then come back to me.'

'While you do what?'

'About Mrs Bordman? I am going to have to think about that. Right now, the obvious thing to do would be to have a chat with Bordman.'

'That would be utterly to betray her confidence.'

'It would be doing my job.'

'Billy, in all the years I have worked for you, have I ever asked a favour?'

Baxter considered. 'Probably not.'

'Then I'd like to ask one now. It won't interfere with your duty. In fact, it will assist you in the carrying out of that duty.'

'Try me.'

'There are two things. One, you think everything she has told me is a lie.'

'I think that everything she told you, she was *told* to tell you.'

'Same difference. However, there is one sure way of finding out if she was telling me the truth. If her father was really an editor in Vienna, of sufficient importance to be arrested by the Nazis, that can surely be ascertained by our people in Switzerland.'

Baxter stroked his chin. 'What do you say his name was?'

'Fehrbach.' Clive spelled it out.

Baxter wrote it down. 'I agree that would be an appropriate thing to do. You said there were two points.'

'I'd like you to meet her.'

'Say again?'

'You'd enjoy it.'

'I'm sure I would. But I don't really move in Bordman-like social circles.'

'I'll arrange a private meeting.'

Baxter studied him for several seconds. 'You mean that your relationship is on-going.'

'I mean that we arranged that she would call me when she got back to England, and whenever it was possible, so that she could find out where she stood.'

'And you would like me to tell her that she stands nowhere, except on the brink of a long prison term.'

'I would like you to meet her before you form that judgement. I don't think that is unreasonable.'

236

Baxter considered this, clearly intrigued at the prospect. 'When will this meeting take place?'

'That I can't say. She is going to call me as soon as she can.'

'And in the meantime she is busy shovelling material out of England to her German masters.'

'I don't think that's likely. She knows she has to provide them with something in the near future, but she's only just taken on the job. They must have allowed her some time to set things up.'

Another brief consideration. Then Baxter pointed. 'You and she have two weeks. If I haven't met her by then, I will initiate an official investigation into her background, in which you will be required to give evidence as to your relations with the lady.'

'I hate to say it,' Ballantine said, 'but I rather like this new maid of yours. Great improvement on that sour-faced witch, Elsa. How did you come by her so quickly?'

'Elsa told me she was quitting on our journey back to Berlin, so the moment I arrived there I put an advert in the paper and the next day there were no less than a dozen applicants. They all wanted to work for an English lady.'

'And you chose very well. She's even quite attractive. No trouble with the visa?'

'The embassy was most co-operative, again because I am Mrs Bordman. And I agree that she is attractive. Would you like to have her?'

What a delightful thought.

'Eh?'

'Well, she is working for us in a strange country. She is not likely to object to anything we propose, especially if the proposal comes from an English aristocrat.'

'My dear girl, the things you do come out with. That idea is positively medieval.'

'Now you are angry with me. I'm sorry. My only wish is to see you happy, and I know I alone cannot satisfy you forever.'

'My darling, you satisfy me more than you will ever understand. Especially as, well, perhaps I shouldn't say this, as I know what a sad occasion it was for you, my darling, but you are looking positively radiant since your return from Berlin.'

'Well,' Anna said, pouring coffee and realizing that all reality was in the eye of the beholder: if she definitely felt happier than at any time in the past eighteen months, as he had been at her virtually all night and every night since her return, she was feeling utterly exhausted. 'I am sure you realized that Papa and I were not very close. He was always engaged in suspicious financial deals. And...' Her voice became a hiss. 'He was a Nazi.'

'Good God! You never told me.'

'I didn't want to upset you. But you can imagine how often we quarrelled over that. And then,' she went on, following her inflexible rule that when one is making up a lie it should be as big a lie as possible, 'he ill treated poor dear

238

Mama. I am sure he was responsible for her early death.'

'What a bounder. I didn't want to tell you this before, but I never did like him. Still...' He drank coffee. 'I presume he left you pretty well off.'

'He left me nothing.'

'Eh?'

'There was nothing to leave. He had been living on borrowed money and those shady business deals.'

'But that apartment ... the castle in Bavaria ... your sable?'

'The coat was on tick. Do you know they tried to get it off me before I left Germany? And the properties are mortgaged to the hilt.'

'Oh, dear me.' He eyed her sapphire ring speculatively.

'Is it important?'

'Oh, well ... it would have been nice to have a little injection of capital. But not to worry. We'll manage.'

The bastard, she thought, he was after my money as much as me.

'It would be a good idea, though,' he went on, 'not to mention the ... ah ... situation to anyone. I mean, it's none of their business, is it?'

'No,' she agreed. 'It's not.'

'Well, then...' He met her gaze, flushed, and looked at his watch. 'Good lord! I'm late.' He came round the table, leaned over to kiss her forehead, but for the first time since their marriage did not complete his usual farewell

239

fondle: a quick caress of her breast. 'I'll be home at five.'

'So you can work at home?'

'I thought you wanted me to do that? As opposed to staying late at the office.'

'I do, dearest. I do. Hurry back.'

He left the bedroom and she finished her coffee. Gehrig waited for the front door to close before coming in.

'He seems to be very much in love with you.'

'Yes, he is,' Anna said disconsolately. 'I offered him you, as I know he fancies you, but I doubt he'll ever do anything about it.'

'You did *what*?'

'Wouldn't you like to be seduced by an England aristocrat? Oh, I was forgetting, you have never been seduced by anyone, have you? Any man, I mean.'

Gehrig glared at her. 'I don't think you want to forget that I am you superior officer.'

'I'm not likely to forget that, Hannah. I was just wondering if you might like to broaden your horizons.'

'My horizon, and yours, is to fulfil our duty to the Reich.'

'I hope I can continue to do that.'

'What do you mean?'

'I have just discovered that Bally is broke.'

Gehrig looked from the silver coffee pot and serving dish to the Persian carpet on the floor. 'You cannot be serious.'

'He is certainly very upset that I have not inherited a fortune from the Count von Wider-

240

stand. I suspect all of this,' she waved her hand, 'is either mortgaged or on tick.'

'Is not his father a wealthy man?'

'He is supposed to be. But then, everyone seems to have supposed that *my* "father" was a wealthy man.'

Gehrig considered for a few seconds, and then she said, 'Well, as long as he is employed by the Foreign Office, and you are his wife, we can continue with our work. Now, I heard him say he would be home early. Will he bring work with him?'

'He usually does.'

'Excellent. The sooner we get something back to Berlin, the better. Now, I am to arrange a meeting between you and the man Schmidt.'

'Whatever for?'

'You have met him before?'

'It has not been necessary. It is not necessary now.'

'You told Colonel Heydrich you did not like him.'

Anna remembered desperately. 'I told Colonel Heydrich I did not like him. I never said I'd met him. I was going on Elsa's description. She made him sound like a slimy little rat.'

'Most men in his line of work are. But what you have just said makes it more important than ever that you meet him. I also need to do this. I have his address. I will go out this morning and make contact with him, and arrange a meeting with you.'

Anna suppressed a sigh of relief; she had

241

anticipated some difficulty in getting any time to herself. But it was necessary to continue playing her role. 'You understand that this meeting cannot be anywhere public. My face is very well known in this country.'

'I will be discreet.'

'Well, run me a bath before you go, please.'

Gehrig made a face, but drew the bath, and Anna soaked until she heard the front door close, then she got out of the bath, wrapped herself in a towel, and picked up the phone.

It was raining, which suited Anna very well. She put her hair up beneath an unflattering floppy waterproof hat, and wore a very ordinary raincoat over her dress.

'You're going out?' Gehrig demanded, instantly suspicious. 'In this weather?'

'I am going to my hairdresser for a shampoo,' Anna informed her. 'And this is England; if I were to wait for it to stop raining I could be here for weeks.'

'I will shampoo your hair for you.'

'I feel like going to the hairdresser,' Anna insisted and, as Bowen was hovering, Gehrig had to accept her mistress's decision. She took the Rolls and was driven to her usual Mayfair salon.

'It may take some time, Basil,' she told her driver, 'and I wish to do a little shopping afterwards. I will take a taxi home.'

'Of course, Mrs Bordman.' The car drove away, and Anna went inside.

'Mrs Bordman!' the receptionist said. 'How nice to see you. But...' She looked anxiously at her appointments book. 'Did you make a booking? Of course, we can fit you in...'

'That won't be necessary,' Anna said. 'I just wish to walk through your salon and out of your back door. Will that be possible?'

'Of course, Mrs Bordman.' The girl adopted an arch expression. 'I'll show you.'

Having gained the next street, Anna hailed a taxi. She had herself dropped a corner away from the address she had been given, and walked briskly to the block of flats, located the name Bartley, and pressed the bell. As always when going into action, as it were, she was both anticipatory and apprehensive. Clive had warned her over the phone that she would have to meet – and convince – his boss, which was a challenge, but he had also warned her not to be taken in by any apparent innocence on Baxter's part, and that he wanted no coquetry or acting, but for her to be entirely natural. As if he had any idea what or who an entirely natural Anna was. But did she, now? She only had to remember that failure today was inconceivable.

She pressed the bell, and said simply, 'Anna.'

The door unlocked with a click, and she stepped into the hall. There was no elevator, and Clive's apartment was on the third floor. She arrived slightly out of breath, but to her great relief Clive was standing in the open doorway. He didn't speak, but held her hand to lead her into the room. Can he have already forgotten what it is like to hold me naked in his arms? she wondered.

Baxter was standing in the middle of the lounge, looking somewhat untidy, as usual. 'Mrs Bordman,' Clive announced, closing the door. 'Née the Countess von Widerstand. Née Annaliese Fehrbach.' Anna shot him a glance. 'I can have no secrets from Mr Baxter,' he explained.

He was being very correct. 'Well, then,' she said, 'may I take off my coat? It is very wet.'

'Please.'

She pulled off her gloves and handed him them along with the coat and her hat, fluffing out her hair as she did so, and allowing it to tumble past her shoulders. Then she smiled. 'So, Mr Baxter, you seem to know all of my secrets, and I know none of yours.'

'Do I know *all* of your secrets, Mrs Bordman?'

Anna sat in the centre of the settee and crossed her knees, which were exposed as the skirt rode up. 'I am a woman, Mr Baxter. No man should ever know *all* of a woman's secrets.'

'Touché.' Baxter sat in an armchair opposite her. Clive remained standing by the door. 'May I say, first of all, that none of the many photographs I have seen of you do you the least justice.'

'That is very kind of you, sir.'

'But I'm afraid I am going to have to pry into just one or two more of your secrets.' Anna waited. 'I would like to know your age. I mean,

244

your real age.'

'I was born on the twenty-first of May, 1920.'

'So you are actually only just nineteen. Dare I say, then, God help the world when you turn twenty-one. But you do look older now.'

Anna made a moue. 'Someone once told me that, in a woman, that is an asset up to the age of twenty-five, and a liability thereafter.'

'And of course, you have had a fairly traumatic life. I should inform you that I am having your father investigated by our agents.' He studied her as he spoke, but if he had been hoping for any kind of panic or even concern he was disappointed.

'If you can tell me anything about the health and whereabouts of my mother and father, and my sister, Mr Baxter, I will be forever in your debt.'

'But you claim they are in the custody of the Gestapo.'

'No, sir. I understand them to be in the custody of the SD, which is a far more serious matter. I was told this by the commander of the SD, Colonel Reinhard Heydrich, who is also a senior officer in the SS.'

'And for whom you are now working.'

'He is employing me, yes.'

'And you understand the risk that you, and your family, are taking if you betray him and are discovered?'

'I have no alternative now.'

'Because he had you tortured? Isn't that a rather emotional reaction?'

Anna allowed her gaze to flicker towards Clive. 'I am an emotional person. Sometimes.'

'I see. Now, before we continue, I wish you to understand one thing very clearly. If I employ you, and you ever decide to betray me, I will see that you go to prison for the rest of your life.'

Anna gazed at him. 'I understand this.'

'And betrayal means ever revealing a word of what has been said here today, to anyone not now present.'

Again Anna glanced towards Clive. 'I understand,' she repeated.

'I am prepared to allow Mr Bartley to continue as your control. This is not for your convenience, but because he is your sponsor, as it were, and is therefore responsible for you, and because, as I have explained, the fact that we are employing you must be a very limited secret, but again you should understand that, while I cannot oversee your time together, should your relationship ever, shall I say, get out of control, I will regard that as a betrayal.'

'Yes, sir.'

'Very good. Now, tell me what your specific task is.'

'To find out if Chamberlain will go to war over these guarantees he has given to Poland and Romania, and, even more importantly, to find out if he is capable of going to war – that is, if your armed forces are ready for war, and if the British people would support such a step.'

'And your masters think you can obtain all of

this information through your husband?'

'Quite a lot of it. Bally brings work home, and I have obtained the combination of his safe. But I am also required to circulate at parties, meet people, discuss the political situation, obtain their views ... People like to talk with me,' she added ingenuously. 'To confide in me.'

'I can believe that,' he said. 'Well, Anna, on this occasion you are not going to work too hard. I would like you to tell your masters – to *convince* them – that not only will the Prime Minister implement his guarantees, but that our armed services are absolutely ready for war at a moment's notice, and that the country is one hundred per cent behind him.'

'I will tell them that, sir.'

'But there is something else I wish you to tell them. You have discovered that we are in the process of concluding an alliance with Soviet Russia, to the effect that should we find it necessary to go to war in defence of Poland, they will come to our assistance with all possible power.'

Anna gazed at him, and he flushed. 'Just for the record, Anna – as I am sure the Nazis know – there is a joint Anglo-French mission in Moscow at this moment.'

Anna nodded. 'I will tell them what I have "heard".'

'Very good. Now, how do you tell them that? Or anything?'

'I have a contact here in London to whom the information is given. How he gets it back to

Germany, I do not know.'

'You give him this information personally?'

'Not up till now. I have never met him. The information is conveyed by my maid.'

'The woman, Hannah Gehrig?'

Anna frowned. 'You know of her?'

'I know what Immigration knows of her. Is she also employed by the German Government?'

Anna drew a deep breath. 'Frau Gehrig is a senior officer in the SD. She is...' She gave Clive a quick smile. 'My German controller.'

'But you do know this man's name and address.'

Anna hesitated. 'If he is arrested, my position is compromised. In fact, it will be destroyed. And me with it.'

'He will not be arrested, as long as you are working for us. But you cannot have any secrets from us.'

Anna made a moue. 'His name is John Smith.'

'How frighteningly original. And his real name?'

'Johann Schmidt.'

'His address?'

'I do not know his address. I will know it, after I meet him, and then I will tell Clive.'

'Very good.' Baxter stood up. 'Let's hope all this works out.' He glanced at Clive. 'I imagine you two have things to discuss, so I'll leave you to it. Just remember, Mrs Bordman, that we require that information, especially concerning our alliance with Russia, to be in German hands just as rapidly as possible.'

'Yes, sir. You understand that I am placing my life in your hands?'

'My dear Anna, your life has been in my hands from the moment you indulged in pillow talk with Mr Bartley. Good day to you.'

Clive closed the door behind him, then faced her. 'His bark is worse than his bite, providing he trusts you.'

'Did you also tell him how I moaned with ecstasy when we were in bed?'

'He knew we had had sex the moment I outlined the circumstances of our meeting. I didn't have to tell him anything more, and he didn't ask for details.'

'I should still slap your face.'

'You're probably right. Be my guest.'

She gazed at him for several seconds, then shrugged. 'I would rather have a bath. I am soaked with sweat.'

'So am I,' Clive said. 'I'll join you.'

Eight

Calamity

'I thought you were thirty-five,' Belinda remarked, sitting up in bed and lighting a cigarette. 'Or have you been pulling the wool over my eyes for all of these years?'

Clive nuzzled her side and the bottom of her breast. 'I'm sorry. There's been so much on. And these things do happen.'

'So I've heard, although it's never happened to me before. I thought the male menopause didn't set in until after forty-five.'

'Look, I'm just over-tired.'

'I know there's a lot happening. I do read the papers. Do I gather that you've dropped your German friend?'

'Eh?'

'Mrs Bordman. You haven't asked me to chase her in weeks. Not since you came back from Germany.'

'Ah. Yes. That was actually a fruitful trip. I discovered that she was genuine, after all, and we've decided it is no longer necessary to investigate her.'

'That must be disappointing for you. How-

250

ever, I have to tell you that I am in an aroused but totally dissatisfied state. So, if we are going to get any sleep, I strongly suggest that you replace dicky-boy with your tongue and do me a service.'

'Nothing would give me greater pleasure,' he said, sinking beneath the sheet as she slid down the bed.

But his heart wasn't in it, and having bathed after his departure in the morning, she found herself brooding in front of her full-length mirror. She was thirty-four years old, and perhaps there was the odd sag here and there, but she was still very presentable. The fact was that she and Clive had been together now for four years, but she was not really in the mood to give him up. Presumably she had been foolish to reject his early proposal of marriage, but she was a career woman, and while she liked to be sure of seeing a man, her man, at least three times a week, she had absolutely no desire to have him around the house all the time, which would involve such things as washing his socks and cooking his meals on a regular basis. So what was she going to do? The annoying thing was that she had no evidence that he was actually seeing anyone else: his sudden lack of sexual enthusiasm could merely be the result of over familiarity.

She had an early appointment at Fortnum & Mason to view some new designs, and had completed this, still unable to get her domestic problem out of her mind, when she emerged on to the pavement to look for a taxi. At that moment one drew up in front of her. She waited to get in when the occupants got out, and found herself face to face with Anna Bordman, who was accompanied by another woman.

'Why, Mrs Bordman!' she exclaimed without thinking.

Anna gazed at her. 'Excuse me,' she said. 'Have we met?'

'Well, no, actually,' Belinda acknowledged. 'I've tried to see you, several times, but you've never been available. I'm Belinda Hoskin, Fashion Editor of the *Pictorial*.'

'Ah,' Anna said, and made to step past her.

Belinda took a stab in the dark, not quite sure what she was aiming at. 'I'm a friend of Clive Bartley.'

Anna's eyes flickered, briefly, but she retained her composure. 'I know no one named Clive Bartley, Miss Hoskin.'

'Oh!' Belinda *was* disconcerted. But she had already been taking a card from her handbag. 'My card. I would so like to interview you, when you can spare the time.'

Anna put the card in the pocket of her summer coat without looking at it, and entered the store, Gehrig at her shoulder. 'I do admire your élan,' she remarked.

'If I were to become upset by all itinerant newspaper people seeking interviews, I would be a nervous wreck.'

'But if she is associated with the man Bartley...'

'Coincidence.' Anna smiled at the floor-walker.

'I have discussed the matter with Schmidt,' Gehrig said a few days later, when they were alone in the drawing room.

'What matter?' Anna asked absently. She was reading the newspaper, trying to get some inkling of what might be happening in Germany. She had delivered all the information required by Baxter, and heard nothing further. Now she had to find an appropriate time to telephone Clive, and not only to receive her next set of instructions.

'The matter of that Hoskin woman.'

Anna dropped the paper and sat up. 'You did what? Without consulting me?'

'You sometimes seem to forget, Anna, that I am in command of this operation. I make the decisions. Now explain to me why you never told me you had reported the matter to him.'

'When she kept calling – this was before my visit to Berlin – I asked Elsa to have Schmidt find out something about her. He reported back that she was a genuine fashion editor.'

'But he also reported that she was a close friend of the man Bartley. And he says that you refused to do anything about it, although he offered to take care of the matter for you.'

'That would have been madness,' Anna snapped. 'This is not Berlin, where we are protected by the Reich. The one big mistake we could make would be to have the British police become interested in us.'

'There could be no possible connection between an accident to this woman and us.'

'You think not? If she *is* investigating us – me – and she suddenly has an accident, don't you think Bartley is going to begin his investigation right here? Once he starts that, God knows what he may turn up. And I have been proved right. Her visits, her interest in me, have ceased. Either she was genuinely interested in my clothes, or Bartley has concluded that there is nothing wrong with me.'

Gehrig regarded her for several seconds. 'I shall consider the matter,' she said at last. 'But it should have been fully reported at the time. The decision was not yours to make. Kindly remember that in the future.'

'This has just come in from Basle.' Amy placed a coded telegram and transcript on Baxter's desk. 'And Chief-Inspector Grattan is here.'

'Oh, yes? Well, you'd better ask him to come in. Mustn't keep the Special Branch hanging about.' He studied the transcript.

Johann Fehrbach, Editor of the Way Forward, *anti-Fascist Viennese newspaper, arrested by the Gestapo with his family – wife and two daughters – 12 March 1938. They have not been heard of since, and are presumed to have been executed.*

He frowned as he reread the words, and then hastily slid the sheet of paper under his blotter as the door opened. 'Good morning, Freddie.

Don't tell me one of my boys has been upsetting your people.'

Chief-Inspector Frederick Grattan was a tall, thin man with a long nose and an expression that suggested he had a stomach ulcer. Baxter wouldn't have been surprised if he did. The policeman lowered himself into the chair before Baxter's desk. 'I assume you have a full team operating inside Germany?'

'It's not as full as we would like, but we do have some agents, yes.'

Grattan nodded. 'I would like you to tell me what you know about Mrs Bordman.'

'What?'

'I am talking about the ultra-glamorous young woman who has had all London by the balls for virtually the past year. Don't tell me you haven't noticed her photograph in the papers. *Tatler* devoted an entire page to shots of her at Ascot.'

'I have seen her photo, yes. And I agree that she is easy on the eye. But why should she interest me?'

'She's German.'

'That is not correct, Freddie. She is actually Austrian...'

'Same difference.'

'And she is, and has been for several months, a naturalized Englishwoman.'

'So you do have a file on her.'

'We have an enormous number of files on an enormous number of people, Freddie. I still have no reason to regard Mrs Bordman as other than the very beautiful wife of one of our more prominent diplomats. You will have to give me a reason for changing that opinion.'

'Her maid is German. You are not going to claim that she has been naturalized?'

'Not to my knowledge.'

'This is in confidence.'

Baxter inclined his head.

'I'm sure you are aware that relations between Whitehall and the Wilhelmstrasse are in a state of what might be termed terminal decline.'

'I am, and my people are doing all they can to discourage the Reich from doing anything rash.'

'I'm sure you're doing your best. However, the Home Secretary takes a pessimistic view of the prospects for continued peace. We have been given instructions to locate every German alien in this country – and in the present state of affairs that includes Austrians – and to prepare to place them under restraint immediately hostilities commence between Great Britain and Germany, should that occur. We are to use our discretion as to which of these people should be placed under surveillance in advance of such an event.'

Baxter reached for his pipe. 'You're proposing to place Mrs Bordman under surveillance?'

'She is in a very sensitive position. Who knows what items of political significance Bordman lets slip beneath the sheets of the nuptial bed.'

Baxter started to fill the pipe. 'I find that somewhat obscene.'

Grattan shrugged. 'It goes with the job. I am certainly considering having the maid watched.'

'Why?'

'Simply that she is worth watching. I had one of my women do a quick survey of her and her habits. She only arrived in this country in April, as a replacement for Mrs Bordman's previous maid, a woman called Elsa Mayers. This Mayers woman accompanied Mrs Bordman into this country when she married last October. She remained in her service until Mrs Bordman returned to Germany in March to attend the funeral of her father, and indeed accompanied her. But on that trip she suddenly resigned her position. Mrs Bordman was only in Germany a fortnight, yet when she returned, she had a new German maid. Just like that. Doesn't ring true.'

'So what do you think happened?'

'I think the woman Mayers was made to resign, and this woman Gehrig put in her place.'

'Forced by whom?'

'I think that is something you should find out.'

Baxter struck a match and puffed his pipe for several seconds. 'You are accusing Mrs Bordman of being a spy?'

'I wish to be able to scratch her name from my list of *potential* spies.'

'Quite. Tell me what this female Sherlock

257

Holmes of yours discovered.'

'Mostly straws in the wind. Gehrig appears to live a very private life. Even on her days off she never goes out to a pub. If she goes anywhere, it is to a second-hand bookshop run by a man called Smith. She sometimes browses there for up to an hour.'

'So she likes second-hand books. I assume she buys one, occasionally?'

'Just about every time.'

'Well, then, don't you think you are being just a little paranoid? The woman can't help being a German.'

'On two occasions, Gehrig was accompanied to the shop by her mistress.'

'You mean you have been keeping Mrs Bordman under round-the-clock surveillance. I assume you have authority for this?'

'I have been given carte blanche by the Home Secretary to do whatever I consider necessary for the security of the country.'

'I see.' Baxter knocked out his pipe slowly. 'Well, Freddie, the security of the realm is my business as well, as I am sure you understand. So I am going to have to ask you to lay off the lady.'

'You're going to have to give me a reason.'

Baxter gazed at him. 'Mrs Bordman is in my pay.'

'You are saying she is an MI6 agent?'

'Not exactly. She is co-operating with us. She comes from the very highest social circles in Germany, and that means, today, the very highest Nazi circles. Let me make it quite clear that she is not a Nazi herself. She detests the regime. But the wives of many of the high Party officials are her friends, and she is in constant communication with them. Now, she shows us those letters, and she puts in her replies whatever items of news from here that we feel would be appropriate. She is proving of immense value in helping us keep up to date with current political opinion in Germany, and even obtains the occasional snippet of military significance.'

Grattan studied him for several seconds. 'Why is she doing this? Is it because of Clive Bartley?'

Baxter raised his eyebrows.

'Mrs Bordman has been observed calling at his flat,' Grattan explained.

And they wouldn't give me permission to keep a tail on her when it mattered more, Baxter thought bitterly. 'Very well, Freddie, as you seem to know so much about it, yes, Bartley turned her because of a physical attraction.'

'Risky. Physical attractions can go as quickly as they come. Did he seduce the maid as well? She's not bad looking, even if she's not quite in the class of her mistress.'

'As far as I am aware, the answer is no. But I will take responsibility for the maid. Now, will you lay off them?'

'Very well, for the time being, and providing no evidence against them turns up. What about the bookseller?'

'What about him?'

'He is certainly a contact. If he's not yours, then he's somebody else's.'

'I would like you to lay off him as well.'

Grattan stood up. 'I think you're playing a dangerous game, Billy. But then I suppose you people always do. I'll lay off, for the time being, and providing nothing changes for the worse. But the file is open, and I intend to add to it wherever I can. I'll be in touch.'

Baxter waited for the door to close, then he pressed his intercom. 'Come in here, please, Amy.'

She appeared immediately.

'Has he left the building?'

'He's on his way downstairs.'

'Right. Get hold of Clive Bartley. I wish to see him. Now.'

'Shit!' Clive commented. 'How bad is it?'

'It could be very bad, for your girlfriend.'

'But if they're laying off...'

'They're not actually going to arrest anyone at this stage. But as he said, they're keeping the file open. And I'm pretty damn sure he intends to continue investigating Smith. He has nothing on him at the moment, but if he keeps probing he is going to find out about the man's German background. Then I am going to have a hell of a time keeping him out. When are you seeing Anna again?'

'She's coming this afternoon. She has some material to send. Do I put her in the picture?'

'It may be necessary to do more than that.'

Clive frowned. 'Would you explain that?'

Baxter took the sheet of paper from beneath his blotter and gave it to him.

Clive scanned it. 'Well, thank God for that. At least we know she's bona fide.'

'I'm afraid that telegram proves quite the reverse. It says her father was anti-Fascist; she told you he was a Nazi sympathizer.'

'Well, perhaps he found it necessary to appear anti-Fascist to sell his newspaper. Certainly to keep his job. Our man in Basle supposes that because Anna was arrested at the same time as her family, she has therefore suffered the same fate, which is logical.'

'Try reading it again, and tell me the date of the arrest.'

'Ah, March twelfth...'

'1938,' Baxter said. 'Just about a year before she claims to have been approached and coerced by the Germans, who just to make their point, arrested her family.'

'She could've made a mistake about the date.'

'Oh, for Christ's sake! She's a genius, isn't she? Now look, you got me into this mess, and you're going to get me out of it. Your lady friend has been useful, I hope. We don't know yet if she's served any real purpose at all. But she's playing some game of her own. I want to know what it is. And if I don't like what it is, her entire file goes to Grattan with my apologies. And if he arrests her and then has her deported back to Germany, where she is almost certainly wanted for murder...'

'She's a British citizen.'

'Well, then, she has an alternative, hasn't she? She can return to Germany and have her pretty neck separated from the rest of her body, or she can stand trial here and have the same pretty neck stretched by the hangman's rope.'

'I think you're being quite unnecessarily vicious about this,' Clive remarked. 'Anna cannot be hanged, even if she were to be convicted of spying for Germany. We're not at war.'

'I would regard that situation as somewhat fluid. Sort it out, Clive. Your neck may not be on the line, but your job sure as hell is.'

Clive nodded. 'May I have that transcript?'

Baxter held it out. 'I have a copy. Clive, there's just one thing.'

Clive waited.

'I know you regard Anna as the best piece of work the Almighty ever did, but I would like you to remember that you have seen her kill a woman with a single blow.'

Clive grinned. 'I'm bigger than Elsa.'

Clive wished he could be sure of his mood as he went home. It seemed evident that Anna had lied to him. But to what extent? It seemed true that she was an Austrian adventuress named Fehrbach, and that her family had indeed been arrested by the Gestapo. While if he could not be certain that she had been tortured with electricity, there could be no argument that she had been viciously caned on her naked but-

262

tocks, only shortly before she had shown him the weals. But she had considered it necessary to drop a year from her life. She would have been seventeen in the March of last year. What had a girl that young been doing – been *able* to do – that required her to lose a year? Of course, it had only been six months before she had seduced Ballantine ... but that in itself had been an incredible performance by an eighteen-year-old girl. He knew he hadn't given it sufficient thought before, because for all his attempts at professionalism she had effectively seduced him as well. And she had still been eighteen, then. As Baxter had said: God help the world when she became an adult!

And now it was his business to decide whether she *was* going to grow up or not. Was he capable of making such a decision?

She had said she would come at two. He reached the flat at twelve thirty, had a quick bath and changed into casual clothes, wondered if she would have lunched. He did not feel very hungry himself; his stomach was churning, but he forced himself to eat a sandwich while he waited, then sat down and tried to relax.

The tap on the door startled him. The street bell had not rung, and it was only quarter to two. How on earth had she got in? He got up, went to the door, but before he could release the latch, it too had turned and Belinda entered the room.

'Surprise!' She peered at him. 'You could try looking pleased to see me.'

'You nearly gave me a heart attack.' He had forgotten that Belinda possessed keys to both the street door and the flat. He had given them to her. But she very seldom used them; she preferred her own place. 'What on earth are you doing here at this hour?'

'I happened to find myself free this afternoon, and I thought it might be nice for us to get together. I called the office, and they said you had also taken the afternoon off and gone home. So I thought, what a happy coincidence, and here I am. Aren't you going to kiss me?'

He did so, looking at his watch behind her head. 'It's lovely to see you, darling, but I have not actually taken the afternoon off. I was just about to go out.'

Belinda stepped back to regard him. 'Dressed like that?'

'Well...'

The street bell rang.

'Aren't you going to answer it?' Belinda asked.

Clive picked it up, trying to get his brain into gear.

'Anna!' the voice said.

'Ah ... right.' He released the latch.

'I can see that I'm an encumbrance,' Belinda said, her voice like drips of ice.

'Look, this is a professional matter,' Clive said. 'So I can't explain it to you. But—'

There was another tap on the door. Belinda herself opened it and the two women stared at each other. Anna was wearing her cloche, with

264

her hair tucked out of sight and, as it was a hot, and for once dry, late August day, had no coat over her summer frock. She looked, as always, immaculately cool and utterly beautiful.

Now she frowned. 'I know you ... The fashion editor!'

'And I know you, Mrs Bordman. I feel like slapping your face. But it'll keep.' She stepped past her and went down the stairs.

Anna gazed at Clive. 'What should I say?'

'Perhaps "oops" might be appropriate. Come in.' He closed the door behind her.

'You knew I was coming,' she said, taking off her hat and shaking out her hair as she liked to do as a sign of intimacy.

'And I didn't know she was,' he agreed. 'I was trying to get rid of her.'

'I'm sorry.'

'It wasn't your fault.'

'But if she knows we are seeing each other, and you once sent her to investigate me...'

'Forget it. She won't do anything about it until she's had a chat with me. We have to talk.'

She sat down, stripped off her gloves, opened her handbag, and took out a roll of microfilm. 'I don't know how important these are. They're mainly concerned with Foreign Office worries about this visit of Ribbentrop to Moscow. Can I use them?'

'I think so. If you are going to use anything.'

She frowned. 'What do you mean?'

'First, empty your handbag on the table.'

Now she raised her eyebrows, but she obeyed.

He flicked through the contents, which were nothing more or less than he would have expected in any handbag.

'Now get off the sofa and kneel, placing your arms on the cushion and your head on your arms.'

'Kinky. But it sounds interesting.' She got down on her knees, her back to him, skirt pulled up, and rested her head on the settee. Clive raised her skirt and petticoat to her waist, and used his hands to spread her legs. 'Oooh,' she breathed, 'I've never been buggered. Will it hurt?'

He slid his hands up her sides and over her stomach, reached her breasts, and released her. 'You can get up,'

She turned to sit on the settee; her cheeks were pink. 'You were searching me!'

'Yes, I was.'

'Do you think I carry a gun? In London?'

'I had to be sure.'

'Why?'

He gave her the transcript. 'You did realize that Baxter would have your story confirmed, as far as possible?'

She studied the paper. 'And this confirms it. So why the angst?'

'There seems to be a small discrepancy in your opinion of your father's politics, not to mention the dates, wouldn't you say?'

She frowned at the words again. 'Shit!'

'And you could be in it. Right up to your very lovely neck. I had the devil of a job to stop

Baxter handing you over to the Special Branch there and then. But he wants the truth. No more games, Anna. Or you could wind up in prison, at the very least.'

She gazed at him. 'You mean you no longer trust me?'

He sat beside her. 'God knows, Anna, I want to trust you. I've just about fallen in love with you, as I think you know. But I can't protect you if you're not absolutely straight with us.'

Another long stare, and he knew her brain was working overtime. 'So I did not tell you everything,' she said. 'You came to me in Berlin when I was in a very upset and emotional state. You cannot blame me for not telling you everything, then. I hardly knew you.'

'You know me now.'

'Yes.' She held his hands. 'The dates on this paper are correct. We were all arrested on the day the Nazis occupied Vienna. And Papa *was* an anti-Fascist. I was separated from my parents and told I must work for the Reich or they would be executed. The Nazis sent me to school, and taught me how to be what I am. How to seduce men. How to...' She bit her lip.

'How to kill?' he asked gently.

'That too. When they felt I was fully trained, they ... they turned me loose.'

'On Ballantine?'

'There had been others before him.'

'But none you slept with.'

Anna shook her head. 'I was forbidden to sleep with anyone unless commanded to do so

267

by my controller.'

'And he commanded you to give yourself to Ballantine?'

'If Bally wanted it, yes. They were desperate to know if Britain would go to war over Czechoslovakia.'

'And he told you we wouldn't. While lying naked in your arms, no doubt. Well, I don't suppose we can blame him. You got me the same way.'

'I did not *get* you, Clive. I told you, I was desperate. Do you have any concept of what it felt like to be strapped over that bar, and...' There were tears in her eyes, and he could not stop himself squeezing her fingers. 'I was afraid that if I told you everything you would reject me.'

'But the truth of the matter – the only truth that is going to matter to my superiors – is that you have been sending secret information to Germany since last October.'

She hunched her shoulders. 'I do not think much of it was important. One of the reasons they punished me was that they felt I had not informed them soon enough that you *would* go to war after the seizure of the rest of Czechoslovakia, if there were any more acts of aggression.'

'You claim to hate these people. Is that true?'

'I hate them more than you can possibly imagine. If there was some way...'

'But you never considered rebelling against them, and hang the consequences. You're too

268

cold-blooded for that.'

She pulled her hands away. 'How can you say that? The girls who rebelled, or even did not complete the course to their satisfaction, were sent to SS brothels. I would have died had that happened to me.'

'So instead you were prepared to kill.'

She refused to lower her eyes. 'Yes, Clive. I was prepared to kill.'

'How many times?'

'I have killed three people.'

He swallowed.

'Each time I have hated what I have been forced to do, hated myself for doing it. Except Elsa. I hated her. And besides...' Her eyes flickered. 'I was protecting you.'

Clive held her hands again and stood up, lifting her with him.

'What are you going to do with me?' she asked.

He released her hands to slide his arm round her shoulders, stooped to put the other arm under her knees, and lifted her from the floor to carry her towards the bedroom. 'The only thing I can think of, right this minute.'

Her arms went round his neck.

Anna paid off the taxi a block from her flat, as always, and walked the rest of the way. This was both therapeutic and gave her nerves time to settle down. It was half past three, and although she knew that Gehrig had been going to the bookstore this afternoon, which was why she had been able to get out herself, there was always the chance she might be home by now. She wondered what Gehrig would say, or do, if she knew where her charge had spent the afternoon. Or how close they had both come to catastrophe. She thought it was rather a pity she could not tell her, for apart from rousing her undoubted sexual jealousy, she would have loved to hear her reaction to the news that she had just told all to a British policeman, without jeopardizing their position at all. In fact, she thought she had strengthened it, while also going a long way to ensure her personal safety.

All because Clive was so madly in love with her. She wished she could convince herself that she loved him back. She did know that she enjoyed sex with him more than with anyone else ... But the only 'anyone else' was Bally. She also liked him as a man, though he was a lot older than she, and even if he shared her antipathy for the Nazis he was still basically her enemy. She could not see that there was any prospect of a happy ending there. But was there any prospect of happy ending anywhere for her?

She went up the steps to the apartment block and heard a voice say, 'I'd like a word, Mrs Bordman.'

Anna turned. She hadn't immediately placed the voice, although it was familiar.

'Why, Miss ... I never did catch your name.'

'My name is Belinda Hoskin, as I think you

270

know very well.'

'And you have followed me here from Mr Bartley's flat?'

'I didn't have to. I knew your address, so I simply came here and waited for you. You were gone quite a long time.'

'We had a great deal to discuss,' Anna said. 'Now, if you'll excuse me...'

'You and I need to have a chat. I would like to come in with you.'

'I don't think that would be a good idea at all.'

'If you don't let me in,' Belinda said, still speaking quietly, 'I shall scream so loudly the entire street will turn out, at which time I will tell them that the German-born Mrs Bordman is having an adulterous affair with Mr Clive Bartley of the British Secret Service.'

'I don't think Clive would like you to do that.' Anna also spoke quietly, but her brain was racing.

'I am sure he would not. But if I have lost him anyway I have nothing more to lose, have I? While at the very least your marriage would be in the firing line. I don't know exactly what game it is you are playing, but I imagine that too would be severely jeopardized. So...' She began drawing deep breaths.

The woman obviously wanted something, and whatever it was must be sorted out in private, and on her own ground. 'Very well,' Anna said. 'You may come in.'

She unlocked the street door, waited for Belinda to follow her, and closed it again

271

behind her, then gestured to the stairs, reflecting with some amusement at Clive's reaction could he know that his mistress had willingly placed herself entirely in the hands of a trained killer, on the mistaken assumption that she held all the high cards. Not that she intended to harm this intense little creature unless she was forced to it. As she had reminded both Elsa and Gehrig, this was not Berlin. On the other hand, she had an idea that no one knew Belinda Hoskin was here at all, and she knew that both Bowen and the cook were out and would not return until five at the earliest, while Gehrig should be back well before then.

They went up the stairs side by side. 'I believe you would like to see my clothes,' Anna said, taking off her hat and allowing her hair to come down.

'I am really not susceptible to your charm, Mrs Bordman,' Belinda pointed out.

Anna made a moue, led the way across the lobby, and unlocked the door, waited for Belinda, and closed the door. The maisonette, as she had expected, was absolutely quiet. 'Straight ahead,' she said.

Belinda opened the inner door and went into the drawing room. 'How the other half live,' she commented. 'You would not like to have to give this up.' She picked up one of the porcelain ornaments from a side table, looked at it, and put it down again.

'I don't think Ballantine would like me to do that,' Anna said equably. 'Do sit down. And would you like something to drink?'

'Thank you, no.' Belinda sank into an armchair.

Anna looked at her Cartier wristwatch. 'I suppose it is a little early for tea. Perhaps later.' She sat opposite, crossed her knees. 'You said you had something to discuss?'

'You really are an amazing woman.' For the first time Belinda revealed some evidence of the tension she was trying to control. 'You sit there, as cool as a cucumber...'

'I am actually quite warm,' Anna confessed. 'It is a hot day. I think there may be a thunderstorm later. It was forecast.'

'Oh...' Belinda got up, moved restlessly round the room. 'How old are you?'

'I was nineteen on the twenty-first of May.'

Belinda stopped her perambulation to stare at her. '*Nineteen?*'

'I know,' Anna said sympathetically. 'A lot of people think I look older.'

'Do you know how old Clive is?'

'He has never told me.'

'He is in his thirty-sixth year.'

'He's very fit.'

'As I am sure you have personally ascertained. Do you know he has had you investigated, because he thinks you are a German agent?'

'He has never told me this.'

'You mean you just fell into his arms by accident?'

'We met in Berlin last October, and he was attracted to me.'

273

'You mean you seduced him at the same time as you seduced Bordman.'

'I attract men,' Anna said ingenuously.

'Does Bordman know about this?'

Anna shrugged. 'We have never discussed it.'

'You are absolutely shameless. Well, it is going to stop. I will not have you making a fool, and a possible scapegoat, out of Clive.'

'You mean you do not wish me to take him away from you.'

Belinda flushed. 'I mean it has to stop. If you see Clive again I am going to break the story in my paper.'

'Ballantine would sue you for libel.'

'Let him. Mud sticks. And I am sure your German employers – as I am equally sure that you do have German employers – will be very interested.' She turned her head as they both heard the front door opening. 'Who is that?'

'I think that will be my maid.'

'Well, get rid of her.' Belinda retired to the far side of the large room, out of the line of sight from the door.

Which now opened. 'All hell is breaking loose,' Gehrig announced, in German. 'I'm to return to Berlin immediately. While you—'

'We have a visitor,' Anna said, also speaking German.

Gehrig turned her head, gazed at Belinda. 'My God!' She opened her shoulder bag and drew a Luger automatic pistol.

Belinda gave a little shriek and backed up against the bookcase.

'You fool,' Anna snapped.

'She is an English agent. And she heard what I was saying.'

'She does not understand German,' Anna said, as was evident from Belinda's expression of bewildered fright.

Gehrig glanced at her, then back at the petrified Belinda. 'Well, it is done now. Fetch a garbage sack from the kitchen. We can dispose of the body later.'

'Are you mad?' Anna shouted. 'This is London. Listen, put that gun away and get out. I will explain it to her.'

'You are working with her,' Gehrig said. 'You are betraying the Reich. You...'

Anna left the chair in a fast movement. She was several feet away from Gehrig, and knew she would not make it in a frontal assault, so she went to her left, throwing out her hand to snatch a vase from an occasional table and hurl it with all her force, before running forward.

The vase struck Gehrig in the face and she stumbled, but fired as she did so, the explosion thunderous in the enclosed room. Anna felt the impact without immediately feeling any pain, but it did not check her forward movement, although she fell to her knees as she reached her target. Being considerably the taller woman she closed her hands on Gehrig's bodice as she fell, so that the two women went down together. Gehrig fired again, but the bullet smashed into the ceiling. Anna wrested the gun from her hand, and, as they wrestled, used all her skill to

275

hit the SD officer again and again. Gehrig had obviously received the same training as herself, but at least twenty years earlier, and Anna was also that twenty years younger and stronger. Besides, she was not merely trying to defend herself; she knew that after what had happened, Gehrig had to die. Her savage blows left the woman temporarily senseless, and Anna seized her head and banged it on the floor to completely knock her out. She heard Belinda shouting at her, and hands were tugging at her shoulder, but she threw them off and, sitting astride her victim, skirt pulled to her thighs, seized her head again, one hand holding the back of the crown, the other grasping her chin, and as Gehrig's eyes opened again, twisted with all of her strength. There was a dreadful click, and Belinda screamed. Anna subsided, as did Gehrig's body, and she looked down at the blood seeping from her dress to soak Gehrig's.

'My God! I just can't believe it!' Belinda sat in a chair, knees pressed together, elbows on knees, her chin on her hands. 'Is she going to be all right?'

'The lady is dead, madam,' Inspector Earnshaw pointed out.

'I think Miss Hoskin is referring to Mrs Bordman, Inspector,' Clive remarked.

'You were here when this incident occurred, sir?'

'No, I was not. Miss Hoskin telephoned me to tell me what had happened. I called an ambulance first, then Scotland Yard, and then came here myself.'

'May I ask why Miss Hoskin called you in the first instance, instead of us or the ambulance service?'

Clive felt in his pocket, took out his wallet, and showed something to the inspector. This was only to be used in cases of emergency, but he reckoned this could be one.

Earnshaw peered at it and gulped. 'Yes, sir.'

'It is a matter involving the wife of a very important man,' Clive said carefully, 'who also happens to be a personal friend of both Miss Hoskin and myself. Where is Mr Bordman, anyway?'

He turned to Bowen, who was standing in the doorway with a police constable, looking green. He had come home before the ambulance men had removed Gehrig's body, and the carpet was still soaked with Anna's blood. 'I telephoned Mr Bordman's office, sir,' Bowen said. 'He was in a meeting with the Foreign Secretary, but his secretary promised to get word to him as soon as she could...'

'I suppose affairs of state must take priority even over wives with bullets in them,' Clive remarked.

'Is she going to be all right?' Belinda shouted. 'She saved my life. That woman was going to shoot me.'

'The medics think she will be all right. She has a couple of broken ribs where the bullet entered, but fortunately it exited again before getting at anything vital. Her principal problem is loss of blood, but they were going to give her a transfusion in the ambulance.'

'You understand, sir, that I must carry out an investigation,' Earnshaw said. 'Shots have been fired; a woman has been killed...'

'Of course, Inspector. I am not going to interfere. But I would like to remain.'

'Ah ... as you wish, sir.' Earnshaw did not look very happy at the prospect of a secret policeman breathing down his neck, but he understood that there might be political implications in this case, about which he knew nothing. 'Sergeant.'

The sergeant sat at the dining table and produced his notebook.

'What I would like is for Miss Hoskin to tell me – tell us – exactly what happened.'

Belinda looked at Clive, who was thinking rapidly. He knew the business had to be hushed up, but that was a matter of timing. More importantly, Belinda's innocence had to be established beyond any doubt. 'I would also like to know that,' he said. 'Take your time, Belinda.'

'Well,' she said, obviously understanding that he wanted her to be as economical as possible with the truth. 'I bumped into Mrs Bordman – Anna – in the street, and she invited me back here for a cup of tea.'

Earnshaw looked left and right.

'It was actually too early for tea,' Belinda explained. 'Anna said that her maid would be in shortly, and she would make the tea. So we sat and talked, and then the maid came home. She seemed quite reasonable when she first came in, but when she saw me, she started shouting. Anna tried to calm her but then she suddenly produced this gun and levelled it at me. I was terrified. But Anna jumped at her and wrestled the gun away from her.'

'Being shot in the process,' Clive reminded her.

'Yes. She was terribly brave.'

'And also killing the maid while doing this,' Earnshaw pointed out.

'Well, what was she to do? The woman was obviously intent on killing us both.'

'It is still an unusual, and unlikely, skill for a lady to possess: the ability to kill with her bare hands. And you said she had taken the gun away from the maid?'

'Did I? I was speaking figuratively. I don't think she actually got the gun away from her until she had laid her out.'

'You mean until she had killed her?'

Belinda licked her lips. 'Yes. That's what I mean.'

'I see. And having disposed of the would-be assassin, what did Mrs Bordman do?'

'She fainted. From loss of blood, I think.'

'Very probably. Now, Miss Hoskin, will you tell us what the maid was shouting, before she drew the pistol? And what Mrs Bordman was saying to her, to calm her down?'

'I don't know what they were saying to each other. I don't speak German.'

'Ah. Well, yes. I see. Thank you, Miss Hos-

279

kin. We will have this typed up into a statement, and then we will require you to sign it.'

'I understand. May I go home now?'

'Of course.' The inspector looked at Clive.

'I'll take her,' Clive said. He followed Earnshaw and the sergeant into the lobby. 'What do you intend to do?'

'I will have to take advice, sir. The facts are plain enough. The question at issue is whether Mrs Bordman used excessive and unnecessary force in dealing with the maid.'

'My dear inspector, she was confronting a woman armed with a gun, who had just shot her.'

'Agreed. And I doubt any jury would convict her of anything more than involuntary manslaughter.'

'But she will have to stand trial?'

'That will be for the DPP to decide, and may well hinge on Mrs Bordman's evidence, whenever we can obtain it. But the fact is that she did kill another human being, which in this country has to be proved to be legal. And there is also the question of how, and why, a woman like Mrs Bordman came to be so proficient at unarmed combat.'

'Well, you'd better take it up with Mr Bordman.' While I take it up with Billy Baxter, he thought, as the front door opened to admit Ballantine.

'What the hell is going on?' he demanded. 'I received a message that my wife has been shot. How the hell did that happen? Who shot her?

280

Bartley? What are you doing here?'

Earnshaw sighed, as he realized that his afternoon was only just beginning.

It was six o'clock that evening before Clive, having dropped Belinda home and promised to return to her as soon as possible, got to the office; he had gone to St George's Hospital first, but had been unable to see Anna, as he was not family. Mrs Bordman, he was informed, was in intensive care. Her condition was critical but stable, and he was assured that there was no question of it being life-threatening.

To his surprise, MI6 Headquarters was still a blaze of light and filled with agitated people. 'Where have you *been*?' Betty, his secretary, demanded. 'We've been trying to get you all afternoon.'

'What's the flap?'

'All hell has broken loose. Mr Baxter wants to see you; he said the moment you came in.'

'And I want to see him as well.' He hurried upstairs.

'Where the hell have you been?'

'Busy. Something rather big has come up.'

'Big? My God!'

'Do I gather you have a problem as well?'

'A problem? The news came through at lunch time. Ribbentrop and Molotov have signed a non-aggression pact between Germany and Russia.'

Clive sank into the chair before the desk. 'Nazi Germany and Soviet Russia have signed a non-aggression pact? That can't be true, Billy. Oil and water simply do not mix.'

'This lot does, apparently. Stalin has done a dirty on us. We don't know the details yet, but the implications are pretty plain. Our guarantees to Poland and Romania are pretty well known. If Stalin has opted out of any agreement with us, he's giving Hitler a free hand.'

'But surely he can't afford to allow Germany to take over Poland, because that would bring the Reich border up against his.'

'You can be sure there's a huge quid pro quo. However, we are acting on the assumption that war is imminent. They are shutting down the Berlin embassy now, and we are instructed to pull any of our people who may be known to the Nazis out of Germany. We are hoping to keep a few in situ. But this also applies to our other agents, and in your case this means Mrs Bordman. How soon can you contact her?'

'At this moment, I can't.'

Baxter reached for his pipe. 'Why not?'

'Because she's in hospital.'

'Don't tell me the silly bitch has got the mumps or something.'

'The silly bitch has got a bullet in the gut. Actually, I understand it has exited, but it left a few broken ribs and some collateral tissue damage behind. She is in intensive care and as I am not a relative I cannot gain access.'

Baxter stuffed tobacco into his bowl. 'How in the name of God did she get herself shot?'

'She was shot by her "maid", who you will

remember is, or was, actually her SD controller here in London.' Clive snapped his fingers. 'I've got it now. Gehrig quite obviously had just heard the news from Schmidt, and had been told to get out of England while she could.'

'Anna told you this, after being shot?' Baxter was incredulous.

'No, no. Belinda told me this.'

'How the hell did she get involved?'

'It's a long story. The point is, she was there, with Anna, when Gehrig showed up. She apparently did not realize that Belinda was in the room and started shouting at Anna. Belinda does not know what she was saying, because she does not speak German. But Anna tried to shut her up, indicating that there was someone else present, whereupon Gehrig lost her head completely, produced a pistol from her handbag and levelled it at Belinda. She knew who she was, of course.'

'But she shot Anna?'

'Because Anna jumped her, and very gallantly saved Belinda's life.'

'So where is Gehrig now?'

'In the police morgue.'

'Holy cows! Anna?'

'Well, she has her little ways, as you well know. But don't you see she had to get rid of Gehrig because if any word of this were to get back to Berlin, she would be done. And her family.'

Baxter struck a match. 'You said the police morgue. So it's an official matter?'

'Well, there was a dead body lying about.'

'So has Mrs Bordman been arrested?'

'Not as yet. I think I convinced Earnshaw that it had to be self defence, but he obviously felt she had gone beyond the use of reasonable force. He was also interested in how a glamorous young socialite should come to be so lethal with her bare hands.'

Baxter puffed, not the least contentedly. 'She used one of her karate chops, did she?'

'Well, yes, she did, to lay Gehrig out. But having done that she twisted her neck until it broke.'

Baxter dropped his pipe, but caught it before it hit the floor. 'And you have been to bed with this woman? I'm surprised you could make it. And what precisely is Earnshaw doing about it?'

'He agrees with me that there should be no question of a conviction, but he feels obliged to send the matter to the DPP for a decision.'

'Well we can put the kibosh on that. What is Bordman's position?'

'Difficult to say. I mean, he appeared even more confused than usual. Unfortunately, he is the only one at the moment who is allowed to see her, as obviously she has no family in England.'

Baxter regarded his pipe as though it were a loaded gun. 'You think she'll confess to him?'

'Not if she's compos mentis. She has a very cool head on those lovely shoulders. But if she's half out on drugs I can't guarantee what

284

she is likely to say.'

Baxter considered this for several seconds. Then he sat up straight. 'Right. I have someone on the inside at St George's. I'll get him to check on that. I'll also get him to wangle you in to see her the moment she is lucid.'

'But if the police...'

'I'm going straight to the top. The story will be killed. Anna was showing Belinda how the gun worked and it went off. You will have to make sure Belinda understands that.'

'Hold on,' Clive said. 'She made a statement which is probably being typed up now.'

'That is going straight into the incinerator. You coach her, and Earnshaw will be along to take another statement. She was too hysterical to make sense when he first saw her.'

'And Gehrig?'

'Was sacked and went home to Germany.'

'You can swing all this?'

'If the boss goes along with it. He may have to go to the Home Secretary, and it is possible – you must understand this, Clive – that they may decide to throw her to the wolves. I think I can persuade them not to do so, for three reasons. One: by insisting how valuable she has been and will be to us. Two: by pointing out that, as this is not Nazi Germany, if she goes to trial she will be defended publicly by the best lawyers money can buy and it will be impossible to estimate what may come out under cross-examination. And three: she did save Belinda's life, at the risk of her own.'

285

'Billy, you are my friend for life. But what do you think will be Berlin's take on this? And Schmidt's?'

'I agree that it's tricky. But if we handle it right, the ball will be in their court. Gehrig is their woman. If you are right, and I believe you are, that Schmidt told her to get out of the country while she could, and she just disappears, he will have to assume that she has done just that. The fact that she never turns up in Germany cannot possibly be related to Anna; the most likely scenario is that she decided to get right out while she could. It's a pity we don't know if Schmidt had any instructions for Anna as well, but, speaking as a professional myself, if I had managed to insert an agent into the very heart of Berlin and got her German nationality, I would be in no hurry to pull her out and waste all that time and money. That is the assumption we are going to work on, anyway.'

'If they assume she will continue working for them, they will wish to contact her again.'

'And now there is no go-between. Schmidt will have to come out of the woodwork, at least to a certain extent.'

'And when he discovers that she is unavailable because she has a bullet in her gut?'

'He isn't going to discover that. There is going to be an item in all the gossip columns relating how the beautiful Mrs Bordman fell down a flight of steps in her maisonette, broke several ribs and is expected to be in hospital for some time.'

'Billy, you are a raving genius. But there's one more problem: Ballantine.'

'How we handle him depends upon just what she tells him before you can get to her. But I intend to see him myself, as soon as possible.'

'If he finds out either that she cold-bloodedly seduced him and has been his loving sexual partner for ten months only on the orders of the SD, or that she is a double agent, he is very likely to have a heart attack.'

Baxter actually smiled.

'Is what you are telling me true?' Belinda asked.

'Every word of it.'

'And you have merely been shagging her in the line of duty?'

'Life isn't all bad.'

'You are a lying, deceitful bastard. I ought to scratch out both of your eyes.'

'It happens to be the truth.'

'Oh, I'm sure it is. But you're trying to pretend you didn't enjoy every moment of it.' She glared at him.

'I am a lecherous bastard. But you've always benefited from that. And think about this: Anna is going to be in no condition – and I would say she is certainly not going to be in the mood – to shag anybody for some considerable time to come. So you will have to fill the bill.'

'Ha!'

The telephone rang. Clive picked up the receiver. 'Mr Bartley?'

'Correct.'

'Carroway here, sir. If you could be at St George's in thirty minutes...'

'You have it.' Clive hung up and reached for his coat.

'Just where are you going?' Belinda enquired.

'To visit the sick,' Clive told her.

Clive was at the hospital by ten o'clock and even the summer evening had faded into darkness. Carroway was a little man who wore a white coat. Clive couldn't determine whether he was a doctor or simply an orderly, but he knew his way around the hospital.

'We must be quiet, Mr Bartley,' he whispered. 'This is very irregular. Almost everyone is asleep, but there is a sister on every ward.'

'Including the intensive care?'

'Especially the intensive care, sir.'

'And this dragon will let me in?'

'I have arranged it, yes.'

'How?'

'She knows you are one of Britain's top secret agents and she is a romantic. I have told her – if you will forgive me, sir– that you and Mrs Bordman are lovers. She finds this terribly exciting.'

'Out of the mouths of babes and sucklings,' Clive commented.

'Sir?'

'Just an old family saying. But Mrs Bordman is lucid?'

'I understand she is under heavy sedation, and

is therefore somewhat drowsy. But I believe she is lucid, yes. Ah, her husband spent most of the evening with her, and he seemed very pleased.' He cast Clive an anxious glance as they reached the end of the last corridor.

'We know each other very well,' Clive assured him.

'Oh, Mr Bartley! It is very irregular, you know.' The sister was a tall, thin, efficient-looking woman, but she was positively simpering. 'And all so hush-hush.'

'We made it so.'

'Oh, yes! Only half an hour, please. And she must not, in any circumstances, be agitated.'

She led him along another corridor, Carroway remaining by her desk as a kind of sentry. Sister stopped outside a closed door. 'Hold on a moment,' Clive said. 'Does she know I'm coming?'

'Well, no, sir. I felt that might agitate her.'

'And you don't think my sudden emanation out of the woodwork is going to agitate her?'

'I am sure she will be pleased to see you, going on what Mr Carroway had to say.'

She opened the door. There was a faint glow from a heavily shaded bedside light, and the room, like all hospital wards, smelled of antiseptic. Sister stood beside the bed and very gently stroked Anna's eyebrows. Anna sighed, and opened her eyes.

'I have a visitor for you,' Sister said softly, and with her other hand beckoned Clive. Then she withdrew, closing the door behind her.

Nine

Spies

'Clive!' Anna whispered. 'Oh, my dear Clive. I did not expect to see you again.'

'It's my business to be where I'm not supposed to be,' he reminded her, and kissed her forehead. 'How are you feeling?'

'Like shit.'

'You are going to be all right.'

'You mean I'll live. What then?'

'That's why I'm here. How is Bally taking it?'

'Not very well. He knows there is, or was, something going on that I never told him. But he seems prepared to wait until I'm a little better.'

'What did you tell him?'

'That I don't really remember much about it, save that for some reason I do not understand, Gehrig attempted to kill me and I defended myself.'

'Good girl. However, he is going to have to be put in the picture – at least, some of the picture. Baxter is going to handle that.'

'He'll divorce me.'

'He is not going to be allowed to do that, at

least at the moment. The only way we can keep you out of prison is to keep you working for us. That means that for Germany's consumption, you are still Mrs Bordman, and once you are back home you will continue sending them appropriate information.'

'But they'll know what happened.'

'No they won't. You fell down a flight of stairs, broke several ribs, and will be in hospital for some time. Damned bad luck, but it could happen to anyone.'

'Gehrig...?'

'Has disappeared, having been recalled to Berlin. Finding her whereabouts is their problem.'

'Schmidt?'

'Will know nothing more than anyone else. He will have to be patient until you recover, when he will undoubtedly attempt to contact you. We intend to make this easy for him.'

'But if I also have been recalled...?'

'We don't think you will have been. Heydrich planted you here and you are a British citizen; he is hardly likely to undo all of that careful planning, even if there is a possibility of war. Your business is just to relax and get well and start functioning again. And remember, MI6 is looking after you.'

Her fingers were tight on his. 'Will I see you again?'

'I'm still your controller. While you're in here it may be a little difficult, but I'll manage it. But once you're out it's business as usual.'

'I'm so looking forward to that. But Clive, what's the end? Can there be an end? I mean a happy one?'

'If there is about to be a war, that's a difficult question for any of us to answer. But if we can get through it, I believe there'll be sunshine all the way.' Behind him he heard the door open. 'Time. I'm counting the moments.'

'I have to say,' Ballantine declared, 'that you are putting me in an intolerable position, Mr Baxter. You are asking me to take this ... this self-confessed scarlet woman, this reincarnation of Mata Hari, this woman who has made me the laughing stock of London...'

'Only you can do that, Mr Bordman,' Baxter pointed out. 'You are regarded with utter sympathy as the most unlucky of men whose so beautiful wife has had a most unfortunate accident. The only people who know the truth are the PM, the Foreign Secretary, the Home Secretary, one of his top policemen, the head of MI6, me and three of my most trusted operatives. We intend to keep it that way. If you betray the truth to anyone, you will not only be making yourself that laughing stock, but you will also be in breach of national security.'

'As you say,' Ballantine grumbled, 'the Foreign Secretary knows of it. Every time I enter his office, he looks at me ... well...'

'Well, sir, at least you know he cannot fire you. You have to sit it out. We all do.'

'No you don't. Not in the way I do. What happens when Anna comes home? Am I supposed to hug her and kiss her and rush her off to bed?'

'I am not cognisant of your domestic arrangements, Mr Bordman. The odd hug and kiss in public would, I feel, be useful. As for the rest, I believe there is more than one bedroom in your home; I know that Anna will wish to accept whatever arrangements you care to make.'

'When I think how she seduced me, my blood boils.'

'As I understand it, sir, you were very happy to be seduced.' Ballantine opened his mouth in outrage, but Baxter hurried on. 'However, I should emphasize one point: Mrs Bordman has a very important job to do. However angry you may feel, she is not to suffer any physical harm.' Quite apart from the fact, he thought, that if you tried to beat her you would wind up with a broken neck.

'Oh, get out!'

Baxter stood up. 'I'll bid you good day, Mr Bordman.'

The telephone jangled. Ballantine picked it up. 'Yes?' he snapped. 'I said I was not to be interrupted until after this gentleman has left ... What? Is that confirmed? My God! I'll be right down.' He replaced the phone and stared at Baxter. 'Germany has invaded Poland!'

'How did he take it?' Clive asked.

'Not very well,' Baxter said. 'I assume you are referring to his situation vis-à-vis his wife and not Germany?'

Outside, the church bells were ringing for Sunday service.

'What is the situation vis-à-vis Germany?'

Baxter looked at his watch. 'The PM is making a speech on the wireless in half an hour's time. I imagine it will include a declaration of war.'

'Shit!'

'It will mean a realignment of our people on the continent, certainly. But it should not immediately affect Anna, except that they may be more anxious than ever to get in touch with her. How much longer is she going to be in hospital?'

'She's doing very well, but it is likely to be a week or two yet.'

'So they'll have to be patient ... Yes, Amy?' he said as his secretary appeared in the doorway.

'Chief-Inspector Grattan, sir.'

It was Baxter's turn to mutter. 'Shit! Well, show him in.'

Clive got up. 'I'd better be off.'

'Hang about. I think this may be in your court. Chief-Inspector! All systems go, eh?'

As usual, Grattan looked in pain. He also looked disapprovingly at Clive.

'Clive Bartley,' Baxter explained. 'One of my senior men.'

'This is confidential,' Grattan remarked.

'So is Clive,' Baxter assured him. 'Do have a seat.'

Grattan sat down. 'You understand the situation?'

Baxter looked at his watch. 'Fifteen minutes to bang.'

'At which time,' Grattan said, 'we intend immediately to implement our plan for rounding up all German and Austrian aliens.'

'There will have to be exceptions,' Baxter said.

'No exceptions can be allowed.'

Baxter pushed a card across the table. 'You will have to call that number. Whatever your feelings on the matter, Mrs Bordman is still my operative. And she is a British citizen.'

'Which will make it easier to put a rope around her neck when the time comes.'

'*If* the time comes,' Baxter said equably.

'However,' Grattan went on, 'the man Smith has got to go. We have a full dossier on him. You know his real name is Schmidt? He came here in 1934, changed his name and opened his bookshop. He has never applied for British Citizenship, although he pretends to it. We have not found out how he gets his information back to Germany, but it obviously will be of great value to us to do so.'

'It will be of no value whatsoever to you – and more importantly to me – if you close it and him down,' Baxter said. 'And to do that would blow Mrs Bordman, as those who consider themselves her masters in Berlin, will assume that you got on to him through her.'

'Do you suppose she is his only operative in London? The man has been here for five years. Pulling him in may finish an entire network.'

'That may be. I'm sure we'll get them all eventually. But for the time being Mrs Bordman must not be compromised. I hate to pull rank on you, Freddie, but you have to use that phone number and do what they will tell you. Or not, as the case may be.'

Grattan regarded him for several moments, then looked at Clive, picked up the card, and left the office without a word.

'He is not a happy man,' Clive suggested.

'Neither am I,' Baxter pointed out. 'Switch on the radio, Amy,' he called. 'We had better hear what the man has to say.'

Anna stared at the ceiling. She had been moved from the intensive-care ward, but was again in a private room, surrounded by flowers and gifts and as much comfort as was possible. Her sedation level had also been reduced; it remained sufficient to leave her with only a dull pain, and was increased at night to make her sleep, but for the most part her brain was clear, although she did nod off from time to time.

But she did not always want her brain to be clear; there was too much to worry about. Bally came almost every day, but once the nurse was gone he made it perfectly clear he was only doing what he had been commanded to do for public consumption. For the rest, he had nothing to say, and preferred to read his newspaper than meet her eye. She had been assured that he knew nothing of her relationship with Clive. It was sufficient that he'd had to accept that she had never loved him as he had supposed, but had seduced him in the most cold-blooded fashion. She reckoned that upset him more than the idea of her being a German spy, or that she was now a double agent. But most of all, she knew that he resented the way in which she had flown out of his orbit. From being, he had supposed, an innocent and therefore vulnerable girl utterly dependent on his position in society, she had become an important member of the SIS, totally beyond his reach or control. She simply could not imagine what their domestic life was going to be like when she went home.

On the plus side, because it was out in the open – if only between a very select few – Clive was also permitted to visit her at regular intervals. The hospital staff had been given to understand that he was an old friend of her family. She also understood that they would be able to enjoy a much more open relationship after she left hospital, in that he would come to her home to decide what information she would send to Germany instead of her having to sneak off to see him. These visits would obviously take place when Ballantine was at the Foreign Office, which promised all manner of delights.

But, however pleasant a prospect, this thought brought into focus her real concern. She had absolutely no idea what was happening in Berlin, what they were thinking, what they were planning. They could have decided to write her off, in which case the lives she had spent the last year and a half desperately trying to save would also be written off. Clive seemed certain this had not happened and that as soon as she was up and about, Schmidt would be in touch with her. So, not for the first time in her life, she just had to be patient.

A gentle knock, and Sister came in. 'I have a visitor for you, Mrs Bordman,' she said.

'Oh!' Anna sat up, which she could now do with only minimal discomfort, and arranged her nightdress. In the middle of the afternoon it could only be Clive.

'If you will come in, please, Mother,' Sister invited.

Anna stared in astonishment as the nun, clad in black from head to foot, entered the room. Sister gave almost a little curtsey, and closed the door.

'Mother...?' Anna asked.

The nun pulled up a straight chair beside the bed and sat down. 'I am Mother Celestina,' she announced.

'I'm afraid I am not a very good Catholic,' Anna said apologetically. 'It is some time since I last went to confession.'

'I am sure your sins will be forgiven,' Mother Celestina promised her, and lowered her voice. 'Is this room bugged?'

Alarm bells jangled in Anna's brain. The wooden crucifix round the woman's neck was certainly genuine, but was anything else? 'The English do not bug their hospital bedrooms, Mother.'

'Not even when they contain a master spy?'

'Were I a spy I would be in prison.'

'You are very confident.'

'I am the Honourable Mrs Bordman. I have no reason not to be confident.'

Celestina gazed at her for several seconds. Then she said, 'I have come to see you at the request of a friend, who is most anxious about the state of your health. His name is Reinhard.' She waited.

'It is so very kind of dear Reinhard to worry about me,' Anna said. 'I'm afraid it will be a few days yet before I can be up and about. And then, I am told, I need some time to recuperate. I have lost a lot of weight.'

'I can see that,' Celestina agreed. 'Were you not so unnaturally beautiful, one could say you look like a skull. However, I am sure you understand that this is a most inconvenient time for you to be out of action. The Polish campaign is virtually over. Which means, as far as we can see, the casus belli no longer exists. If the English determine to continue the war, it will be as a senseless act of aggression. But as they have so far confined themselves to dropping leaflets over our cities, and as the French have done nothing more than probe the frontier, it is our belief that they will be pleased to get out of an impossible situation. The Fuehrer intends to give them every opportunity to do so, but as always it would be greatly to his advantage to know what English public opinion – I am talking about the upper classes of course – feel about the situation. Can you obtain this information?'

'Certainly. As soon as I get home. But I have lost my go-between, who was also my controller. She was ordered back to Germany immediately before the outbreak of hostilities and she has not been replaced. This may be because my accident occurred soon after she left. I'm afraid I was so upset by her sudden departure that I just was not looking where I was going on those stairs.'

'We know about this. Did she give you no idea where she was going before she left?'

Only that it was straight down, Anna thought. 'Isn't she back in Germany?' Her tone was her most dulcet.

'She never returned to Germany. We very much fear that something has happened to her. This is worrying, because if she was taken by the British Secret Services, she may well have been tortured into revealing the truth about you.'

'I think that is unlikely,' Anna said. 'For the simple reason,' she hurried on, 'that if she had, as you say, been tortured into confessing, I would surely have been arrested by now.'

'The English are very devious,' Celestina mused. 'They could be, how do they say, playing you like a fish on the hook. Still, we must give General Heydrich the information he requires.'

'General Heydrich?'

'He has been promoted, and is now head of all the German secret police. Under General Himmler, of course. So I am to be your go-between. Not surprisingly, after your accident, you have turned back to religion. There is no need to go to confession or mass if you do not feel like it. But I will be a regular visitor, to talk with you, and soothe your nerves. Whatever you have for Schmidt you can give me then.' She stood up. 'It has been a great privilege, Mrs Bordman. Goodbye.'

'Well,' Clive said, 'that is good news.'

'I'm glad you think so,' Anna said.

'It shows that they still consider you to be theirs, and this was bothering us, after such a long break.'

'She gives me the creeps.'

'You, Anna? I did not suppose that there was a human being alive who could give you the creeps.'

'The trouble with you, and with Heydrich, and with Baxter, and with Bally, and with Gehrig, and all the rest of them, is that you don't think I am a human being at all. You think I am some kind of robot whom you can programme, twiddle a few knobs, and send me off. And if I don't work properly you simply change the fuse.'

'I'd hate you to include me in that group, although I am sure you're right about the rest of them.'

She laid her hand on his. 'I'm sorry, Clive. Doctor Waldren told me this morning that I can go home on Friday. The thought of being alone in that place with Bally also gives me the creeps. I have not been instructed as to what I do if he wants sex.'

'Do you think he will want sex?'

'He is a very virile man in his own little way. And when I start to put on weight again, I would say he is almost certain to find bits of me to interest him.'

'Well, any wife is entitled to say, "not tonight, Napoleon, I have a headache."'

'Night after night, ad infinitum? I am his wife. I do not suppose – if it got out via Bowen or the maids that I am refusing to have sex with him – that it will earn me any sympathy from anyone.'

'Um. That is a tricky one. I'll have to take advice. But in the meantime, please try not to break any of *his* bits, especially his neck. That would not go down very well. But maybe it won't happen. I got the impression he was rather off you.'

'That has absolutely nothing to do with satis-fying either his lusts or his male ego,' she said darkly.

'They've cancelled the Cheltenham Festival!' Ballantine said with disgust.

'Well,' Anna said, 'there is a war on.'

Ballantine snorted. 'You wouldn't believe it. Not a damn thing is happening. Hitler keeps making these preposterous offers of peace ... You know all about that. Do you think he's serious?'

When they sat together of an evening, like this, it was almost as if nothing had ever happened. The utter stiffness of the first few weeks after her return from hospital had long faded. The fact was that Ballantine was an intensely gregarious man, and if he had taken up spending as much of his spare time as he could at his club, and as little as possible at home, he had to be there some of the time, and he couldn't stop himself talking. But, to her enormous relief, he had maintained at least a façade of cold indifference to her as a woman. Except, briefly, at Christmas when he had actually kissed her cheek. But he had been full of champagne.

For the rest, he equally did not investigate what she and MI6 were doing. He continued to bring papers home, as instructed, and he knew that Clive regularly called to sift through them and decide which were to be sent to Germany, but the papers he brought home had, in any event, been vetted by the Foreign Secretary. He did not know, and he did not enquire into, the method she used to send the papers on. He had no idea that Mother Celestina existed. And if Bowen was aware of this, he no doubt thought that his mistress was moving in a proper direction, as he certainly disapproved of Clive's visits.

So, except for those visits, she had lived a very private and indeed lonely life over the winter. The acquaintances – she could not really consider them friends – she had made before her accident regularly invited her to tea, and she and Ballantine continued to move in the cocktail party circuit, but she was aware always of being surrounded by hostility. Of course, none of their social circle had the slightest concept of the truth, but the fact was that she was German, even if naturalised, and no one had any doubt that, however quiet things were at the moment, they were engaged in a conflict that might last a very long time.

So most of the time she pursued her own path. The winter having been one of the coldest in living memory, she had seldom been able to go riding, but she attended the gymnasium regularly as her health and strength returned, and used the swimming bath at every opportunity. She was now back to her very best, she felt. And in two months' time she would be twenty. There was a thought to conjure with!

Meanwhile, niceties. 'I very much doubt that anyone in Germany knows what really goes on in Hitler's mind,' she said. 'I certainly have never had a clue.'

'Were you really forced into this by threats to your parents?'

Anna looked up. This was the first time he had ever discussed her situation, at least with her. 'Yes, I was.'

'And what do you think has happened to them?'

'I have to believe that Himmler is sticking to his side of the bargain, as long as I stick to mine. So far as he knows.'

He gazed at her for several seconds, then

304

flushed. 'It must be damned difficult for you.'

'Thank you.'

Bowen appeared in the doorway. 'Mr Bartley, sir.'

'At this hour? He's not supposed to come at this hour. Can't a fellow have a moment's peace?' He looked at Anna, undoubtedly blaming her for the intrusion.

'It is unusual,' she agreed. 'Something must be going on.'

Clive appeared in the doorway. 'I'm sorry to disturb you, Mr Bordman,' he said. 'But it is very necessary that I speak with Mrs Bordman.'

Ballantine snorted. 'We were about to have dinner.'

'It is urgent, sir.'

'Hm. I'm out of place in my own home. I'll be in the study.' He stamped out of the room.

Clive waited for him to disappear. 'You're looking very lovely tonight. Are you dining out?'

'We always dress for dinner.' Anna stood up, her long white gown settling about her. 'Bally insists upon it. What is happening?'

Clive took her in his arms and kissed her. 'Ballantine has not mentioned the cabinet meeting today?'

'Not yet.'

'Well, the decision was taken to mine the Norwegian coastal waters to restrict the German iron ore trade, which is using them.'

'Can they do that, legally?'

'No. But war is not a legal business. It's the

First Lord's idea. One can't help wishing he was running things, instead of the PM. Actually, he is. Chamberlain follows his advice in almost everything.'

'But won't it mean war with Norway?'

'I don't think, in the context of this war, that Norwegian sensibilities come into consideration. What they are hoping is that it will bring out the German fleet, such as it is, so that we can take it apart. But Jerry has to know of the plan as rapidly as possible or he might not respond. When next do you expect your nun?'

'She was here last week. She won't be back for at least a fortnight.'

'Then you have to go to Smith yourself. Tell him you consider this information of such importance that it cannot wait for the normal procedure.'

Anna swallowed. 'Will I get away with it?'

'We will see that you do.'

She nodded. 'It should keep them happy. Clive...'

He shook his head. 'I can't stop. Mustn't upset Bally. Can you do this tomorrow?'

'Yes.'

'Then I'll be in the day after. Two o'clock.' He kissed her again. 'I adore you.'

Ballantine signalled Bowen to pour the wine. 'Are his visits always that brief?'

'Not all of them.'

He brooded on this, and she toyed with her meal. She was still feeling quite breathless. It was some time since she had had to go into the field herself, and even Clive's assurance was not completely comforting. They finished their meal in silence and then Ballantine followed her into the drawing room, carefully closing the doors behind him. 'And when the visits are not brief, what happens then?'

Anna sat down and crossed her knees. 'If they are not brief it is because we have more papers than usual to go through.'

Ballantine poured them each a glass of port. 'I don't believe you.'

Anna took the glass and raised her eyebrows.

'When he came in tonight you looked, well, almost as if you were waiting to be taken out somewhere. You actually looked happy, for a moment.'

Anna sipped her drink.

'I think you're having it off with him,' Ballantine declared.

'Oh, really, Bally. He's a secret policeman.'

'And you are a secret-service agent, so they say.'

Anna finished her drink and stood up. 'The operative word is *secret*. Good night.'

To her surprise, as she made to step past him he grasped her arm and swung her round to hold her against him. 'You are my wife,' he said. 'I have been told that you have to remain my wife for the foreseeable future. Well, by God, if you are to be my wife you will bloody well *be* my wife.'

'Oh, really, Bally, don't let's have a scene.'

307

'There won't be a scene unless you make it.'

To her consternation he released her arms and dug both hands into her décolletage to pull down with all his strength. There were only two straps, and these offered no resistance. As the dress collapsed about her waist, her muscles instinctively tensed as she knew the killing urge. But she had been forbidden to hurt him, simply because Baxter, who appeared to be asexual, had assumed her husband would never again wish to have sex with her. So she slowly relaxed.

Ballantine had been looking into her eyes, and again released her. 'Do you know, for a moment, I thought you were going to hit me?'

'I was tempted.' She made no effort to retrieve her dress, but left her breasts exposed; she was in the mood to be cruel. 'But I have been forbidden to hurt you.'

'You, hurt me? You're just a girl. I could—'

'No, Bally. I could. Do you not know how Gehrig died?'

'Of course. She fell heavily and hit her head. The police said so.'

'She died when I broke her neck,' Anna said. 'I would hang on to your neck if I were you, for as long as possible. The time may come when my orders are rescinded.'

He stared at her with his mouth open as, still leaving her bodice hanging from her waistband, she walked away from him and left the room.

Anna used the Rolls: she had determined that

her safest course was to be entirely above board.

'Dodgy neighbourhood, Mrs Bordman,' Basil commented.

'It is, rather,' Anna agreed. 'But apparently this chap Smith's shop is the only place I am liable to find the book I want. That's it, over there.' The car pulled in to the kerb. 'I shouldn't be very long.'

'Of course, madam.'

Basil got out and opened the door for her. She smiled at him, and entered the shop. Although the exterior was distinctly shabby, which was true of all the houses and shops on the street, the interior was surprisingly large, with books of every size, description and condition scattered in every direction, on ceiling-high shelves, on tables, and even piled on the floor. There were several customers browsing, most of whom appeared to be university students of both sexes. Anna went to the desk where a middle-aged woman was reading a novel. 'I'd like to see Mr Smith, personally,' she said.

The woman looked up. 'He's cataloguing. He doesn't like to be disturbed.'

Anna opened her handbag and took out her card. The woman looked at it and raised her eyebrows. 'Of course, Mrs Bordman.' She rose from her chair, went through an inner door, and a moment later a rather small, round-shouldered man with thinning grey hair emerged to peer at her over his pince-nez.

'Mrs Bordman! This is indeed an honour.

May we be of assistance?'

'I am looking for a rather rare first edition,' Anna said. 'And I was hoping you might be able to save me hunting through all these thousands of volumes.'

'I shall do my best. Will you come in?' He held the door for her and she went round the desk into the inner room, where even more books were carelessly scattered around. Schmidt closed the door behind him. 'This is most highly irregular.'

'It is very urgent, and I have no means of contacting Celestina.'

'I see. Will you sit down?' Anna sank on to one of the two straight chairs in the room. Schmidt took the other, which was in front of the table. 'It had better be urgent.' He waited.

'The British Cabinet yesterday took the decision to lay mines inside Norwegian territorial waters in order to restrain the iron ore trade from Sweden.'

Schmidt frowned. 'You are certain of this? The British Government has always been most careful to maintain the utter legality of their position.'

Anna shrugged. 'Perhaps they are getting desperate. I was told this by my husband at dinner last night. I am sure you agree that is a most urgent piece of information.'

'Indeed it is. I will get it off immediately. But I sincerely hope it is not a false alarm. That could have serious consequences.'

'It is not a false alarm. How soon can it reach

Berlin?'

'Three, perhaps five days.'

'That long?'

'It is not just a matter of picking up a telephone, Frau.'

'How exactly is it done?' Anna asked, at her ingenuous best.

Schmidt gave a brief smile. 'I do not think that is something you should know, Frau. Now I think you had better leave. This is the one you want.'

He handed her a book and Anna got up and left the office, found her way back out onto the street, and went across it to where the Rolls waited. To her surprise, Basil, who was behind the wheel, did not get out to open the door. Instead the door was opened from within, and before she understood what was happening, her wrist had been seized and she was plucked into the interior. She fell across what appeared to be several knees, dishevelling her coat and dress and leaving her breathless.

She gasped, and her hat came off. 'What the sh—' She choked off the expletive as it was hardly language that should be used by Mrs Bordman.

She found herself sitting between two men, who, in their belted raincoats and slouch hats, reminded her uncomfortably of the Gestapo. And while the British were always savagely denigrating the methods used by the German secret police, she had no actual knowledge of the methods employed by their British counter-

311

parts. However, both men were looking very apologetic.

'You must excuse this behaviour, Mrs Bordman,' one said, 'but we did not wish to be obvious.'

Anna got her breathing under control. 'Then perhaps you will explain exactly what you *are* doing?' Her voice was cold. 'Do you know these people, Basil?'

The car was now hurrying away from the shop. 'Well, madam...'

The man who had first spoken now took out his wallet and showed Anna his warrant.

'What have I to do with the Special Branch?'

'You are a name on our list, Mrs Bordman, and so is John Smith. When two names on our list come together we are required to take action.'

'For heaven's sake,' Anna snapped. 'I do not know this man. I have never seen him before today. I was looking for this rare book, and I was advised that my best chance of finding it was in that shop.'

'Madam, I should advise you to say nothing until we reach Scotland Yard. Then, if you wish, you may require your solicitor to be present.'

Anna stared at him; she could not believe this was happening: Clive had promised her his protection. 'Are you arresting me?'

'Not at this moment, madam. We are merely asking for your assistance. We feel sure that the wife of the Honourable Mr Ballantine Bordman will be more than happy to help HM Government to bring this war to a successful conclusion.'

'The Honourable Mr Ballantine Bordman to see you, sir,' Amy said.

'Shit!' Baxter muttered. What in the name of God had gone wrong now? 'Show him in.' He stood up. 'Mr Bordman! This is an unexpected pleasure. Tell me what I can do for you?'

Ballantine sat before his desk. 'You can try telling me the truth about what the hell is going on between my wife and that fellow Bartley.'

Baxter sat down, and found himself instinctively reaching for his pipe. 'I'm not with you.'

'You told me that in April of last year my wife decided that she was fed up working for the Nazis and, happening to encounter Bartley on her visit to Berlin, offered to change sides. I found it a bit thin at the time, but frankly I was so confoundedly upset by everything else I was being told at the same time, I really didn't think too deeply about it. Now I want the truth.'

Baxter began to fill his pipe. 'That is exactly what happened.'

'You are expecting me to believe that my wife made the decision to change sides, happens – *accidentally* – to run into Bartley, and, without a moment's hesitation, says, "here's the very man I want."?'

Baxter struck a match. 'He was someone she had known for some time. She met him at your wedding, or perhaps earlier, during your visit to

313

Berlin. She felt he was someone she could trust.'

'Balderdash!'

'Mr Bordman?' Baxter puffed smoke.

'They were lovers. They are lovers. They have been lovers for God knows how long. Perhaps from that first meeting, when he was so anxious to put me off marrying her.'

'Oh, come now, sir. That really is going over the top. I happen to know that Bartley has a long-standing lady friend.'

'So maybe he runs a *ménage a trois*. I can tell you that last night I saw them together, and they are in love with each other. I am not a fool, you know.'

'Ahh . . .' Baxter decided against following that line of reasoning. 'You say you saw them together? Were they ... ah...?'

'Of course they weren't. I was present. It was the way they looked at each other.'

'I see. You really have nothing more than suspicions. I'm not sure what you wish me to do about it.'

'Suspicions! I know what's going on, and let me tell you, Mr Baxter, I do not intend to put up with it any longer. Last night when I asked her about the matter, Mrs Bordman all but attacked me.'

'But she didn't,' Baxter said, peering over his desk, as if expecting to see an arm in a sling, or a pair of crutches.

'No, she didn't. But I do not wish her in my home any longer. I don't care how valuable she is to you people, I am filing for a divorce.'

'On what grounds, Mr Bordman?'

'Adultery.'

'I'm afraid the publicity would be unacceptable.'

'I don't give a damn.'

'Well...' Baxter looked up as Amy appeared in the doorway. 'I don't want to be disturbed, Amy.' He frowned at her expression. 'Is something the matter?'

Amy drew a deep breath. 'It's Mrs Bordman, sir.'

'Here?' Both men spoke together, in mutual alarm.

'No, sir,' Amy replied. 'She's at Scotland Yard. She's under arrest.'

'Come in, Bartley.' Grattan did not rise from behind his desk, but he gestured Clive to a seat. 'Bit of a snafu, what?'

'That, sir, is the understatement of the year,' Clive said. 'When my man telephoned to say he had seen Mrs Bordman being taken off by your people, I damn near had a heart attack.'

'They have assured me they were very discreet,' Grattan protested.

'If my man could see them and understand what they were doing, so could anyone else. Including the man Schmidt.'

'He wasn't there.'

'With respect, sir, it's his store. And he lives above it. How do you know that he, or an associate of his, was not watching? Her position

315

could be irretrievably compromised. I was under the impression that we had an agreement that no move was to be made against either Mrs Bordman or Schmidt until and unless we gave the go-ahead.'

'Yes. I know. But she is on our list, and my people were, shall I say, overzealous. I do apologize.'

'They should not have been following her in the first place.'

'I simply cannot have MI6 telling my people how to run their business.'

Clive stood up. 'Well, sir, you may have to. Where is Mrs Bordman now?'

'Waiting for you.'

A plain-clothed woman unlocked the door of an interrogation room, opened it and stood aside. She looked vaguely apprehensive, but Clive nodded pleasantly enough as he went in. Anna sat at the table, her elbows resting on the wood. She looked composed enough, but stood up as he entered. He closed the door behind him.

'Are you all right?'

'That depends on what you mean by "all right".'

He went up to her, took her in his arms. 'They didn't, well...'

'They have not harmed me. I did not expect them to, really. But they made me very aware that they considered me an enemy. The man who was interviewing me until he was suddenly called away felt it necessary to remind me that if I had been engaged in espionage for Germany, I would be hanged.'

He kissed her. 'They're all a bit paranoid right now. Do you have anything to collect?'

She took a deep breath. 'Only myself. They searched me, you know.'

'Damn! Someone will get a reprimand.'

'Oh, it was nothing like it would have been in Germany.' She smiled. 'Or as you once searched me, remember? It was done by two women and they were very polite.' She freed herself and picked up her handbag. 'And they virtually took this apart.' She opened it to show him the torn lining.

'They'll replace this.'

She shrugged. 'It's not important.' She closed the handbag. 'They also photographed me and took my fingerprints.'

'We'll have those back.'

'It wasn't bad, Clive.' She gave a little shiver. 'It was the memories they stirred. Having to go to the toilet with a woman standing at the door. Not knowing what was going to happen next.' She glanced at him. 'I don't suppose anything like that has ever happened to you.'

Clive held her arm. 'Let's get you out of here.'

The waiting woman escorted them down a side corridor to a door leading on to the street where the car was parked. She did not speak, and did not look the least apologetic.

'They think I'm guilty,' Anna commented as she sank on to the cushions.

'It's their habit. They are assuming that you have been set free because you have friends in high places.' He smiled at her. 'Which you have.'

'Where do you wish to go, Mr Bartley?' the MI6 driver asked. 'Mrs Bordman's residence?'

Clive glanced at Anna, who gave another little shiver. 'I cannot possibly face Bally right now.'

'My flat, Harry.'

The car moved away.

'But how did it happen?' Anna asked. 'You said I would be fully protected.'

'A balls-up. My man was watching you, but he knew they were Special Branch men butting in, and he wasn't sure he had the right to interfere. So he telephoned Baxter. As for the police, they were just being bloody minded. But there are some loose ends which need to be addressed. Were you using your own car?'

'Yes. They brought me here in it.'

'Is it waiting for you?'

'I have no idea. I think they sent it away.'

'Is your chauffeur a gossip?'

'In the kitchen, maybe.'

'Mm.'

'I really wouldn't like anything to happen to him. He's by way of being a friend.'

'We'll sort it out. Now there's the million-dollar question. I take it you managed to deliver the message?'

'Yes. He was shaken rigid.'

'But he's sending it off?'

'Oh, yes. He said it should be there in under

318

a week.'

'Mm. Did you manage to find out how he handles this stuff, gets it out of the country?'

'He wouldn't tell me.'

'Right. Now do you think anyone in the shop saw what happened on the street?'

'I doubt it. Apart from half a dozen students, there was only a woman on the desk and that was at the back of the main store. Schmidt himself was in an office beyond that.'

'Then we'll keep our fingers crossed. We won't know for certain until the next time your religious friend calls.'

'Do I have to go back home?'

'I'm afraid it is necessary. Quite apart from maintaining the façade of your marriage, it's where Celestina will come looking for you.'

Another shiver. 'The façade of my marriage. Last night, after you had left, Bally tried to rape me.'

'Jesus! Is he all right?'

'I'm very good at resisting temptation. But he was livid.'

They had reached his flat. 'That'll be all for now, Harry,' Clive said. 'I'll call you when Mrs Bordman is ready to leave.'

He escorted her upstairs. 'I feel like a drink,' she said. 'And please don't tell me it's only four o'clock in the afternoon. This day has been going on a very long time.'

He poured two whiskies, gave her one, and sipped his own. 'But you still look marvellous.'

As she drank deeply colour filled her cheeks.

'I would like a bath. I feel filthy. I always feel filthy when I have been pawed by people I don't like.'

'You know where it is.' He refilled her glass and followed her. She stood, naked, watching the tub fill. 'Do I come under the heading of people by whom you do not wish to be touched?' he asked.

'You are the only person who I wish to touch me, ever again.' She tested the water, turned off the taps and sank into it with a sigh. 'Hostility. For the last two years, I have been surrounded by nothing but hostility, except from Bally for those first few months, and, more recently, from you. But you were pretty hostile to begin with, remember?'

He sat on the toilet lid to watch her soap herself. 'I regret that.'

She extended an arm to pick up her second drink. 'Where is it going to end, Clive? Where can it end for me?'

'Right this minute, like soldiers advancing into battle, we can do nothing more than march forward looking straight ahead. But at least we can do this shoulder to shoulder.'

'And when Germany wins the war?'

'Germany isn't going to win the war.'

She turned her head to look at him. 'That's a remarkably optimistic statement.'

'It's a statement based on fact. In the last nine hundred years Britain has only ever lost one war, and that was to the British.'

'I'll believe you, because I must. So tell me

what happens after Britain wins the war.'

'Your erstwhile employers will all be locked up, at the very least; your family will be rescued, and, if you like the idea, you will marry me.'

She squeezed his fingers. 'Clive, I have killed three people.' And I am consistently lying to you, she thought. She wondered what his reaction would be if he ever found out about Friedemann. 'Do you really think I am house-wife material?'

'I'll teach you.'

'And Belinda?'

'I know.' He sighed. 'I am being an absolute cad. But, as my grandfather used to say, you can't fart against thunder.'

The telephone rang.

Clive sat down with the phone in his hand. 'Now there's a problem.'

'It mustn't be a problem,' Baxter insisted. 'I've tried to talk to him and I'll go all the way up to the top if I have to. However, after what seems to have happened last night...'

'He tried to rape her,' Clive pointed out. 'He's damned lucky to be alive.'

'Absolutely. What I was saying was, you can't really blame him for not wanting to find himself alone with her. I have made it clear that she must have the use of the maisonette, so I understand that he's taking himself off to his club until things can be sorted out. He made it perfectly clear that it's we who have to do the sorting. Where is the lady now?'

'Ah...'

'I assume that means between the sheets. I also assume they are your sheets.'

'Actually, she's in my bath. Correction,' he added, looking through the door, 'she's out of the bath.'

'Well, you put the rocks to her, and I'm not talking about yours.'

'She's fairly upset about both last night and today.'

'I'm sure you'll be able to soothe her. But she must go home.'

'Message understood.' Clive replaced the telephone.

'Is he offering some kind of an explanation?' Anna enquired, going into her awakening lioness mode.

'Well, he's very sorry, but it was about Bally, really. He's raising a stink.'

'*He's* raising a stink!'

'About you and me. He's moved out and is muttering about divorces. Billy reckons he can keep him under control, but you have to go home to be there when next Celestina pops up.'

'And when Bally comes home?'

'I have an idea he's not going to do that, at least for a while.'

'Oh, very well.' She picked up her cami-knickers. 'I'd like another drink before I go.'

'There's no rush.' Clive took the garment from her hand.

The maisonette felt strange. It was not that she was unused to being alone in it, nor was she alone. Aline, her new maid, was there, as well as the cook, Bowen having accompanied his employer to the club. But Aline was still very much a fish out of water, and the cook had always regarded her with suspicion. She smiled at them and let them get on with it.

The strangest aspect of her situation was the knowledge that Bally was not coming home, compounded by the uncertainty as to when he might next decide to. Even if they had virtually lived separate lives for the past eight months, she had always been aware of his presence.

But she could do nothing more than wait. She kept hoping that Clive would appear, but it was several days before he did so, and then he merely telephoned.

'Your message certainly got through to Berlin, but it didn't quite produce the result we had hoped. Have you seen the news?'

'I don't watch the news.'

'Well, do so tonight. Hitler didn't send his ships to fight us off; he's invaded Norway instead.'

'My God! Isn't that a catastrophe?'

'There are two opinions on that. It's a catastrophe for the Norwegians, and it has rather caught us on the hop. On the other hand, we had expected him to make his move against France. This side show is a distraction which should keep him occupied for the summer, and

323

it gives us the opportunity to engage him on the ground.'

'I'm happy you're so upbeat,' she said. 'When can I see you?'

'It'll have to wait a day or two. As you can imagine, there's an almighty flap on. No trouble from Bally, I hope?'

'I haven't seen or heard anything of him. Thank God! But, Clive, I am so lonely.'

'I'll be there, just as soon as I can. I love you.'

She went to bed in a happier frame of mind than she had for some time, awoke in the same mood, and spent the morning listening to the radio that was full of the apparently huge Anglo-French army being escorted to Norway by the Royal Navy.

It was nearly noon when Aline entered the drawing room in her usual anxious manner. 'The nun is here, ma'am.'

'Oh!' Anna felt her heart pounding: she had almost forgotten about Celestina. 'Show her in.'

Celestina entered the room and the door was closed. 'I believe my message got through to Berlin,' Anna said.

'Yes it did. They are very pleased with you. But the Fuehrer is furious.'

'With me?' Anna's voice rose.

'No, no. He thinks you are the best. He is furious with the British effrontery. And particularly this man Churchill. He has long regarded Chamberlain as a ninny, and he recognized that Churchill is the mainspring of British antagonism. He has determined that he must be eliminated.'

'My God!' Anna gasped. 'How is he going to do that?'

'*You* are going to do it, Anna.'

Ten

Assassins

Anna stared at Celestina. 'Are you mad? Are they mad? How am I supposed to do that?'

'It will be the simplest thing in the world. Do you not go to many a reception at which leading government ministers are present? I am told that you have a weapon.'

'Yes,' Anna muttered. Her brain was spinning.

'And you are not searched when you attend one of these functions?'

'No.'

'Very well then. The gun will be in your handbag. You simply walk up to Mr Churchill ... You have met him before?'

'Yes.'

'When you are up to him, you speak with him, you open your handbag, you draw the pistol, and you shoot him. As it is a small gun, you may have to fire more than once. We think everyone around you will be so surprised by

325

what is happening that you will have time to do this. The important thing is that he must be dead before anyone takes the gun away from you.'

Anna felt as if she had been engulfed by a roaring furnace. She could hardly believe it was her own voice she was hearing, speaking so calmly. 'But I will be arrested.'

'Well, of course. There may even be a little rough handling; we understand that he is a popular figure. But the English are basically not into ill treating women.'

You don't know the English very well, Anna thought; certainly when pushed. 'They will hang me.'

'Well, that does seem probable. But again, in England these things are always done with great politeness and as little discomfort as possible.'

'I do think that you have lost your senses,' Anna said. 'You are asking me to commit suicide?'

Celestina shrugged. 'My dear Anna, you are in a position of a storm trooper commanded to attack and take an enemy strongpoint. You know this will almost certainly cost your life, but as a servant of the Reich you also know that you must carry out your orders. In your case, as I have said, death will be as dignified as possible. The English will even allow you to employ the best lawyer in the land. Who knows?' She gave a reassuring smile. 'He may even be able to get you off on the grounds of diminished responsibility.'

'Then I will be locked up for life in a mad-house.'

'Well, that might be preferable to being dead. But the job must be carried out. By the way, I have something for you, sent specially by General Heydrich.' She felt in the pocket of her habit, and took out a square of cardboard. 'He thought you would appreciate having this.'

Anna took the photograph. It was of both her mother and father, and Katerina. The women wore summer dresses, and Papa's shirt neck was open. At their feet lay an obviously contented Alsatian dog. She raised her head. 'When was this taken?'

'I believe about a month ago.'

Anna studied the photograph again. It indicated that the trio were in some kind of wood; there were no guards or restraints anywhere in sight. And Katerina was certainly older than when last she had seen her, two years before. 'Where is this?'

'I have no idea. It is a secret location. But I'm sure you will agree that they are looking well.'

They are looking well, Anna thought. Do they know by how slender a thread their lives hang? 'Will they continue to look well after I am dead?'

'When you are dead, Anna, there will be no further reason to keep them under restraint. General Heydrich asked me to tell you that should this assignment turn out badly for you, as you will have died in the service of the Reich, your family will be returned to their

327

home in Vienna. I'm afraid your father will have to find a job; his newspaper has been shut down.'

It was all so terribly pleasant and civilized. Could she believe a word of it? But she had evidence in her hand that Himmler had so far kept his word. And she had no alternative, other than to believe that he would continue to do so. While she would be in a wooden box in an unmarked grave. But she suddenly saw a straw floating by. 'You are assuming that I am going to be invited to any of these receptions.'

'The social calendar indicates that The Honourable Mr Ballantine and Mrs Bordman are invited to just about every reception in London. You are such an attraction, my dear.'

'You are out of date,' Anna pointed out. 'My husband has left me.'

Celestina frowned. 'When did this happen?'

'A week ago.'

'Why?'

'He thinks I am having an adulterous affair.'

'I hope you are not. That would be a gross dereliction of duty.'

'Of course I am not,' Anna snapped. 'That sort of thing does not interest me.'

'So I have heard,' Celestina mused. 'But the invitations still come here?'

'Yes,' Anna said. 'I pay very little attention to them.'

'Well, when the appropriate one arrives, you will have to attend on your own.'

'That would cause a scandal.'

'My dear Anna, the scandal of your attending a reception without your husband will surely be of little importance beside the scandal of your shooting dead the First Lord of the Admiralty. Now, our people are constantly monitoring these events. I will tell you which one to attend. If you and your husband have become reconciled by then, so much the better. If not, you will go alone and complete your assignment. It will be within a month. I will let myself out.'

Anna remained staring at the wall for several minutes after the door had closed. Her brain was numb. But she had to think, very clearly, and very positively. She supposed she had always known that one day the Reich would demand her life. But she had not anticipated it quite this soon. She was only a month away from her twentieth birthday!

She did not want to die. If she could not yet be sure that she loved Clive, that she could love Clive – and more importantly, that he could love her in view of her past, once his infatuation with her body wore off – he was showing her, and promising her, glimpses of a life without fear or suspicion, a life that could be enjoyed, that could even be peaceful. Supposing that could ever be possible for a woman who, when she fell through the trap, would have several murders to her credit.

When she fell through the trap! She found she was grasping her neck in both hands. But her hands were soft. The rope would be rough. Of course, it would not actually touch her flesh; she would be wearing a hood. They would put the hood over her head and she would be plunged into darkness. She would only feel for the next few moments the noose being put in place, and then...

Perhaps worse than that, she knew Celestina was quite right when she said the whole thing would be conducted with the utmost politeness and perhaps even sympathy. But then, Blaner and Gehrig, and even Heydrich, had been utterly polite as they had conducted her to the room where she was then savagely tortured.

All of that, for this. She got up, went to the sideboard and poured herself a drink. It wasn't as if she could accomplish anything to save her family. But as she had thought, once she was dead there was absolutely no reason for them to be kept alive. Therefore, if they were all condemned to death, there was no reason for her to carry out the Reich's orders and improve their position. She entirely agreed with the Fuehrer that Churchill was far and away his most implacable enemy in the British Government. So why not go out in a blaze of glory, destroying the entire network? Save that the only parts of the network she knew were Schmidt and Celestina. She did not doubt that she could kill them both. But she also did not doubt that the German network in England was like a Hydra, and would immediately grow other heads to replace those struck off.

She felt a crack in her fingers and looked

down to see blood mingling with the whisky, dripping on to the carpet. She had actually broken the glass she had been squeezing so tightly. She threw it into the waste bin under the sideboard, went upstairs to her bedroom to wash away the blood, and applied antiseptic and plaster to the two cut fingers. Then she sat on the bed. She supposed she was the loneliest woman in the world. It was a burden she could no longer bear. Whatever happened, she had to look for help. She got up, went to the table and picked up the phone.

'Well,' Baxter remarked, 'however you look at it, it seems like curtains for your lady friend. Damn shame. But that's life.'

'And death,' Clive said. 'It can't happen, Billy.'

Baxter sighed. 'Clive, she is in a cul de sac from which we cannot extricate her without blowing wide open everything we have done for the past year. You're not suggesting we let her shoot Winston?'

'Of course not. We can easily make sure she can never get to him. But if she had intended to get to him, she wouldn't have told me.'

'So, she doesn't carry out her assignment. We can be pretty certain that Jerry will then write her off.' He stroked his chin. 'I suppose we could put her away somewhere safe, but she'd be of no more value to us.'

'She can't accept that,' Clive said, 'as long as there is the remotest chance that her parents are still being held as security for her behaviour.'

'Then, as I said, she's done.'

'Listen.' Clive leaned forward and put his elbows on the desk. 'She can still be of enormous value to us. Let's be rational. We cannot allow her to carry out her assignment. But if she does not carry out her assignment Jerry will, as you say, at best discard her, at worst dispose of her. So either way, her value to them and to us is at an end, here in England. But if she were to be betrayed by her own people here, blown before she can carry out the assignment, and managed to flee the country before being arrested, they should welcome her back in Berlin as being the victim of circumstances.'

'You mean you would send her back to Berlin? I thought you had something going for her.'

'I have everything going for her, Billy. More than you could ever know. I am trying to save her life and her reason. If by any chance her family is still alive – and she can't help praying that that is so – and we close her down and keep her here while they are hanged, well ... She's a tough cookie, but I don't think there is a cookie that tough.'

Baxter reached for his pipe. 'And she'll do this if you ask her?'

'She'll do it because she wants to do it. And she's prepared to be contacted by our people on the ground.'

Baxter, opening his tobacco pouch, laid it down again. 'It's a brilliant concept, Clive, on both of your parts. But there is one small problem you seem to have overlooked: which one of her people, if any of them, is going to betray her?'

Clive rubbed his nose. 'All of them.'

'Eh?'

'They don't have to stand up in court, Billy. Will you leave it with me?'

Baxter picked up his pouch again. 'If I'm thinking what you're thinking, I can't know the facts. Nobody can know the facts, except ... Who and what do you need?'

Clive considered this. 'A couple of open warrants. She has her British passport. That should get her into Switzerland, and from there she should be able to reach her SD controllers. And a thousand pounds cash, in lire.'

Baxter, busily making notes, raised his head. 'You're using Italy?'

'Southampton–Naples. Italy is officially neutral. They won't ask any questions about an English tourist, and if there is any problem she can go to the German embassy. Once she makes herself known, they'll take care of her. And when once she gets to the German border she'll be home and dry.'

Baxter wrote. 'Anything else?'

'Curtis. He's the best we have and he's absolutely reliable. When it's over you will have to take it from there, but from your point of view it will all be straightforward.'

Baxter carefully laid his pipe beside the pouch. 'My wife thinks I should give this up, and maybe she's right. You're dicing with both

333

death and your career, Clive. All for the sake of a pair of legs. You want to be damned sure.'

Clive got up. 'You've never seen the legs, Billy. I'll pick the warrants up this afternoon.'

Curtis was a short, heavy-set man with sleek black hair and a black pencil moustache; his comrades often called him Hitler. He pulled the car in to the kerb and glanced at Clive.

'Straight in,' Clive said. 'No one must have any doubt this is a simple raid. You are loaded?'

'Yes, sir.'

Clive checked his own Browning; all nine chambers were filled. He restored the gun to its shoulder holster, opened the door and got out. Curtis joined him, and they walked across the pavement together. It was a bright, sunlit early May afternoon, but inside the shop was gloomy. There were the usual half-dozen browsing customers, but none took any notice of the two quietly dressed men.

They went up to the desk, where the woman looked up. 'Mr Smith in?' Clive inquired.

'Yes, sir. Who is calling?'

'We'll announce ourselves,' Clive said and stepped round the desk. Curtis raised his hat and followed.

The woman stood up. 'You can't go in there,' she snapped, but Clive was already opening the inner door.

Schmidt rose from behind the book-covered table. 'What is the meaning of this?' he demanded.

Curtis closed the door in the woman's face. Clive produced a manila envelope from his inner pocket. 'Johann Schmidt, alias John Smith. I have a warrant here for your arrest, on a charge of espionage for the German Government. You do not have to say anything, but anything you do say may be given in evidence.'

Curtis took out a notebook, holding it in his left hand; he did not use his right hand to hold a pencil.

Schmidt got up. 'This is an outrage. And a total mistake. I will sue you in every court in the land.'

'When you have the time,' Clive said. 'And if you can manage it before we hang you.'

'You ... What proof do you have?'

'The full confession of your associate, Mrs Bordman, alias the Countess von Widerstand, alias Annaliese Fehrbach.'

Schmidt stared at him in consternation. 'You ... That bitch!' His head half turned.

Clive saw the movement and drew his pistol. Curtis followed his example as another inner door opened and three men entered the room. They were also armed, but the Englishmen fired first. One of the opponents went down with a shout. The others returned fire. Curtis also gave a shout. Clive dropped to his knees before the table, and behind another pile of books.

The door behind them opened, and the woman came in, also carrying a gun. Clive turned on his knees and brought her down with a single shot. The other two men had been firing virtually at random; books were dissolving in every direction. Clive could see their legs beyond the table. He fired three times himself, and they screamed in agony as their trousers became bloodied. Then a huge weight crashed on to his head.

For a moment Clive was dazed, and in that moment Schmidt ran for the inner door. One of the wounded men shouted something in German and Schmidt replied. Then there was another explosion and a cry, followed by a thump. Clive pushed himself up, still holding his pistol, and looked over the table. One of the men was definitely dead. The other two were lying on the ground in a spreading pool of blood. Now they both held up their hands.

'Don't shoot! We surrender.'

Clive stood above them. 'Do you want to hang?'

'*Nein, nein.* We will tell you everything.'

'But we know everything,' Clive pointed out. 'This is much better for everyone.' He shot them both. 'Are you all right?'

'I'll survive,' Curtis said. There was blood on his sleeve. 'Marksmanship is not these chaps' forte.'

'Luckily for us,' Clive observed. 'And the lady?'

Curtis stooped over the woman. 'Straight through the heart. They could learn from you.'

Clive was kneeling beside Schmidt. 'Very satisfactory.'

Curtis stood above him. 'Didn't you want this one alive?'

'I wanted him dead,' Clive said. 'They tell no tales.' He looked at the crowd gaping in the doorway. 'Don't just stand there,' he said, 'call a policeman!'

Anna looked at the clock. It was six; Clive had said he would be there by seven. She poured herself a drink. Her valise waited by the settee. She could take no more than two changes of clothing, and he had said not to wear her sable; she had to be totally inconspicuous. So her hair was tucked up beneath her cloche, and she wore the most ordinary of her cloth coats. It was a great shame, having to abandon all her beautiful clothes and her jewellery, but she had always known they were only on loan.

The maisonette felt eerie in the absence of the servants. She had given them both the afternoon off and it was the first time she had been alone; on that disastrous afternoon when she had been shot, if the place had been empty she at least had been accompanied by Belinda.

She carried the drink to the settee, sat down and immediately stood up again. She could not keep still. She knew she was following the only course open to her, but she still could not be certain that she was not going, willingly, to her death. She simply had to believe, both in herself and, ultimately, in Clive.

The front door opened. She faced the drawing-room door, taking deep breaths as it also opened. She gave a little gasp and stepped back. The back of her knees touched the settee and she sat down involuntarily, spilling her drink.

Celestina was today wearing a dress instead of a nun's habit, and she was not alone; two men stood behind her.

'What...?' Anna gasped, almost refusing to believe her eyes.

'Bitch!' Celestina spat. 'Treacherous bitch! She is probably armed.'

The two men moved, one to either side of her, each drawing a Luger automatic pistol as they did so.

Anna's brain, acting with its usual lightning decision, had already determined that she had to gain time; Clive would be here at any moment. Surely. 'I do not understand,' she said, making her voice quaver. 'What am I supposed to have done?'

'You have betrayed the Reich. You have betrayed the organization. You have betrayed your position. You have betrayed me.' Her tone left no doubt that she considered the last the most heinous offence.

'How am I supposed to have done that?' Anna cried. 'The invitation arrived yesterday, as did your note, saying this was the one I should accept. I am prepared for it,' she said bravely. 'I am prepared to die for the Reich.'

Celestina's lip curled. 'Then tell me why, an hour ago, Schmidt and his bodyguards were shot dead in a police raid?'

Anna stared at her. 'How do you know this?'

338

'I was *there*! I was in the shop and by the time I realized what was happening, Schmidt was dead. I saw him from the doorway. They did not know who I was. There were quite a few people who came in from the street when the shooting started.'

'And you think I betrayed him? How can I have done that? You know the hold the SD have on me.'

'I also know that Johann had lived and worked in London for six years without there ever having been the slightest indication of suspicion about him. But the day after you receive your final instructions from me, he is killed. Get up.'

Anna slowly rose to her feet. 'What is to happen to me?'

'We are going to send you back to Germany. You will have to travel in a trunk, and it will be very uncomfortable. But not as uncomfortable as what will happen to you when you get home. Now, will you come outside to the car quietly, or would you like us to soften you up a little first? I think my friends would enjoy that.'

Another moment for an instant decision. She did have her pistol in her handbag, but she knew she would never be allowed to draw it. On the other hand, they did not seem to wish to kill her here, and it was obvious that none of them, including Celestina, had any idea of what she was capable.

She moved to the door. One of the men stepped in front to open it for her, and she knew that

Celestina, who was not carrying a gun, was immediately behind her, thus carelessly impeding the other man. She drew a deep breath and, as the door opened, swung her left hand with all her strength. The man had been looking up at her, and with her invariable accuracy, the edge of Anna's hand crashed into his Adam's apple.

He fell against the wall and went down with a ghastly wheezing sound. As soon as he hit the floor Anna was on her knees, taking the pistol from his grasp, turning, and emptying the magazine.

Celestina had been shouting and reaching for her, and took three bullets in the stomach. As she fell, the man behind her fired, but his shot went into the half-open door above Anna's head. By then he was already dead, a further six bullets having slammed into his head, chest and belly.

Anna drew several deep breaths. The man by the door was gasping, and although his face was suffused, he might well recover. Anna stood up, put the empty pistol on the table, and picked up the other man's gun. She fired twice into the stricken man's body. Then she laid down the gun, went to the sideboard to pour herself a drink, and looked at her watch. Ten past seven.

At that moment there was a knock on the hall door. She went into the lobby, opened the door and smiled at Clive.

'You're late,' she said. 'Almost too late.'

* * *

Clive peered at her. 'Trouble?'

She waved her hand at the inner door; he stepped forward and gazed at the body lying in the doorway. 'Shit!'

'Keep going,' she suggested.

He stepped over the man and his mouth dropped open. 'Holy shit!' He gasped. 'You did this?'

She followed him into the drawing room. 'Well, I didn't have much choice. I was alone here, and they wanted to send me to Berlin ... in a trunk.'

Clive took out a handkerchief and wiped his neck. 'But ... three people? What were they doing?'

'They were dying,' Anna said patiently. 'It only took me ten seconds.'

'Jesus!' Clive sat on the settee.

Anna poured him a drink. 'You don't understand. Nobody does. These people, and you, and I suppose your people as well, are all trained to use guns, or knives, to protect yourselves, and, if necessary, to kill. I was trained to kill without consideration or hesitation, using whatever weapon was nearest or my hands if necessary. Not having to *decide* whether to kill or not makes a difference of perhaps a fraction of second in response time, but a fraction of a second is the difference between living and dying.'

Clive gulped his drink, and mopped his forehead as he realized that if she had been one of Schmidt's bodyguards he would be dead.

341

'You're quite sure they were Nazis?'

'Quite sure. I told you, they had plans to send me back to Germany to be tortured to death. Did you want that to happen?'

'My God, no!' She was standing beside him, and he put his arm round her hips to bury his face in her groin. She was not even sweating. 'But you do take a little getting used to.'

'Can you handle this?' she asked.

'Yes. But you do realize it is the plan to give your escape maximum publicity.'

'Just so long as it works.'

From his breast pocket he took a folded piece of paper. 'These are your contact instructions. Memorize them and then burn them. And wait.'

She kissed him.

The black-out meant that Southampton docks were dark, and there was only a glimmer of light from the steamer alongside; she already had steam up. Clive escorted Anna to the foot of the gangplank where a sailor stood sentry. He held her valise in one hand, and her hand with the other.

'I am sending you to hell,' he remarked.

She turned to face him. 'I came from there, remember. Am I going to stay there, Clive?'

He put down the valise and took her in his arms. 'Only until we get this business sorted out.'

'I will count the minutes.'

He held her close and kissed her. 'As shall I. I love you, Anna.'

'And I look forward to loving you, Clive.'

'But it's not on at this moment?'

She continued to hold him close. 'Until I see you again, Clive, I am only concerned with survival. But please make it soon.'

She released him, picked up the valise, and went to the gangway. The sailor saluted, and she went up into the darkness.

'Have a look at these.' Baxter held out a sheaf of newspapers.

Clive took them, somewhat gingerly.

SPY DRAMA IN CENTRAL LONDON. SPY RING DESTROYED.

NAZI AGENTS KILLED BY BRITISH POLICE. AMAZING STORY OF MRS BORDMAN. GLAMOUROUS SOCIALITE WAS NAZI SPY. DISAPPEARS AND MAY HAVE FLED COUNTRY.

'SHE WAS A SPY FROM THE BEGINNING,' SAYS CHIEF SUPERINTENDENT GRATTAN OF SCOTLAND YARD. 'SHE FOOLED US ALL, AND ELUDED US AT THE END.'

'Nice of him to carry the can,' Clive said.

'Well, we're a secret department,' Baxter pointed out. 'And if he let one get away, he's taking the kudos for breaking up the ring.'

'So tell me,' Clive said, 'how is Ballantine?'

'The Honourable Ballantine Bordman is in

hospital suffering a nervous breakdown. He is being retired from the Foreign Office for health reasons. I think he had it coming. If he hadn't gone completely off his rocker in the first place at the sight of a sexy girl half his age, none of this would have happened.'

'Ah,' Clive reminded him, 'but if he hadn't gone for Anna, as Schmidt was already operating here, we might never have found him.'

'And you would not have had some of the best sex of your life, I would suggest. In view of what you now know of her, do you think you would ever be able to sleep with her again?'

'Life is full of risks. And what a way to go!'

'It's open,' Clive said into the street phone.

He sat down and gazed at the door. He actually dreamed for a moment that it might be Anna.

'Am I welcome?' Belinda asked, closing the door.

'Very. I need a shoulder to weep on.'

She went to the bar and poured two whiskies.

'That is,' he said, 'if you forgive me.'

She handed him his glass and sat beside him. 'I tell myself that it was all in the line of work. And I've always known that you enjoy your work. But she is gone, isn't she? You don't have her shacked up somewhere?'

'She's gone. She's where she came from.'

'But you're hoping she'll survive?'

'She has to survive. She is unique.'

Belinda sighed. 'And beggars can't be choos-

344

ers.' She put down her drink and got up. 'Shall I fix us some dinner?'

The car drove into that so familiar, so frightening courtyard. The door was opened by a uniformed officer, who stood to attention and saluted.

'Heil Hitler!'

Anna got out and responded.

'The General is waiting for you.'

'Thank you.' Anna stepped past him and walked towards the doorway, waiting for his hand to close on her arm, or at least to hear his boots immediately behind her. But he had apparently remained by the car. The door was opened for her by a sentry and she stepped into the hall. There was the usual number of people, men and women in uniform, hurrying to and fro. One or two recognized her and gave nods of greeting, but most ignored her; there was an air of tension.

About her? But no one was making the slightest move towards her. She went up the main staircase on to the wide gallery, remembering how she had been forced down that staircase just over a year ago, and went to the huge double doors. These were opened for her by yet another waiting sentry, and she was in the outer office. There were three women secretaries, all of whom stood up as she entered.

'General Heydrich said you were to go right in, Frau Bordman,' one said, hurrying in front of her to knock and then open the inner doors.

345

'Frau Bordman, Herr General!'

Feeling quite breathless, Anna entered the room. Again, she had not been in here since the day he had so calmly told her she was to be tortured. She raised her hand. 'Heil Hitler!'

There were three men in the room, two standing in front of the desk, and Anna's knees felt weak as she recognized Blaner. They all saluted in response, then Heydrich said, 'Thank you, gentlemen, we will continue our discussion later.'

Again they saluted and went to the door. As he passed her, Blaner said, 'Welcome home, Countess.'

The door closed behind them and Heydrich came round his desk. 'Anna!' He advanced towards her, arms outstretched, held her close, and kissed her on the mouth. 'It is so good to see you. Come, sit down. You have heard the news?'

Anna sank into the chair before the desk. 'I know there is something going on, Herr General.'

Heydrich sat in his chair. 'Yesterday, the Wehrmacht invaded Holland, Belgium and France.'

Anna clasped both hands to her neck.

Heydrich smiled. 'It is stupendous, isn't it? It is the start of the greatest battle in the history of the world.'

'But ... can we win it? Are we strong enough?'

'We are sweeping them aside like chaff. It will be over in a month. But there is another item of news which will amuse you. Also yesterday, the British House of Commons threw out Chamberlain and put Churchill in his place. You were supposed to stop that happening.'

Anna's heartbeat quickened; she had no idea how much he knew. 'I do not understand. How was I to prevent it?'

'By killing the man!'

Anna stared at him. 'I was supposed to do that? I received no instructions.'

'Or you would have done it?'

'I am a servant of the Reich,' Anna said bravely. 'I carry out my orders.'

'Even if it would have meant your death,' Heydrich said thoughtfully. 'You know, Anna, I believe you. I believe you would. You are a most unusual young woman. But you say you never received the instructions?'

'I received nothing. Celestina said she was coming to see me with vital information, but she never came. Instead, I received a phone call from Schmidt telling me to get out immediately. So I did. I feel so guilty, Herr General.'

'You can hardly be blamed for not carrying out an order you apparently never received. And your own personal exploits in escaping from England has been an enormous propaganda coup. You were lucky that an Italian ship was about to sail, but you have to be congratulated on the speed and decision with which you acted to get to her. You know that Celestina and Schmidt and six others got involved in a gun battle with the British police. How it happened I cannot imagine, and I don't suppose we will find out the truth until the war is over, when we get our hands on the British archives. But, as I say, you are now world famous, and a heroine of the Reich. As for Churchill, as we are about to force Great Britain to her knees, he is really of very little importance.'

Anna sat very still, her knees pressed together; she could feel perspiration coating her neck and shoulders. 'And what is to become of me now, Herr General?'

Heydrich got up and came round the desk. I am sure we will find something to do with a girl of your talents. However, I think you deserve a few weeks' rest. Your apartment has been kept for you, and you will find everything you require already there.'

'Have I really pleased the Reich?'

'I have just said so. The Fuehrer himself wishes to meet you.'

'Then would it be possible to see my parents and my sister?'

'I think that could be arranged. But, I think it would be very nice if you would have dinner with me tonight.'

So I am back in hell, Anna thought. For eternity? As Clive had said, she could only wait to find out.

Epilogue

'The deadliest woman in the world,' I mused. 'That's what they called you.'

'I know,' the Countess said. 'But I only ever killed to survive. That was my overriding aim in life: survival.'

'Which you did so successfully.'

She made a moue. 'Until now.'

'May I ask a question?'

She inclined her head.

'Did you love him?'

She considered for a few moments. Then she said, 'Yes. At the end I loved him. I was heart-broken when we had to say goodbye.'

'Did you ever see him again?'

The Countess smiled. 'That, Mr Nicole, is another story.'